THE LOOKBACK

B. E. BAKER

Purple
Puppy
Publishing

For Mom
Thanks for having a wonderful love story

PROLOGUE: MANDY

Most families have some *thing* that makes them different from other families. The Brooks family boys dominated in most every sport. The Gibbens family found trash that no one wanted and managed to use it for something unexpected. The Davis family loves to cook and bake. The Duttons love to argue.

My family has its thing, just like any other, only, no one knew. Or, whatever they thought our thing was, it really wasn't. From the time I was old enough to understand anything at all about the world, I was taught what it took to be a successful member of the Saddler family.

We were liars. Accomplished liars.

Never in a way that hurt someone else. That was our one guiding principle, really. If a lie stole something, hurt someone, or did obvious damage? No, no, double no. But as long as no one was hurt by the exaggeration, it was not only allowed, it was downright encouraged.

I didn't even find out what my real name *should* have been until I turned eighteen. That's when my mom sat me down and explained that my dad had been a hero—he'd stood up to the Red Army's invasion of our home country, Latvia. But they had eventually lost against the swelling tide of Russians that spilled across our border, eager to trample Latvia in their attempt to face off against Germany.

What really happened when my family left Latvia, no one will ever know for sure. My family's propensity to embellish was too firmly rooted by then for me to have any hope of sussing out the unvarnished truth. But I'm reasonably sure that my father fled Latvia just in time to escape, and that he brought my mother to America right as this fledgling nation was preparing to enter the same war he'd just avoided. He wasn't keen on rejoining it from a new position.

To avoid being sent back to Europe to join the fray as a United States citizen, he entered illegally, somehow finding what I'm quite sure were fraudulent papers on his way out West. Manila was a new town and it needed men badly—my dad could work wonders with leather, especially saddle repairs. Eventually he began crafting saddles himself. Although he also ran cows on our land, the majority of our income came from his saddle repairs. It was only natural that our family should shed its prior name that was bizarre in this country—Liepa—and adopt a new one that people had no trouble with: Saddler.

It was also the best kind of marketing in that era.

And so it was that, when my mother was nearly ready to give birth to me, my father loaded her into our old Ford Standard and started out for the hospital. It was a fluke that Jedediah's mother happened to be almost ready to burst as well, and with her husband needing to watch their older child, little Clyde, we offered to give her a ride over.

When I was born on September 25 of 1944, Jedediah and I were only the third and fourth babies delivered in the brand new Roosevelt Hospital, a solid ninety plus miles to the south of our family ranch outside of Manila. The name my parents put on my birth certificate, just in case anyone was paying attention, wasn't Amanda Liepa. It was Amanda Saddler.

That's how I started my life with a lie, and my parents made sure that I learned to proceed that way whenever the truth would be inconvenient, embarrassing, or in any way undesirable.

It took me a very long time to realize the error of that line of thinking. A *very* long time. I've always said that no villain can do as much damage to a person as their own family, and that's not a lie.

I still blame them for the worst lie I ever told. As with most things, I didn't realize it was such a damaging lie until long after I told it.

HELEN

The start of summer in the Wasatch Front is literally the only time it becomes even a little bit habitable. I mean, sure, New York City gets cold, but other than walking from your brownstone to a cab, you're never exposed to the elements for long.

This entire area's just rotten with outdoors. In fact, it's the only thing that draws new people, usually, and the tourists who come to see the Flaming Gorge barely spend any time *inside*, so having the weather warm enough that the mounds of snow melt and the sunshine actually warms your face is absolutely lovely.

All the mud that squishes and squelches everywhere, because the horses and cows that everyone else seems to love greedily gobble up anything at all that tries to grow, isn't quite so wonderful. Still, when Abby told me that Amanda and Mandy had both already signed the contracts and that I could come pick them up, I knew she'd probably be outside, so I wasn't even annoyed when that's where I found her.

I've been staying with Ethan at the Brooks ranch—I stuck around when Steve and Abigail moved to a remodeled version of Steve's house—and it's a little lonely if I'm being honest.

Ethan's gone all the time. He's either out with cows or he's preoccupied with Beth. Even when he's around, he's not much for elevated conversation, in spite of my best efforts.

I honestly wonder sometimes how Abigail and her relatively intelligent first husband Nathan created a kid like Ethan. He's not dumb, but he's so unmotivated. His hopes and dreams couldn't even fill a salt shaker—and most of them, he's already realized at the age of nineteen, right here in this cowtown. I just don't understand how a person could be that *satisfied*. What does he strive for?

Nothing. That's what.

"Oh, you're here." Abigail smiles and waves from where she's standing along the split rail fence. The baby on her hip turns toward me and smiles a gummy grin. For some reason that no one has been able to explain to me, they have to tell people how old he is in *weeks*. Thankfully, I've broken their code, so I know that he's six months old as of last week. It's a decent age—he's young enough that no one tries to fob him off on the women who know nothing and have no interest in babies, but he's old enough that he can sit up on the floor and play with things to keep him from crying. He's young enough he can't talk your ear off with inane babble yet, and old enough to chew on soft objects as his teeth come in. That'll happen any day now, hopefully. I find his gummy smile a little disturbing, if I'm being honest.

But most importantly, he holds his head up on his own.

The few times I've been forced to hold him, I was always terrified that his neck would give out and his head would just roll right off his shoulders. Baby-holding should come with some kind of mandatory neck-cradling training. Anyone who hasn't had that training yet should never be allowed to touch them.

"Where did you say the contracts are?" I'm being polite. I've been here more than a minute already and she still hasn't told me.

2

"They're doing some work on the closet in the master, so I had to put them in that cabinet beside the microwave so no one would spill anything on them or, you know, use them as an oversized coaster."

I can't help pulling a face. I do occasionally get a little lonely living with Ethan after staying with Abby for a while, but it's the lesser of two evils for sure. Her house exists in a perpetual state of barely managed chaos. "Well, I'll go rummage around until I find them, trying not to get in the way of the cabinet people."

When I glance up, I see why Abigail's waiting on the fence line.

As usual, if Steve's not at the hospital, he's on a huffing and puffing horse. This one appears to be young or stupid or both, because it keeps trying to rear back. Meanwhile, Emery, Izzy, *and* Whitney are doing something quite strange, making serpentine, twisty, follow-the-leader back and forth movements from one end of the arena to the other.

"That's the wrong lead again, Emery," Steve says, already sounding a bit winded himself. "Why do you girls think that she keeps getting the wrong lead on a horse who knows them?"

"It's because she's letting his shoulder collapse," Izzy says. "That's also why her turns are so wide they almost crash into the rest of us."

Emery looks ready to cry.

Steve's talking to her rather sternly now, which is probably for the best, and he's stopped riding, which means he thinks something major is wrong. Either that, or he senses an upcoming meltdown. "Izzy, keep your eyes forward. If you don't look where you're going, you'll wind up way off when it matters. You can't look at the ground and hope to find your destination."

Emery starts moving again, and she looks fine to me. At least her turns are sharper.

3

"That's still the wrong lead. That's what? Thirteen times, now?" Steve sounds a little annoyed. "That horse knows his leads cold, Em."

And now she's bawling. Loudly.

Thankfully, it's not my circus and not my monkeys. I turn to walk off when Steve's reddish horse decides to bite the back of Whitney's dark brown one, and Whitney's horse bolts—without her on its back.

Abigail exhales. "Here."

Before I know how to say no, she's thrusting her drooling, gummy-mouthed baby at me and ducking between the rails of the fence. "Whitney, are you alright?"

As if he's figured out that Whitney's fine and an amateur now has him, baby Nate scowls at me. Then, predictably, his entire face turns bright red and he starts to howl. "Ma-ma!" He's reaching and twisting for Abigail like someone gave him water after midnight. Or was the no-no food after midnight and water poured directly on him?

Either way, I'm literally holding a gremlin straight out in front of me, and I strongly consider just setting him down on the ground. If it wasn't quite so muddy between me and the edge of the arena, I might do it. I've seen him sitting up on his own in the family room. He'd be up to the task.

But Abigail's still talking to Whitney, who's now standing and brushing off her pants.

"I'm sorry," Steve's saying. "I've never seen Danke bite before so I wasn't expecting it."

"It's fine." Whitney nods. "I can get back on."

Unfortunately, in spite of her reassurance, it takes them several more minutes to calm the dumb brown horse down enough for Whitney to swing back on—which you could not pay me enough to do—and my shoulders are well and truly sore by the time Abigail finally starts back toward me. My ears are also quite sick of the screaming.

"Here." She's not quite through the gate yet, but I hold

the little nightmare out and bounce him a little so he knows she's coming.

Abigail stops short of the rails and smirks. "I'm sorry, but do my eyes deceive me? Or is the great Helen Fisher distressed about having to hold a baby for three minutes?"

"Was it only three minutes? I'm not sure I've heard that much crying in my entire life."

Abigail's laughing as she swings through the fence and takes little Nate back. Being demon spawn, he immediately collapses against her chest and sighs, like I was somehow abusing him. "It would help if you held him more like an acquisition agreement and less like a sack of moldy potatoes."

He *smells* more like the potatoes, but I'm feeling generous, so I don't point that out. "It must be less stressful taking care of a child once you get used to doing it."

Abigail shrugs. "Not really, but you get used to the stress, like someone with a chronic ulcer becomes accustomed to the burning feeling."

"Like you know anything at all about ulcers." Marrying a doctor has expanded her analogy repertoire, at least.

"I probably know as much as you do about children." She's still smirking as she walks with me into the house. "You're around someone who has one, at least."

It's a good thing she comes with me, because the contracts are not in the cabinet I thought she was talking about. There are very few people in the world whose company I enjoy, and Abigail is one of them, but spending time with her is way less fun when she's shackled to a drool factory who poops his pants on the regular.

"Steve's off tomorrow," she says. "I can meet you to go over the documents on that seed deal first thing."

That seed deal.

It's such a typically Abigail way to refer to a multi-million dollar deal that I'm smiling as I leave. That seed deal, as she calls it, is the newest hostile takeover that I've been scouting, and I'm more excited about it than I have been about anything in a while.

Vitality Plus, a relatively new agricultural startup company I've been looking into, was backed by Gonzago, which is one of the largest global food engineering and production companies in the world. Lately, it has come under increasingly uncomfortable fire for some of its reverse engineering practices, and it's taken a beating in both the media and to its bottom line.

It's been bad enough that it cut a few of its pet projects loose, and now they're all floundering. I love to look for baby ducks whose mother has lost track of them, and this certainly qualifies. Without consistent revenue to fund its growth through new research, Vitality Plus had to make an IPO that didn't go well, just to stay in operation. In spite of its early shove into maturity, it has consistently turned a profit. It's in a reasonably good position, but thanks to a few ongoing management blunders, it's worth less than half what it could be worth, and if its pending tech breaks through?

It'll be meteoric.

It's an investment someone else made that they dropped on the ten-yard line, and I can't *wait* to snatch it out from under their nose. I'm practically salivating, thinking about how much easy money I stand to make. I've been buying up shares from a dozen different holding companies, and inside of another week, I'll have enough to make a decent proffer. I don't usually go for takeovers by proxy, because proxy fights can get ugly fast. If they go wrong, they wind up costing even more than an up-front purchase offer, but in this case, with Gonzago holding onto so many Vitality Plus shares, it's probably my only play.

The worst part of a proxy fight is meeting with all the major stakeholders and feeling them out without tipping my hand. I've done my research, and I know quite a lot about one of the biggest. Even so, it's almost impossible to really know what the people you're petitioning want until they're right in front of you. I like to go in with every angle covered, and that's just not possible in this circumstance. It makes me uneasy.

I'm about to get on the plane to head for Los Angeles for the meeting when my phone buzzes.

CAN YOU SWING BY BEFORE YOU LEAVE? David never asks like that. He'll say he misses me. He'll tell me that he can't wait to see me again. But he never asks me to "swing by," because he knows that it's a thirty-minute drive each way to his resort in Dutch John. In this area, most things are five to ten minutes—but he put down roots a half an hour away. It's irksome.

I want to tell him that I'm already heading out, but he knows I own the jet. It'll leave when I tell it to leave, and he knows it. I mentally groan, but I change directions and head for his place instead of the local hangar.

I'm reviewing the basics of my position for tomorrow morning's meeting as I drive, and I feel pretty confident that I can sway Mr. McFarland. I've never met him in person, and it took us three weeks to track him down, but I'm prepared to make him an excellent offer. I'm confident he'll either sell me his shares, or agree to vote my way if and when I call for a vote of no confidence.

After all. . .who wouldn't prefer to bring in Tom Brady over Eli Manning, really? Not that I know a lot about sports, but I try to keep important figures straight so I can understand the guy talk that permeates the boardrooms.

When I reach David's resort, the staff wave as I waltz through the door, except for the men with earpieces—they nod and smile. I jog up the steps in an attempt to get some movement in before sitting on a plane all day, and then I hang a right around the corner to his office, entering the code to walk through the otherwise locked stairwell door.

I always walk through this way—not to take him off guard

anymore, but because it's the quickest way to reach his hippie cubicle space.

"Ms. Foster," David's assistant Ysandre says with a curt nod. "Mr. Park is currently in the conference room."

I sigh and spin on my heel, thinking about the first time I came and how different it feels to visit now. But when I walk into the conference room, a rush of adrenaline floods my system just like it did that first day when I stormed his resort, looking for blood.

Because David's not alone.

If I'm not mistaken, the people waiting for me in that conference room with him, shocked expressions on their faces, are his parents.

MANDY

manda has no real business experience, and she often misunderstands basic principles until someone takes the time to explain them to her. She's also doggedly determined to do things her own way, even when her way is just bad. It's frankly a miracle that she managed at all after her first husband Paul died.

But she does have something going for her that most people don't—the uncanny sense of a bloodhound in sniffing out when something is just a bit *off* in really any aspect of life.

I should've guessed that, after I put them off for several days, she and the girls would show up at my door, but they've been so busy that I thought I had a little time before it happened.

When I open the door, I'm careful to make sure I sound breezy and comfortable. "What on earth are you three doing here? I thought you were too busy to accost old ladies these days." I lean against the doorframe so they can't just push past me without taking a risk of knocking me over.

"You've been putting me off, and it's weird you never want to meet here." Amanda arches an eyebrow.

"What?" I ask. "No way. I may not be a newlywed with

dogs and kids, but I also have things to do. I've just been busy."

Emery swivels her phone around so I'm looking at my own text to her about why I wasn't available to pick her up for breakfast yesterday. "You weren't washing your hair all day." Emery folds her arms. "You could have squeezed me in. And anyway, isn't that a lame excuse women gave for being busy like, a hundred years ago?"

I press my hand to the back of my hair, hoping that the subtle color I got to darken it from fading grey to a slightly richer and more luminous grey isn't too obvious. "I didn't say I was *washing* my hair. I said I was doing it. And I did."

"It does look nice." Amanda narrows her eyes. "Did your friend already get here?"

My laugh isn't totally normal, but hopefully they won't notice. "My friend? Are you still going on about Tommy?"

"See?" Emery jabs Maren. "He is real."

"We were beginning to think Emery had made him up," Maren says. "She said that when she answered the phone, he said he was coming to visit, but it's been months, and no one has ever shown up." Maren narrows her eyes. "We've been watching."

Like hawks, in fact, which is just more motivation for me to keep Tommy away from them. They're too interested. "He's real," I say. "I just haven't had the time or energy to want to host anyone lately."

"But now school has started up again," Maren says. "We've been so busy, how would we even notice if he did come?"

She's often overlooked as the pretty one, but she has a surprising amount of insight in some areas, just like her mother. I like to think that Maren's the one who surprises you, like a sneak attack. I paste a smile on my face. "I'll be sure to let you know if Tommy ever does make it out to Manila. You can count on that."

"Why haven't you invited us in?" Amanda asks. "We've

been standing here like traveling Bible salesmen for five minutes." She's peering around my shoulder now.

Curse her and her stupid bloodhound instincts.

I shake my head. "I was going through some things and the house is a terrible mess."

Jed, my black and white potbelly pig bumps at my leg, opening the door just a hair wider.

"It looks fine to me." Emery peers around my shoulder. "Except for that huge painting? I've never seen it before. Is it new?"

I grit my teeth. "It was in storage. I thought I'd try it out."

"Ooh, I want to see it." Amanda tries to push past me, inadvertently stepping on Jed's foot when I refuse to budge.

Jed starts howling like, well, like a stuck pig, and Amanda's scowl deepens. "Why won't you let us in? What's going on?"

"Just give me a few days," I say. "I'll explain what's going on then."

Amanda folds her arms and huffs. "Why? Are you sure you won't be *dead* in a few days? Skipping town again, are you?"

"I promised I'd never do anything like that again." I still refuse to regret it, but that decision definitely caused a major breach of trust I'm still paying for today. "I'm not doing anything bad. I just need a little space." I can't help muttering, "Something that seems to be in short supply around here."

Amanda backs up, gesturing to the girls. "Let's be respectful of her wishes and just go." Her sigh is beleaguered, but it sounds like defeat. Thank goodness.

I'm locking the door with an exaggerated sigh of my own when Jed heads for the fridge, clearly wanting treat compensation since I didn't let him play with the girls. I'm rummaging around looking for a plum—I'm almost sure I had one left—when I hear a strange rustling on the back porch.

Before I even realize what's happened, Amanda bursts through my back door and shouts, "Aha! I guess you forgot that I have the back door key." It only takes her a few seconds to blink and shuffle forward to let the girls in before her jaw drops. "What in the world is going on with your house?" She spins around on Emery. "A painting? That's all you noticed?"

"You just can't let anything go." I want to kick her, but the person who really deserves a kick is me. The back door. It's such a basic move. I should have seen it coming and done the deadbolt.

"You're being so weird," Maren says. "Almost as weird as Mom."

Emery's pointing, her eyebrows raised. "I told you the painting was of the Eiffel Tower, and look! It's huge!"

The painting now hanging over the sofa fills half the wall. I had no idea it would be that large when I ordered it, which is really at the heart of the problem with all internet ordering. Unfortunately, Manila is still a complete dead zone for home decor. Unless you want a t-shirt that says, "I run like the Wind(ed)," or a sign for your laundry room that says, "Please excuse the noise and mess. The kids are making happy memories," you're pretty much out of luck. That's all the True Value carries.

"The wooden giraffe is stranger than the painting," Maren says. "And what's up with the huge gourd vase things?" She's grimacing and turning around slowly. She has never looked more like her mother in her entire life.

"Is that a *tiger* rug under the coffee table?" Amanda can't decide whether to laugh or cry, and I'm not sure which would be worse.

"I'm old," I say. "I like to change things around now and again. I only have a little time to enjoy myself before I die."

"It looks like Pier One threw up in here," Amanda says. "And not in a good way."

"Do people ever use puke analogies to describe something good?" I wish I could shoo them out, but now I'm pretty much stuck with them attacking everything.

"Is that a plaid blanket?" Maren starts for the family room, her hand outstretched.

This is only going to get worse. "I can tell you don't like my new decor, but it's not really—"

"This has something to do with Tommy, doesn't it?" Emery's question is soft, as if she wanted to ask it at a level that's just for my ears.

It freezes me.

I've spent a lifetime trying to be different from my parents. I don't lie about everything, especially to people who matter. Except for the whole dying thing, I guess. But that was really important.

And so is this.

"It is about Tommy," I finally confess. "He's coming to visit tomorrow, and I need you guys to leave me alone while he's here."

Amanda looks hurt—badly hurt. That's what I was trying to avoid. The one time I lied to her, even though it was to help get through her big old pigheaded stubbornness, it almost broke our relationship. I still wonder if we'll ever fully recover.

I decide, in that moment, to let them in on the secret. I hate admitting my lie, but I'm not sure what else to do. It's the only way they might possibly understand, and it's really my only remaining play.

"Can you all just sit?" I point at the family room, cringing a little at the tiger rug.

"Is that a real tiger?" Maren's peering at it as if it might miraculously regain its strength—and skeleton—and attack her, but they do finally all sit, like peas in a pod, all lined up, prim and proper on the couch.

I sit across from them on a chair. "Tommy Collins is, other than Jed, my oldest friend. And unlike Jedediah, we were never romantically involved. Actually, I was never romantically involved with Jed, either. The point is, I know Emery got excited. I understand why. It probably felt like a story from some movie. It's not. He's just an old friend."

Amanda cuts her gaze sideways, meeting Emery and Maren's eyes. "What does that have to do with—"

"I'm getting there," I say. "Just be patient." I stand up, needing to move as I speak. Or maybe it's that I hate the pressure of their eyes, staring at me. "When I was going through all the high school drama—dating Clyde and dealing with Jed hating me during and after, I only had one person to talk to."

"Tommy," Emery says.

I nod.

"And that's when you fell for him?" Maren asks. "Because Emery says he's really good looking."

"Pshaw," I say. "Nothing like that."

"And what does that have to do with all the bizarre decorations?" Amanda pokes the carved wooden elephant on the coffee table with her foot. "Because *none* of this goes together, and you are *so* not helping me with any design stuff at the resort anymore."

"I gathered these things myself on my extensive travels," I say.

"What extensive travels?" Amanda asks. "And how can that be?" She frowns. "None of this was here when we lived here, and all the stuff you'd collected and stuffed in boxes burned up with the shed when you left."

I clear my throat. "This stuff was in a storage room at the time."

Maren blinks. "There's a room we didn't know was—"

Amanda stands up, spearing me with a glare. "Make some sense, please, or we're taking you to the hospital to get you checked out. This is exactly the kind of nonsense someone who's losing function would say."

I collapse into the chair. "You all know that I haven't traveled anywhere. I spent my entire pathetic life right here, but while I settled in after high school, helping my parents and running the ranch for them, my best friend Tommy went out into the world. He would write me letters each week, and after a few years, he started threatening me."

"Like, some kind of murder threats?" Amanda blinks. "Why?"

I snort. "Nothing like that. No, he said he would come back home and tell Jed how I felt, unless I did it myself."

"He—what?"

"I couldn't risk him doing that, so at first, I told him that I wasn't even home. When I was younger, I always talked about wanting to see the world, and he knew that. So I started sending him letters recounting my travels."

"You. . ." Amanda sits again, shaking her head. "You told him you'd been. . .where exactly?"

"Oh, you know, everywhere. Africa. Europe. India. Asia. South America." I scrunch my nose. "I had to put him off for a while. Every time I said I came home, he'd threaten to come tell Jed again."

"And you supposedly got all this horrible stuff on those trips?" Maren frowns. "Because it all looks brand new. It's not even dusty."

"Well, I stored it carefully in the spare room." I can't help my growl. "And dust wipes off, which you would know if you ever cleaned."

Emery peels a sticker I missed off the back of the elephant. "I suppose Tommy might not have noticed this." She hands me the price tag.

I snatch it out of her hand and shove it into my pocket. "I knew you wouldn't understand."

"Let me get this straight," Amanda says. "Your oldest living friend thinks you spent the last sixty-something years traveling around the world?" She shakes her head. "How dumb is he?"

"No," I say. "He thinks I went to all those places, and then. . ." I sigh. "Look, I can't ask you to lie for me, so I think it's better if you just don't meet him. He's only coming into town to sell me his old family land. He's hung onto it all this time, but he's ready to sell, finally."

"I think there's something else," Amanda says. "I think you told him something worse than the lie about the traveling, something so bad that you don't even want to tell us what it is." She leans toward me, bracing her hands on her knees. "Spill it, Mandy, or we'll be sure to stalk your house like, well, like *tigers* until we figure it out." She holds up her hands like they're paws next to her face and says, "Rawr."

I wouldn't put the stalking past her. It's not much worse than sneaking through the back door when I'd already kicked them out. My nostrils flare, and I ball my hands into fists, but that bothers my arthritis. The problem is, if they figure out my bigger lie by coming here and visiting with Tommy, he'll probably realize it's not true as well.

I'm stuck, really.

I've already been caught.

Now all I can do is mitigate the damage.

"How about I go ahead and make you a deal?" I ask. "I'll create a college fund for both Emery and Maren, and in exchange, you guys never ask me about this again?"

"Like you're not going to do that already." Amanda frowns. "Out with it. What horrible lie did you tell him?"

"I think I already know," Emery says.

Everyone stares at her. "You can't possibly," I say.

She frowns. "You lived with him when you faked your

death. You've known him for a long time. You told him you were traveling around the world. You wrote him letters every week. He was looking at you just like Jed was in that photo. . ." She shrugs. "I think he liked you a great deal, and I think he left because it was too hard to watch you pining after Jed."

"That's ridiculous," I say. "First of all, he left when his father died, and secondly, there's no way that Tommy—"

"He told you he'd come out here and tell Jedediah how you felt if you didn't do it, right?" Emery arches one eyebrow.

"I said that already." I fold my arms.

"So you told him that you did tell Jed, and the obvious next step is to tell him that you're getting married—you and Jed, I mean."

I can't help my gasp. "You must have snuck in here and read my letters." I want to throw them out. I want to break something. "There's no way you could have guessed that without—"

Emery shakes her head. "Tommy Collins was in love with you, but you didn't know it. The only thing that kept him from coming out and telling you that. . .was your lie about Jed."

She's right about my lie, but not about Tommy. He was just being a good friend, and in his mind, it worked. "I did tell him Jed and I were together," I say. "But you're wrong about the other part. I'm absolutely sure that Tommy Collins never liked me."

Amanda sits down again, slowly. Then she pops her feet up on the coffee table. "I'm going to need you to sit down."

I drop my hands on my hips. "Why?"

"Because you have some explaining to do if you want to convince us that you're right, and that much pacing might overload your heart."

🦋 3 🦋

HELEN

My own mother has come to visit me exactly three times in my forty plus years of life. She emailed me about the visit several times—once to get permission—before each of her trips. I did convince her to ambush Abigail in an attempt to stave off the Steve blunder, but otherwise, the Fosters aren't big on surprises.

"Helen!" David's mother opens her arms wide like she thinks we're going to *hug*.

I was led to believe Koreans were a little more reserved, especially the wealthy ones. Did K-dramas lie to me? "Mrs. Park," I say. "What a wonderful surprise."

Mr. Park steps toward me, one hand extended. "We like to surprise David sometimes, and now that means you as well."

I shake his hand, happy to see that at least they know the normal American etiquette for someone you've never met. "Like an unplanned audit."

Mr. Park's laughter is loud and booming, an exaggerated version of his son's, honestly. And he has aged well—really well, since he has an older daughter too.

"We wanted to check over the business, of course, because you mentioned an acquisition on the phone, but then we never heard anything more about it." Mrs. Park gestures toward the conference room table.

I sit, but I can't help noticing that David has been entirely quiet since summoning me. "Surely David mentioned that I was on my way to Los Angeles for a meeting?" I glare at him. "A meeting that was hard to get."

"Isn't that why we have private jets?" David's smiling, but it looks a little pained.

"We told David that just a few hours of your time would help us feel much better about things." Mrs. Park sits across from me, like we're about to discuss a business deal. Then she looks at me expectantly.

Are we talking about business? "I'm sorry—what things exactly do we have to discuss?" I hate feeling like I failed to read a memo that was marked urgent.

"My son isn't young, and you're even older than he is." Mrs. Park leans closer. "You called me a few months back and told me that you were getting married, but we haven't heard a single peep about it since. We've been patient, but as far as I can tell, you've made no progress whatsoever in pinning things down."

Pinning things. . . "Do you mean, like setting a date?"

Mrs. Park blinks. "Surely you two have chosen a date already."

"Helen and I both have busy schedules," David says. "We were just so happy to be engaged that—"

Mrs. Park grabs my hand, pulling it toward her. "What is this?" She's peering at the ring David had custom made for me at Tiffany's. It's supposed to be a tiny shackle. "What on earth is this?" She snaps her head toward her son, who's now sitting beside me. "No wonder she's not rushing to marry you. You bought her the ugliest ring I have ever seen. Americans care about this kind of thing. You've embarrassed her."

"Mom, it has a special meaning." David's *finally* starting to look a little annoyed, but he's about an hour late, if you ask me. Which Mrs. Park will surely do any minute.

"What's the meaning?" She tilts her head. "Does it symbolize that your relationship is mechanical? Or is it something to do with garbage?" She purses her lips.

Mr. Park clears his throat. "You're being worse than my mother."

Mrs. Park's eyes fly wide, and she rounds on her husband. She's speaking Korean far too fast for me to understand what she's saying, but he sure earned himself an earful. At least he freed my hand. I was about two seconds away from gnawing it off at my wrist just to escape.

"Listen," I say in a short lull. "David and I aren't even sure that we're getting married."

Mrs. Park freezes.

So does her husband.

David grunts next to me.

"If you think about it, from a business perspective, unless an acquisition by my company makes sense to grow your group, there's really no reason for us to get married. When David and I looked into the numbers, your strengths and ours. . ." I shrug. "I mostly acquire undervalued companies so I can sell them off or fix them up and *then* sell them off. You have a totally different growth strategy, which is admirable, and your company isn't undervalued, so—"

"You can't sell our company off." Mrs. Park's consonants are clipped.

"Exactly," I say.

"So you're breaking up?" Mr. Park frowns.

David laughs. "No, Dad, we aren't breaking up. She's just not planning to acquire our American branch at this time."

Mr. Park blinks. "And because our company isn't undervalued, you're not getting married?"

"The only good reasons to get married are to solidify an

unequal merger or acquisition," I say, "or if you're having children."

"Exactly." Mrs. Park smiles. "Most Americans don't understand, but your parents raised you properly."

I frown. "Which is why we don't need to get married."

Now Mrs. Park and Mr. Park are both frowning. "Are you saying you never plan to have children?"

"I've been very clear with David that I don't want—"

"To be forced into anything," David says. "We're going to let things happen as they happen." He stands up. "And on that note, my lovely girlfriend has a meeting in the morning and there's a long way for her to go before she gets there."

"Right." I stand up, not as relieved as I expected to be. "Yes, I do need to go."

"And while she's hard at work, I'll show you around the resort," David says. "I think you'll find that everything meets the international standard. . .or exceeds it."

"Forget the international standard," Mrs. Park says. "You're too old to be taking things as they come." She stands, bracing her hands against the top of the table. "How old are you exactly? Because with every year you go past forty, the chances that you'll have a child decrease. You should be involving the best doctors in the country. You need to work on this immediately."

"If you don't want to get married, well." Mr. Park shakes his head in disgust. "But at least think of the next generation."

"Of course we're doing that, Mom," David says. "Helen is the smartest person I've ever met—she's the smartest person *you've* ever met. You can be sure that we're handling things in the best way."

He actually winks at me as he ushers his parents out the door. I'm still fuming as I walk out and head for the stairs. Before I can start down them, David jogs down the hall. "Helen, wait."

I whip around, my eyes flashing, I'm quite sure. "What in the world was that—"

He grabs my face with both hands and kisses me. It's irresponsible, it's irritating, and it works far better than it should. With his mouth on mine, I can almost forget his ludicrous show of cowardice and idiocy in that conference room.

Almost.

When he finally releases me, my knees a little weak, my head spinning, I blink once. "What was that—"

"To remind you why you love me."

"Your parents are—"

"Horrible? The worst?" He sighs. "It's a miracle I've kept them away as long as I have, honestly. I thought they'd show up right after you called them from my phone in New York."

"But you told them we're *handling* things," I say. "And we have no plans to get married, much less have *children.*" I'm sputtering. "I have an IUD, David, and I'm forty-four. The chances of me getting pregnant, even without an IUD at my age are—"

He kisses me again, but it's shorter this time. "Helen Fisher, I love you. I love your stubborn streak. I love your passion. I love your fury. I even love when you make that face that warns me that you're about to attack. I know you have no plans for children, but I also know that telling my parents that would set us up for a war I don't want to fight."

I can't help blinking. Several times. "But then. . ."

"I've done this with them my entire life. If you just keep tabling the discussion, you win by default."

"You're not going to tell them that we aren't planning a wedding *or* kids? You'll just keep letting them fly out here and accost us?"

"They're busy a lot. They don't come out very often." He shrugs. "For better or worse, I'm the younger child. Ninety-nine percent of their crazy lands on my sister, who's almost your age, by the way, and still childless. In our culture, we're about the worst two kids you could possibly imagine. So I let her deal with their nonsense and I live my life in peace almost all year long."

"But if you—"

"You don't get it. I win without fighting with them at all. I nod, and I give vague answers, and instead of fuming and threats, they think we're on the same page. Then I do what I want. It's really for the best." He shakes his head. "Don't worry. There's a reason I moved to America and almost never go back to Korea. I like it here—everyone lets kids make their own decisions. They act like we have a right to choose things in our own life." He beams.

He's so gorgeous when he smiles, and he knows his parents better than I do. "Fine." I would never ask him to understand the profound damage my parents inflicted on me and Abby, so I suppose I shouldn't expect to understand how he handles his. "I'm going to LA, and I'm not going to think about babies at all while I'm there."

He's still smiling as he bites his lip. "I mean, don't think about babies, but you could think about practicing making them."

I can't help my laugh. He's a grown man, but he's still a teenage boy. "I'll only be gone for a day. Let's get dinner tomorrow and I'll tell you everything I thought about on my trip."

Only, on the way to my jet, and on the flight to LA, I'm not thinking about David and his impossibly beautiful face or his improbably beautiful physique. I spend most of the flight thinking about what he said to his parents. Thinking about what he said to me.

Any way I slice it, I can't help wondering. . .what if he does the same thing to me? What if, when he agrees with me on things, he's really just saying what he has to say to keep me happy? I've thought this whole time that he was fine with me exactly as I am.

But what if my boyfriend, whom I love dearly, is going to resent me forever because I didn't marry him and pop out a kid? What if instead of placating his parents, all his vague assurances are really for *my* benefit?

It may be time to break up with the glorious David Park, and that thought leaves me feeling very, very broken inside.

4

MANDY

"It's not like I never thought about dating Tommy. He was tall, good-looking, and smart. After Clyde dumped me and left for college, I spent my entire junior and senior year being ignored by Jed, and Tommy was really my only friend. *Of course* I thought about him that way, but I knew he didn't like me like that, so I stopped considering it almost as soon as I thought about it in the first place."

"But how did you know?" Maren asks.

"Yeah, what did he say, exactly?" Emery asks.

"There's no way she remembers after all these years," Amanda says.

She's right of course. Memory blurs things, but there are a few memories that I hold dear. A few memories that are still bright and haven't faded with age. Most of those memories are the ones with Tommy in them.

"Why do you look like that?" Emery asks.

"Like what?" I frown.

"Like you're looking at something we can't see?" Emery cranes her head around, staring at the wall.

"I was zoning out," I say. "Thinking back a little."

"On what?" Emery's half-smiling, and then she claps.

"Ooh, I know. I bet you're thinking about a time when you wondered if he liked you."

My jaw drops. Is she telepathic?

"I knew it." Emery sits again. "Now tell us."

"Tell you what?"

"All about that moment, the one where you thought maybe Tommy liked you back." She's beaming.

Maren and Amanda are staring at me expectantly, and it makes me remember the very first time I ever really *wondered*.

The whole thing started with a news article, actually.

"Did you see this?" Tommy drops onto the seat next to me in the cafeteria and shoves a newspaper in my face. His dad's the only person in town who gets the Salt Lake Tribune. Everyone else does just fine having the Vernal Express show up a few times a month in the mail, but Mr. Collins insists it doesn't have reliable news.

I pick up the paper and scan the page. "The whole Berlin wall thing is really sad, but I don't know Ida, so—"

"No, no, not that." Tommy frowns. "I mean, that is really sad. That woman jumped out of her window to try and get free, but no. I'm talking about this." He taps the article below it.

The King and I Broadway Revival.

Not this again. "There's no way the Bishop's going to approve this for the church's roadshow. You asked last year, and—"

He's shaking his head. "No, not that, you dummy. Mrs. Rasmussen said we could do it for school." His eyes are practically shining. Of all the impractical careers in the world, Tommy wants to be a movie director one day.

"Are you serious?" *The King and I* has been popular for almost ten years, but a play about a man with ninety wives

26

and concubines who then falls in love with a white lady just isn't going to hit well in Manila, Utah, of all places. "I think that's a bad idea."

"It's what the rest of the world has been performing for a decade, Mandy. Can you imagine? Manila could finally catch up."

"I think we should just be happy we weren't drowned." I stand up and grab my bag. "But I'm happy you're happy."

Tommy hops to his feet. "I still can't believe they just made everyone from Linwood move—the dam could have been put somewhere else, and the whole town wouldn't have been flooded out."

We should be pleased—after all the Linwood people had to evacuate their homes, a lot of them moved to our area. Our tiny school grew by a third. "Anywhere they put the dam would have flooded someplace." I shrug. "That's just how life works."

"I guess," Tommy says. "But hey, I need you to help me with the play. I promised Mrs. Rasmussen I'd make fliers and help with whatever she needs."

"That sounds like a problem for you to deal with." I smirk as I head for math.

"Why are you leaving early?" Tommy frowns, clearly annoyed at having to jog along without having eaten his lunch. "You hate polynomials."

"I haven't finished my homework," I say.

"But you can't do it in the classroom. Mr. Ulrike will see you."

I shrug. "You got me. I'd rather get a zero on my math homework than sit in there while you badger me about the play that's never going to happen."

"Actually, it's a musical." He's back to smiling.

I groan. "That's even worse."

"You're the only junior who can really sing." He's skipping now, like the joy in his body simply can't be contained and is escaping against his will. "You have to at least try out for the role of Anna."

"No way." I can carry a tune, but I hate doing it in front of people. His idea is my worst nightmare.

"Come on." He blocks the door into math. "I'll give you whatever you want."

Just then, Jedediah Brooks reaches the door behind Tommy. "Excuse me."

For a split second, I think maybe he's talking to me, but then I realize he was asking Tommy to move. Tommy rolls his eyes, but he shifts so Jed can squeeze past. Before I can follow him in, Tommy whips back into place. "Not so fast." His finger is hovering in front of my face again, waggling toward my nose. "Anything you want, remember?" He's staring at me with wide eyes. "Just name your price."

"Get him to forgive me," I say. "And then I'm in." I mean, it *is* what I'd like, if pigs could fly, but it's also never going to happen. Which means I'll never have to be in the play.

I should have known that Tommy wouldn't give up just because I laid down an impossible gauntlet. I skip the tryouts on principle, but the next day, when they post the roles for the musical, next to the name Anna, it says Amanda Saddler, in big, bold black letters.

"You have got to be kidding me." I round on Tommy so fast that he actually stumbles back. "I didn't even *go* to the tryouts."

"Your reputation preceded you." He's half-smiling.

"Thomas Collins, you can't do that." I drop both hands on my hips. "I am *not* going to be in that musical."

"The cast list doesn't lie." He's beaming.

"Well, the joke will be on you when I never show for a single practice. You can take it up with the cast list."

When he drags me into the corner, one hand over my mouth, I think about biting him. Hard. "Just listen to me for a minute."

I shake my head and shove him off. "Not even for a half a second."

"You didn't see who's listed as the understudy for King Mongkut."

My voice sounds a little too loud and a little too shrill, even to me. But my sense of injustice is now enflamed. "Who cares?"

"It's Jedediah," he whispers. "And I'll get sick on the day of the play."

Wait. It's. . . "*You're* playing King Mongkut?"

He rolls his eyes. "I mean, for now, but only because Jed said he'd only be willing to be the understudy. But think about it! I can just say I'm sick. Then he'll have to take over." He grins. "And then you'll *have* to interact. King Mongkut's Anna's love interest."

"This is a terrible plan."

"He hasn't talked to you in over a year. Do you have a better one? Because I'm sick of watching you moping around."

I can't argue with that. Nothing else I've tried to get Jed to forgive me has worked.

"As an understudy, he has to step in and play the role at one practice a week, too. We can use that as well. He'll have to talk to you—or at least *at* you."

I'm rolling my eyes, but I'm listening. "It's not a horrible plan. I'm surprised he agreed to it."

Tommy's smile is diabolical. "I didn't play fair."

"What does that mean?"

"You know his mother loves plays, so when I bumped into them at Steinaker's Market, I talked to him about how amazing it was that Manila was finally catching up to Broadway, and oh, boy. She was so excited that he couldn't say no to the auditions."

"I know Jed. He could still have said no."

Tommy smirks and drops his voice again. "Not when she

said that she was so disappointed when *Clyde* didn't get a role in *Seven Brides for Seven Brothers*, and that was with *seven* guy roles."

"But they all had to sing, and Clyde can't sing at all."

"You're missing the point," Tommy says.

I'm not, though. He brilliantly used Clyde's failure and his mother's encouragement to goad Jed into auditioning, and then he somehow convinced him to take a role that forces him to interact with me weekly. He may not have granted my impossible wish yet, but he's gotten closer than I thought possible. "Fine."

"Fine. . .as in you'll do it?" His eyes light up, his longish hair falling over his brow again. He sweeps it back over the top of his head in a familiar gesture. "Say yes."

I nod slowly. "I guess so."

He pumps his fist. "Yes. This play is going to be amazing."

I'm afraid he may be dead wrong about that, but it might do something more lasting than any regular play could boast. It might fix things between me and Jed. I'm sure that if he would just start talking to me again, we could at least go back to being friends.

But when rehearsals start, Jed isn't there. When Mrs. Rasmussen starts the practice, pointing at me to start reading through the script, I hiss at Tommy. "Where is he?"

Mrs. Rasmussen shoos Tommy away. "You're not in this scene." I'm stuck practicing the opening act with Tommy and the other members of the cast, and Jed's nowhere to be found.

"What was that?" I finally ask, after practice is over. "You said—"

Tommy grabs my bag and carries it outside. He always does things like that. He's basically taken over doing all the things Jed used to do. "Jed's going to be here every Thursday. It's the only day he doesn't have football or basketball practice."

"But—"

"Look, I know you took this to get Jed to forgive you, but he's an understudy and you still have to do the whole play or it won't work," he says. "It's not like this whole thing's one big sham, and he's the only one not in on it."

I grudgingly admit that he's right. It doesn't make the play rehearsals any less onerous. But when Thursday comes around, Jed's there, as promised, and we work on the *Getting to Know You* song almost the entire time. It's a little frustrating learning dance steps and singing, but Jed's watching, and little kids in the play are cute.

It could be worse. Way worse.

I didn't really want to do this play, but some of the kids actually crack me up. There's this one, the little girl who's playing Princess Yink, King Mongkut's most beloved daughter, who is absolutely adorable. Her name's Dolores Gibbens, and she's obsessed with plants, and she always carries around a little crocheted kitten. At first Mrs. Rasmussen tried to take it away, but she wouldn't practice without it, so she just let it go. I'm not sure whether they had kittens in Siam, but I doubt the audience will know either.

When we finally finish the song and begin to work on the scene where Mrs. Leonowens, which is me, tells the King that she gave his son, the prince, the book *Uncle Tom's Cabin*, and that she's opposed to slavery, Jed's forced to stand up and talk to me. It's written right there in the script.

"Why aren't you looking at her?" Dolores asks. "Shouldn't you be looking at her?"

"Yes." Mrs. Rasmussen drops her hands on her hips. "I heard that you two had a falling out. Are you going to be capable of doing this play, Mister Brooks? Or do I need to cast another, more cooperative understudy? Because *you* are replaceable, but she is not." She arches one eye and compresses her lips.

Jed looks at his feet, still not willing to meet my eye.

"Your mother was just asking me today how the play was going." Mrs. Rasmussen taps the table in front of her with her fingers. "In fact, she told me that her parents are coming to watch on the off chance you get to perform." She arches that eyebrow again. "But I can tell her, when next I see her, that you're just not able to bring yourself to—"

"No." Jed straightens. "It's fine. It'll be fine."

"Well, you'll have to turn toward Mrs. Leonowens, channel your most regal and arrogant thoughts, and speak clearly. Try to remind yourself that this is not Amanda Saddler, it's Mrs. Anna Leonowens. Do you think you can do that?" Mrs. Rasmussen sounds like she has her doubts.

"It's fine," Jed says. "I'll do it."

And when we resume, he does. He looks right at me and says, "Shall Mister Lincoln be winning this war he's fighting at present?" He lifts both eyebrows.

"No one knows, really," I say, staring right back at him.

Jed looks a little uncomfortable when he says, "Does he have enough guns and elephants for transporting them?"

"I don't think they have elephants in America, Your Majesty," I say.

The children all laugh. It irritates Jed, I think, but Mrs. Rasmussen claps. "That was wonderful. You're a natural at this, Jedediah. You have a sort of grumpy energy that really works for King Mongkut. It's why I chose you for the understudy. Keep channeling that sense of indignation, just as you have been, and you'll be perfect."

Jed smiles, then. Everyone loves to be praised, I think, but Jed more than most. All of his parents' attention always went to Clyde. I don't think I realized quite how starved for affection he was until this moment.

Not that I pity him. He's the one ignoring me. But now, when he reads his next line, I see his attendance here for what it is. Hope that he'll get some recognition for once. "No elephants in America?" He sounds horrified.

32

"None." I shrug.

"No wonder he's not winning." Jed sighs like it's the saddest thing he's heard, not to have an army full of elephants for gun hauling and whatever else elephants do in war.

We run through the scene a few times, and he gets better each time, playing on and expanding the things he gets right. A part of me wishes Tommy could just bow out now. A few more practices like this, and maybe. . .

But the second Mrs. Rasmussen dismisses us, Jed shuts down, like a light that's electricity has been cut off. He just goes dark.

"You did great today," I say, trying to get him to look at me again.

He shoves his script in his bag and loops around me.

"Jed," I say. "Wait."

But he doesn't. He's out the door and swinging a leg up over his bike seat before I can even grab his arm.

Tommy's waiting by my bike, already holding my bag—his backpack on front and mine on his back. "Give it time. Rome wasn't built in a day."

"You're not a thousand years old." I huff. "You don't know how long it took."

He's laughing as he hops on his ancient bike and takes off, creaking and squeaking along behind me.

"You should stop taking me to my house," I say. "It's way out of the way for you."

"I don't mind," Tommy says, breathing a little heavy. "My mom would kill me if I didn't."

"If you didn't," I counter, "Jed might actually take me home. He lives next door, remember?"

"And if he doesn't step up, you'd have to go all the way alone, which I won't risk." Tommy said the same thing every single day of rehearsals, and although Jed did get better and better about looking at me and saying the proper lines during practice, he didn't soften at all after Mrs. Rasmussen dismissed us.

Until the day we practiced the scene where someone calls King Mongkut a barbarian. On that day, after seeing how the king's unable to admit when he's wrong, how both of them have to pretend he's right when he's not, I've had about enough of Jed acting like I don't exist when we're not reading lines. He may be playing a prince, but he certainly isn't one in real life.

The second Mrs. Rasmussen dismisses us, I leap in front of him and grab his bag. I'm out the door and almost to his bike when he finally calls my name.

"Amanda!"

"Mandy, that's not yours," Tommy says, as if he thinks I don't know whose bag I'm stealing. He's always been a great liar. It's why he's great at acting and directing.

"Wait, isn't it?" I turn toward Tommy. "Yeah, I think it's mine for sure." I sling the straps over my shoulders. "Now, let's go home. I have homework to do. And we have that big test in English tomorrow. I need to finish studying."

Out of the corner of my eye, I can see that Jed's fuming.

"Unless." I freeze. "Did you want to *guess* who else's bag it might be, Tommy?"

He's suppressing a smile, which is classic. "I think *you* ought to guess, Your Majesty."

"That's enough," Jed says. "Give me my bag."

"Did you hear something?" I ask. "It almost sounded like someone was talking to me, but that can't be. There's no one here who *does* talk to me."

"I can talk to her," Jed says, "but even if I do, it doesn't change anything." He's staring at Tommy. "It'll just make things even harder. Tell her to drop it."

We all stand like that for at least thirty seconds, maybe longer, before I finally toss the bag on the ground in disgust.

"Someone who knows how stupid he's being and doesn't fix it is the biggest idiot of all."

Jed takes his bag, gets on his bike, and pedals off.

"This whole thing is a waste of time," I say.

"The play?" Tommy's shoulders droop, the strap from one side of my backpack sliding off.

He's been trying so hard—the whole thing was his idea. He wants to help, so it's not his fault that Jed's a bull-headed idiot.

Standing outside the school, one hand on his bike, two backpacks strapped to him, Tommy looks like the kind of person who slays dragons. The kind of person who doesn't run away when things are hard. The kind of person who I *should* be spending my time on instead of the stubborn moron who just rode away.

That's the moment when I realize that I might *like* Tommy Collins.

5

MANDY

Since the day Clyde told me he was leaving for college.
. .and we needed to break up, I've regretted going
with him to that homecoming dance. Sure, we had a
fun year. Clyde's like a basset hound set to sniff out excitement, and that makes him the constant center of attention.

When you're with him, people orbit around you, too.

But sometimes when we were together, I still felt
strangely lonely, even while surrounded by a crowd. Everyone's attention was on him, not me, and I felt almost like a
decoration. I didn't like that feeling.

When he left me, I figured Jed would finally forgive me.
He'd take pity on how I'd been cast aside, and he'd come back
around. He never did, of course. In fact, if anything, after
Clyde left, Jed acted like he was angrier. He wouldn't even
look at me in class. He sat all the way on the opposite end of
the cafeteria at lunch. He would pretend he couldn't even
see me.

That made me look at him more, and comparing him to
his brother was something I couldn't help doing. He wasn't
quite as tall, but he was still the tallest boy at Manila High
School. His features weren't quite as sharp or as bright as

Clyde's, and he didn't command the attention of everyone in the room. But he did play basketball nearly as well, and he had a sort of quiet dignity his brother never had.

Clyde scored better than Jed on tests and homework assignments, but I'm not quite sure why. He always knew the answers to every question he was asked, and he was at least as bright. Maybe it was that Jed never cared about his grades, because he had no intention of leaving for college. Either way, once Clyde was gone, I realized exactly what I had lost for my year of fame.

My best friend.

Someone I could trust.

The only person who really saw me.

But none of my efforts—not bribery, cajoling, group project manipulation, or even trying activities he liked in the hopes of seeing more of him—made any difference. Where my best friend used to be, there was a very handsome, very angry brick wall.

Tommy's play actually got the brick wall talking, briefly, but no matter how hard I doubled down, I kept smashing my nose. Until I finally stopped trying to force it. After I tried to steal his backpack and he still wouldn't talk to me, I gave up.

Miraculously, once I stop pressing, he finally seems to relax. In fact, on the one day a week that Jed comes to practice, I can almost pretend that we're like before.

Uncomplicated.

Best friends again.

Healed from my bad decisions.

While we're in rehearsal, he smiles at me when King Mongkut would, and it's the exact same smile I've always known. It's as familiar as my own kitchen counter. As familiar as the bench seat of my dad's car. Something in my heart eases as his anger seems to fade, and I wonder whether we might be making some real progress, finally.

Jed's always been the brother I felt safe with. He was the

brother who cared about me, no matter what. It feels like I'm getting a little bit of that back.

And that confuses me.

At the beginning of the year, I thought I liked Jed. I thought that's why he was angry with me—he liked me too, and I chose wrong. But can I like more than one person? No, right? So what do I feel about Tommy? Liking Clyde is what ticked Jed off last time. As the play approaches, I start to wonder: if I had to pick between them, which one would I choose?

And as it turns out, I do have to choose.

Tommy comes and asks me just before the dress rehearsal to pick one of them. "Do you still want me to 'get sick'?" He makes air quotes with his fingers. "Or no?"

I'm just choosing which one should play King Mongkut, but still, it feels meaningful in some way.

Tommy's a better actor, but he's done several plays. His parents won't care much whether he does the performance or sits out. To Jed, this could change how everyone sees him— his mom, the other students, and maybe even himself. I also agreed to do this whole thing to try and mend the unhappiness between me and Jed.

I ignore the part of me that wants to perform with Tommy. "Yes, get sick so he can do it."

Tommy stares at me calmly. "You're sure that's what you want, right?" His gaze is steady, his eyes intent.

"Right," I say. "That's always been the plan."

"Do you think after the play, he'll quit being so stupid? Do you think doing the whole thing will convince him to forgive you?"

"I think that the one time we really worked on the *Shall we Dance* scene, Jed looked at me—actually looked at me." I sigh. "I think if he'll just let go of his anger, he'll finally forgive me, yes. I don't know whether the play will be enough, but I'd like to try. If nothing else, we'd be working together on something again."

Tommy stands still, frozen for a moment, staring.

"I know you're a better actor," I say.

Tommy frowns.

"But Jed and I were friends for so long." I sit down on the ground, my head leaning against the wall. "We played Monopoly every single day for like three summers. We helped each other with our chores. We studied together. He came to my rodeos, and I went to his basketball and football games and cheered."

"We do those things now," Tommy says. "Well, except for the Monopoly thing."

I realize he's right. He does come help with my chores. And he eats most meals with me—lately, anyway. He studies with me. He rides in rodeos too, but he usually does calf roping, while I do racing. "If he ever gets over himself, you'll like him," I say. "He's funny and smart."

His broad shoulders droop a little, but he says, "I'll go tell him."

I can't help tiptoeing along behind him and peering around the corner when Tommy goes to tell Jed that he's too sick to perform. Jed's brow furrows when Tommy reaches him.

"Hey, man," Tommy says. "We should talk." He grabs his stomach.

Jed presses his lips together, his whole face pale. He looks like he's upset, but what could have made him mad?

"Why?" Jed asks.

"I know I said I only needed you to be the understudy, but you know why we have understudies, right?"

Jed frowns.

"The thing is, this morning when I woke up, my throat—"

Jed doubles over then and pukes all over Tommy's shoes. When he straightens, he's wiping his mouth.

"Are you. . ." Tommy backs up a little. "You're sick?"

The groan Jed makes can't be faked.

"Go home, right now." Mrs. Rasmussen comes tearing around the corner, her eyes wide. She barely stops in time to avoid slipping on the puddle of bright orange puke. "Oh." She throws her hand up over her mouth. "Get Nelson in here. Throw some shavings on it for now, and I'll come sanitize it later. We've got to start if we're going to have time for a full run through."

Nelson, when he arrives, looks like he wants to cry.

I don't really blame him.

"Well." Tommy turns around. "I guess best-laid plans of mice and men and all that."

Which is how, when the curtain goes up—or rather, with our little theater, when it slides to the side—I'm preparing to meet Tommy as King Mongkut, not Jed.

The dress rehearsal goes pretty smoothly, other than two small wardrobe malfunctions for some of the ensemble, but there's always something different about the real performance. You know your lines cold, you're surrounded by people who haven't heard each scene a million times, and all the things you kind of planned to do but don't really practice over and over, you're finally doing.

The full skirt I'm wearing swishes as I grab my son Louis's hand—really a bratty third grader who manages to annoy me constantly by popping his gum, stepping on my feet, and spitting out the wrong lines like a poorly behaved goat.

Luckily he's a tiny kid, so when he bumbles a line in the opening scene, everyone laughs.

When Tommy walks on stage for his first appearance, it's the first time he's been bare chested, his vest gaping wide open, his chest shining with some kind of oil, and I can't help staring.

Tommy plays football, too.

He ropes calves.

He's even on the basketball team, though he's not very good.

I should have assumed he would be in good shape, but I had no idea he was. . . He looks better than Clyde did with his shirt off. I almost fumble a line myself. I catch myself just in time, and the only person who notices is the bratty little kid playing my son.

"You're embarrassing," he mutters.

I squeeze his hand until he squirms. "Think about your own lines," I whisper.

Luckily, even with the bright lights and the stress of the audience, even the children who make up a large part of the cast do quite well. Little Dolores elicits dozens of awws from the audience when she leaps up into Tommy's arms, her father's favorite child. It's an easy transfer for her to be the audience's favorite actress, but it's also well-earned. She nails all the blocking and the lines.

And then it's time.

The King and I isn't strictly a romance, of course, as King Mongkut has more wives and concubines than anyone could ever hope to manage, and Anna Leonowens is a widow from England. But the story definitely shows that the two star-crossed lovers did care a great deal for one another, and that by the end, they respected one another. Indeed, the king changes important behaviors and allows her to teach his children revolutionary things.

I love that it's based on a true story.

So when I sing, "and shall you be my new romance?" I happen to glance over at Tommy, and he's staring at me intently. It makes something inside my stomach flip over.

My voice wavers.

And my voice *never* wavers. That's the one good thing about me. I never flub a song. Not in practice, not in performances, never. My voice is as steady as the sun in the summer.

Except in that moment.

Tommy steps toward me, his eyes wide.

But I forge ahead. I sing my last line or two and dance in circles around him, and then I stop. Tommy tells me to keep going, and I tell him I never dance that way, not at home.

That's when he says, "But you will dance with strange men, holding hands, etcetera."

He sounds so confused, so forlorn, that my half-laugh is genuine. "Well, yes, but not always a stranger. Usually a very dear friend or a loved one."

"Good," Tommy says, walking closer. "Then you'll show me. Teach, teach, teach."

"But I—"

"Teacher teach," Tommy says, his hands out.

"Well," I say. "It's quite simple, the polka. You just count one-two-three." And I take his hands.

I've done this scene a dozen times, but never with his shining chest exposed. Never with a million people watching. Never while he was looking at me like he wants to eat me. When his hands touch mine, it's like something I've never felt before runs through me. Whatever it is makes the hair on my arms stand on end. I inhale sharply, and his eyes fall down toward my mouth.

He noticed.

He's noticed that I'm reacting to him strangely.

But I have to keep going—the piano's keeping us on track. When I sing, "On a bright cloud of music, shall we fly?" my voice *cracks*. It's so embarrassing that I want to die.

Tommy squeezes my hand, and then he takes over for me, singing his part, the one-two-three and the shall we dance stanzas. Until I manage to join him with "Or perchance."

Then we can spin around, doing our own parts and movement until I ask again, "Shall you be my new romance?" And I turn to look at him, and his knowing half smile makes that thing in my stomach flip over *again*. Even harder this time.

Blessedly, I pull myself together well enough to sing the next part, and execute the little misalignments that make everyone laugh. Until then Tommy says, "That's not right. We're not supposed to be dancing holding two hands like this."

My voice is breathy and stupid when I say, "No, as a matter of fact. . ."

And then Tommy's hand reaches for my waist, his eyes intent on mine, and he says, "My hand should be here, like this." His half-smile, with those intense eyes. . .

I lose my breath. I can't even think. I simply stare at him.

"No?" he asks in a deep voice. "Like this?"

I can't even say yes. I just nod.

And he pulls me closer. And closer. Until our faces are right beside one another. I feel the minty cloud of his breath and the heat radiating off his body. I drop my eyes to his mouth, which is just a little open.

"I can't," he whispers. "I want to, but I can't."

"Can't what?" I whisper back.

And then the music surges and he sweeps me in a circle, and then more of them, swirling me around the dance floor smoothly, with the same grace I see when he ropes a calf, when he swings up on his bike carrying two backpacks, and when he forces horses to back up, move out, and spin effortlessly.

I'm barely able to breathe when we finally stop. He stares at me in a way I've never seen—it makes me feel things I've never felt. I can't help being grateful that Jed was sick.

I might have been confused before, but not now. All I can think about is Tommy. I definitely like him. I like him a lot.

He lifts one hand and brushes it against my cheek. "Shall we dance again?"

I'm laughing with joy when the curtain closes, and Tommy's hand is still on my cheek.

"That's enough, now." Mrs. Rasmussen grabs my wrist and drags me away. "Scene change."

But after the play, I'm determined that I will say something to him. I have to at least find out whether it's all just the magic of the play, or whether he might like me, too. I can just ask what he meant when he said he wants to but he can't. That's a normal question, right? It's not a line from the play.

But when the play ends, the audience swarms us. It's normal, for a small town like this, where everyone knows everyone. My parents brought me wildflowers, and even Tommy's mother brought blooms for him.

Jed's mother brought me daisies, and I can't help wondering where she found them. It's not like Manila has a florist. "Thank you so much," I say. "I'm so sorry Jed's sick."

"Oh, dear." Mrs. Brooks wrings her hands. "He told me I had to come anyway, and that the play is really something," she says. "He was so right. He really enjoyed working on it, to be honest. I bet you can get him to try out again for the next one."

By the time I finish talking to her, a half dozen other people are waiting to talk to me, and by the time I've finally thanked everyone for their kind wishes, I can't find Tommy at all.

"You're looking for Tommy, aren't you?" Mrs. Rasmussen asks.

I nod.

"I thought something looked. . .electric between you two." She's smirking, and I hate it.

"No, nothing like that," I say. "I just wanted to tell him that he did a great job."

"I think he left—Jed's mother had already left when we realized his lunch pail was still here. I didn't want him to worry about having lost it, so I asked Tommy to drop it off and tell him how the show went, too."

If I hurry home, maybe I can catch him on the way. Jed's

house is just before mine, anyway. My mom waves, but I point at my bike. "I'll meet you at home," I say.

There's no way I could have explained that I need to be let out by Jed's house. They'd either realize that I liked Tommy, or they'd worry that I liked Jed. Either way, it would have created too many questions I don't want to answer. So when my mom tries to tell me she and Dad can put my bike in the car, I'm stuck being forceful.

"Mom, I need to take a little ride to clear my head."

"But you'll be all alone," Dad says.

"Yes, the cows out here will pose quite the risk." I roll my eyes.

Finally, they relent, and I hop on my bike for the six-mile ride. I pedal like I've never pedaled before, turning a thirty-minute ride into more like twenty, I think. The whole way, I keep thinking about how Tommy looked at me.

It can't just be me who felt that, right?

He has to like me, too.

But when I reach the Brooks house, I still haven't caught up to him. I must have taken so long to leave that he got there and left before I ever even saw him. I just don't understand how I didn't pass him on the way back. The muscles in my legs are burning, and my lungs are heaving when I force myself to start pedaling again, this time, up the final hill to my house.

But just as I'm straightening out, I hear it.

Voices coming from around the back of Jed's house.

I drop my bike on the side of the road and jog across their dark, damp yard. A shiver runs up my spine at the thought that I can wait until Tommy has dropped off the pail, and then say I heard him, and I'm sure he'll insist on biking the rest of the way to my house alongside me.

He always does.

I'm stepping around the corner into the back yard when I realize the voices I'm hearing aren't happy ones.

"I already told you—I know you're sick, but are you also deaf? I *don't like Mandy*," Tommy says. "Most of the time I actually can't stand her, because the two of you are the most aggravating pair I know. More than anything else, I'm just so disgusted by all your back and forth that I could scream."

I want to drop down onto my bottom in the wet grass and cry.

Jed's standing like a statue on the back porch of his house, a dark figure silhouetted by a soft golden light. "You're lying. I saw how you looked at her. You just don't want to make me mad."

"If you think I'm afraid of making you mad, you're even dumber than I thought. I just don't like her—not the way you do," Tommy says. "She sings like an angel, and that's all I care about."

When he turns and walks away, I crouch behind a bush, hoping that the light from Jed's house will keep him from noticing me in the darkness.

For the first time since I set out on my bike, my luck holds. He walks right past me, and he doesn't even notice my bike on his way back down the road.

I trudge back to the road, climb on my bike, and pedal the rest of the way home slowly, ponderously, letting out all my tears and all my angst before I reach my house, where I have to pretend for my parents' sake that all is right with the world.

Even though everything feels so very, very wrong.

❧ 6 ❧

HELEN

My earliest memory is actually fairly clear. I'm not sure exactly how old I was, but somewhere around three years old, because of, well. What I heard.

My parents were arguing, and my mom, who was usually quite reasonable, was being so shrill that it woke me up. I dragged my blanket into the hall and was about to walk into the kitchen to ask them what was wrong, but something Mom said made me stop.

"I didn't even want Helen, but you insisted that I would change my mind."

She didn't want me? Want me to what?

"Well, I never did. You were wrong. And now you've done it *again*. You're going to wreck my chances at getting tenure, all because you can't seem to keep your hands off me."

"We're married," my dad said softly. "And you may not be glad you had Helen, but I'm happy we have her. She's a very smart little girl, just like her mother. And in a few years, when we're older, we'll be glad we had a child. It's an investment in our future happiness."

"Oh? And when's the last time an *investment* in our future

made you throw up in the middle of a faculty meeting? When's the last time you got passed over for a promotion because you were having a baby?" Mom stood. "Never. Which is so unfair. I hated being pregnant the first time, and this time, I'm doing something about it."

"I'm not saying you can't," Dad said. "I'm just saying that we should wait and think about it for a week."

Mom shoved Dad. "*You* wait."

"People say having two dogs makes the whole thing easier. Kids might be like that," Dad said. "Maybe having another one will make Helen easier to deal with. Another child could help level out her tantrums and mood swings."

"I can't believe I thought you were smart when we got married." Mom's eyes flashed. "But the good news is that it doesn't matter what you say. In California, I can do what I want, and what I want is to terminate this pregnancy."

Terminate. It meant to end. I knew that much.

It hit me then, what was happening. A boy at my preschool just had a little sister. They named her Olive. It was a bad name, because olives were gross. But my desire for a sister, which I had previously never realized I had, exploded inside of me.

"No!" I lurched into the kitchen, dropping my blanket so Mom couldn't get angry I was carrying it around. "You can't terminate my sister."

"Helen." Mom's eyes widened. "You—how long have you been standing there?"

"You can't kill her." I realized that tears were streaming down my cheeks. "I want a sister. And I want to name her Abigail. And I want to take her with me to the park. And she can sleep in my room. And I can get up and feed her. Okay? You can work, and Abigail will be my job."

Dad picked me up and cradled me against his chest. "Oh, Helen, you're too small to have a baby as your job."

I shook my head. "I'm not. If you can just have my little

sister, she can be my job, and Mom can work, and you can work too, and I'll take care of her. Okay? Please?"

Mom opened her mouth and closed it again.

Dad just swallowed.

"Please. Please don't kill my sister."

"It could be a boy," Mom said. "We don't even know. The baby's just a speck right now."

But to me, that speck was already my sister. I never let it go. I fought for that speck every single day, hard enough that my mom, who clearly didn't want to have another baby, kept her. Hard enough that when she was finally born, four years younger than me, I took my job seriously. I helped change her diapers. I cleaned up her dirty laundry. I helped make her bottles.

I never regretted fighting for Abigail's life.

But I did learn as I grew older that there were some people who should never have kids. My parents were certainly among them. And after I saw Abigail raise her children, I realized that in spite of wanting a sister so badly that it hurt, in spite of knowing that something was missing from my life, I was one of them, too.

Because I'm nothing like Abigail.

I could never give a child what it really needs. In my heart of hearts, I'm my mother's daughter. I might want to invest in my future happiness. I may wish I could be the kind of person who puts someone else's needs first. But any child that had me as a mother would suffer for it.

No, the babies of the world deserve Abigails, not Helens.

I can't help thinking about how natural Abigail is with her children, with little Nate, with all of them. I can see her, whipping them up in the air, cradling their heads naturally, without even thinking. I see her, patiently setting the contract she's reviewing aside so she can burp a baby. So she can read Gabe a book. So she can direct her kids how to clean up from dinner.

She doesn't snap.

She doesn't resent them for ruining her life.

No, she cherishes them. She sees the fleeting moments for what they are: beautiful and transient. She puts everything else behind what really matters, and those kids all know it in their bones. In their DNA. In a way Abigail and I never did, her children know that they're loved.

Unlike my mother, I'm not willing to be swayed. So if David's secretly trying to tell me that he knows I don't want children, but he thinks he can wear me down, he's sadly mistaken. I will never make the mistake my mother did. I will never bring children into this world only to disappoint and neglect them.

I will always do the thing Helen Fisher is best at doing. That's why I'm here right now. I'm about to convince one shareholder at a time, including the reticent, shy recluse I've tracked down to go ahead and sell me his or her shares so I can take this company over and make it into something great.

And make a lot of money from it. Let's not forget that part.

That's what Fishers do best. We take things over. We succeed. We impress. We exceed expectations. But we do not have children and raise them with love and tender care. Abigail managed it, because in her heart of hearts, she's different than me and Mom and Dad. She's better. She came through all the madness whole and healthy in a way I can't even fathom.

I do like to think I had some small part in that, but I often wonder whether it's true. Yes, I was a little kinder and gentler than my mom, but I was never there for her the way a person really needs. I never offered her what she has shown to her children—comfort, stability, and acceptance. Sacrifice and understanding. Those just aren't things Fishers are great at providing.

When I walk into the boardroom of the hotel this bizarre

McFarland person insisted on meeting me at, I square my shoulders and run through my arguments one last time. Instead of one man sitting at the table, McFarland, or possibly two, McFarland and his lawyer, there are more than six people waiting for me.

"Excuse me," I say. "I may be in the wrong room. I'm looking for a Mister or Missus McFarland. Pratt McFarland."

The men and women stand, but the one who speaks is a tall, handsome man at the front. "We named our group Pratt McFarland in the hopes that people would assume we were a single man." The man grins, and I realize that I know him.

It's Oliver, my business school boyfriend.

My very first boyfriend.

The one who stole my idea.

I was hoping that if I ever saw him again, he'd be fat and bald. If he also had bushy nose hair and a unibrow, well, that would not upset me. Unfortunately, he looks just fine. He also doesn't appear to be the least bit surprised that I'm here, so I assume that he's kept up with where I am and what I've been doing. He knows he'd have been better off helping me with my idea than he was stealing it and giving it to his dad. That gives me at least a small twinge of satisfaction.

I modify my presentation to address the fact that it's not a single person but a group, not letting on that I recognize Oliver or even know who he is. By the end of the meeting, they still won't sell me their shares, but they've at least agreed to vote with me when the time comes.

"It's been disappointing, really," a woman named Alexa Pratt says. "This company had so much promise, but Gonzago's imploding."

"It's time we do something about that," I say.

"I think we all heartily agree," Oliver says.

I don't leave anything to chance, of course, so I pull out the documents I prepared for this contingency. Once I have the proper signatures in place for their proxy, I stand. "It's been a pleasure, *Mister* McFarland." I'm smiling as I turn to leave.

"Helen, wait." Oliver jogs to catch up with me just before I walk out the door.

I turn around, glad I wore my four-inch heels so he's barely taller than me, and look him over as if I'm trying very hard to place him. "Yes?"

"It's me," he says. "Oliver—from Harvard."

"Oh," I say. "Right. Business School." I nod. "I knew you looked familiar."

He frowns. "Surely you remember—"

"I'm kidding, Oliver. Of course I know who you are." He was my boyfriend for nearly two years. He was the first person I thought I loved. I didn't really know what love meant, but losing him still really hurt. "What did you want?"

"Do you have time to go to dinner? I thought we could catch up."

"Catch up?" I lift my eyebrows.

He sighs, finally having the decency to look a little embarrassed. "I could apologize if you'll hear me out."

I purse my lips. "You could apologize for dumping me and then shamelessly stealing my idea, but I'm not sure what good it would do."

"I'll pay for dinner—anywhere you choose."

"Anywhere?" I arch one eyebrow.

He shrugs.

"Citrine and Mélisse," I say. "I loved Citrine, and I hear it's still excellent now that they've moved and joined forces."

He cringes a little, and that makes it worth it. For a split second, I wonder whether I ought to ask David whether it will bother him—me going to dinner with my ex. But then I think about the idea of a grown woman having to ask *permission* from someone to do something, and I want to burn this hotel down.

It'll be fine.

I'm only going with him in order to extract an ounce of flesh from someone who wronged me. Which is why, when I reach the restaurant in my own car and toss the key to the valet, I breeze past Oliver. "I'm not doing the tasting menu." I can't help my tiny smirk. "Prepare to pay through the nose."

"I expected nothing less," he says.

About five hundred dollars in appetizer and dinner selections and a thousand-dollar bottle of wine later, I'm ready for him to grovel.

"You know, I could have squashed your family's little bank into the ground." I fold my arms. "You should really be thanking me instead of apologizing. If I were a vengeful person, you'd be eating at McDonald's right now."

He laughs. "You're pretty impressive, but you're not God."

I whip out my phone. "Just for that, I'm calling Haverly and telling him—"

He grabs my wrist. "Fine. You are god, and my family and I are both very sorry and very grateful for your condescension. Happy?"

I put my phone away. "Is that it? That's the whole apology?"

"You were always a lot for me to handle," he says. "I knew you were glorious, but I was also a little jealous. So when I started telling my dad about your idea, and he thought it was mine. . ." He squirms. "I'm sorry. If I were a better person, I'd have told him the truth, but in that moment, all I could think about was the fact that my dad was finally proud of something I did."

"But he wasn't," I say. "It was never yours to be proud of."

"You can't own an idea," he says.

"You do like to think you can trust your boyfriend not to steal yours and then dump you." Coming here was a mistake. It's been a long time, but I'm still angry.

"Clearly you kept your best ideas for yourself." He picks up his hand like he's going to try and place it on mine, but he thinks better of it, thankfully, so I don't have to claw his eyes out. "You've done really, really well, Helen. Better even than anyone at HBS thought you would."

Luckily, they bring the wine. If they hadn't, I might have punctured the top of his foot with my stiletto as I left.

A glass or two later, I'm not nearly as angry.

"Is it true?" he asks, his cheeks a little rosy. I think he's had even more wine than me. He's totally the kind of guy who would try to drink more than his half of the bottle since he's paying and it's expensive.

Idiot.

"Is what true?" I ask. "About Vitality Plus, you mean?"

He waves his hand through the air dismissively. "No, no. I'm sure you're totally right about that, and I trust you to make us lots of money. I meant about David."

I freeze.

"Are you really dating that guy?" He looks at my hand, and more specifically, at the shackle on my ring finger. "Tell me that's not some kind of bizarre engagement ring."

"It is," I say. "Or at least, it's the ring he had custom designed by Tiffany's when he proposed and I said yes."

His mouth dangles open in a very satisfying way.

"Is it really that surprising? He's handsome, rich, kind, and talented."

"I'm not surprised you like him," he says.

My hands ball into fists. "Do you really want to piss me off again?"

"Oh, I don't mean that. Of course he'd like you. He's always been into women who are even cooler than he is. His sister and his mom run his company, by all accounts. No, I'm surprised you've stayed together, because by all counts, you're uniquely unsuited for one another."

"Unsuited?" I sniff. "You're really not making things better."

The scallops and truffle egg arrive just in time to keep me

from spearing him with my fork. I can't do something like that right in front of a witness after all, and it's so good that I calm down slightly. A moment later, the lobster bolognese comes, too, and it's the best thing I've had here yet. Eating always helps me retract my claws—probably a reflex because I have to be polite to the server.

Now that I look less angry, Oliver decides to do some damage control. "All I meant is that, unless you've somehow changed your mind, it's odd that Mister I-Adore-Children proposed to Miss I'll-Never-Have-Them. That's all I'm saying."

"David adores children?" I blink. "Why do you say that?"

Oliver laughs, and then he laughs some more. He actually has to wipe his eyes.

When the truffle risotto comes, I wonder whether we ordered too many dishes with truffles in them, but one bite and I'm a believer. "I feel like I'm missing something," I say. "I wasn't making a joke. What's so funny?"

"You weren't?" Oliver sets his fork down.

I shake my head. "He's great with my nieces and nephews, and I know his parents want us to have a kid, but he told me he's fine with not having any."

"Oh." He shrugs. "Well, great. If you've talked about it, I'm sure it's fine. Maybe it's all just for show."

But then I think about his parents and how he didn't tell them we aren't having kids. He didn't tell them anything at all. "He knows I'm in my forties," I say.

"Has he heard of IVF?" Oliver sounds incredulous. "Because I read about an eighty-year-old lady getting pregnant, like, in Africa or somewhere."

I roll my eyes. "I'm just saying, if he was really worried, he'd be pushing it now. It's pretty much already too late for me." Or at least, that's what I spent most of the night telling myself.

Oliver holds up both hands, palms facing me. "I call a truce. I didn't mean to pick a fight."

"But why do you think he loves kids so much?" Did he say something while we were in school? Would it even matter if he did? I mean, it's not like Oliver might know more than I do about my own boyfriend. Right? Right.

"I mean, I think everyone knows it." Oliver whips out his phone and starts tapping. He swivels it around. "I figured everyone in the world had seen these."

The video's playing on a tiny phone screen, but it's still quite clearly David Park, my handsome, well-spoken, kind-hearted boyfriend, er, fiancé, talking to the screen. . .while sitting in a room full of children.

"St. Jude?" I look away long enough to stare at Oliver. "You're saying he's, what? A spokesperson for St. Jude?"

"He was their largest single donor for the last three years," Oliver says. "Or, rather, his company was. He does these live fundraiser chats about twice a year, and he always features some of the kids he has met and helped, personally, and then tells people exactly where their money goes."

I snatch the phone out of his hands, and I'm so busy watching the videos I've never even seen that I don't think to taste the Vermilion Rockfish until it's *cold*. When I finally relinquish Oliver's phone back to him, I feel a little sick.

"Maybe he doesn't like kids as much as it seems." He shrugs. "Maybe you two are a perfect match. They always show so many things on television that aren't reality. It's hard to tell."

But the same scene keeps playing on repeat over and over in my head. In one particularly touching moment, a little girl with an adorable unicorn scarf covering her head is laughing, and then she stops. "What about you, Mr. Park?" she asks. "You make all our wishes come true, but what's your wish?"

"One day," he says, "one day I hope to have a dozen little

56

children of my very own." He taps her nose lightly. "And if they're half as cute as you, I'll be a very lucky man."

She sneezes.

And they both laugh.

It's a magical moment, and it totally ruins the rest of my two thousand dollar meal.

7
MANDY

"That's why you think he didn't like you?" Amanda's back to pacing from my kitchen to my family room and back again. "That was such an infuriating story."

"Why?" I stand. "You didn't have to go through it, and if you'd been there, you'd have understood that he was being utterly serious."

"I have so many questions." Maren hops to her feet, too. "Starting with, *you can sing?*"

I shake my head. "I *could* sing. Now I can only croak."

"You're obsessed with singing," Emery says. "It's boring."

"You'd be obsessed too," Maren says, "if Mom and Eddy had turned down not one, but three record deals for you, just because Eddy was an addict."

Amanda looks like she might punch her. "That is not why—"

"That was just one question," Emery says. "But if that's all you've got, then it's my turn." She reaches for my hand from the corner of the sofa. "Sit down, and tell me why Tommy moved to. . .where did you say it was? Montana?"

"Yes, Montana," I say.

"I'm not done yet," Amanda says. "You two are so rude, butting in on conversations that aren't even yours to have."

"I only got to ask about the singing, and she didn't even answer." Maren's scowling at her mother.

"Yes," I say. "I could sing quite well, at least, for Manila I could. It's not as if we have a lot to compare my singing with. I certainly had no real training."

"And what about Montana?" Emery dings me again.

"After his father died of a heart attack, his mom dragged them out to live with her brother." I shrug. "He went, because otherwise she'd have been all alone, and he would have too."

Amanda sits down and tugs me down next to her on the sofa, crowding Emery a little. "You're telling me that after you did that play together, after all that chemistry you felt, you just. . ." She shrugs. "You just went back to normal?"

"I was the only one feeling it," I say. "Clearly he wasn't, so. . .yes. We went back to normal."

Amanda closes her eyes and groans.

"Mostly back to normal," I hedge.

"Wait, what does that mean?" Emery asks. "Something else happened, right?"

"That was only the fall of our junior year," I say. "We had a year and a half before his mom dragged him to Montana, so yeah. More happened."

Maren perches on the edge of the chair I vacated and rubs her hands together. "I knew it. You kissed, right?"

I can't help rolling my eyes. "You young people are all about the lips pressing together."

"I hate to tell you this, but even us older people are all about that," Amanda says. "So did you?"

"It wasn't like that," I say. "When I found out he didn't like me like that, I decided to put my time back into trying to repair things with Jed. But something had made it worse, not better. He was back to totally ignoring me."

"Yeah, he knew what you didn't," Maren says. "That Tommy was *lying*, so seeing you two together every day probably just ticked him off more."

"I'm sure that wasn't it," I say. "But after a blizzard ruined our homecoming dance, everyone decided to take the budget from that and make our prom dance for my junior year *huge*."

"Wow," Emery says. "What does huge mean?"

"Well, with a graduating class of thirty-eight," I say, "huge is relative. But we were having Miss Lou's famous meatballs, pigs in a blanket, *and* cheesecake as refreshments, and we found a local band to come play for us. In Manila, those were all the ingredients for a really rocking party."

"Please tell me you're kidding," Maren says.

I shrug. "Most everyone was planning to go—freshmen all the way up to seniors. That made it the biggest event of the year. Only, I had no one to be my date."

Maren and Emery look at each other. "So, wait. Who did you go with?"

"It was a week before prom, and no one had asked me yet." I nod slowly. "I was actually thinking that I wouldn't go. Or if I did go, I'd hide behind the refreshment table with the excuse that I had to serve people."

"Isn't this kind of the same situation that got you into the whole mess with Jed the year before?"

I nod slowly. "Two years, but yes. Something like this."

"Oh, no," Emery says. "And I'm guessing this one didn't go much better?"

"Well." Before I can say anything, someone knocks on the front door.

Without thinking, Emery hops up to answer it.

"Wait," I say, but it's too late.

She's already opened the door. "Oh." Emery turns back around slowly as if she's just realizing how strange my whole house looks right now. "I thought it was a package." She turns toward me slowly, as Abigail peers around her.

60

"You two are both here. That's a stroke of luck. Helen's coming back today, so once I have all your signatures—" She freezes. "What's wrong with your family room?"

I groan. Once Abigail has even gotten a whiff of something, you may as well just surrender.

It takes us almost an hour to catch her up on Thomas Collins, his impending visit, and how I'm a big, fat liar.

"But I still don't understand *why* you told him that you and Jed got married," Abigail says. "Or why you said you were touring the world, before that, either."

"You've never met an ex while your hair was in a messy knot on your head and you were wearing sweatpants with a big zit on your nose, have you?" Amanda asks.

Abigail frowns.

"Of course she hasn't," I say. "It's perfect Abigail."

"Come on," Abigail says. "Of course I've run into people when—well. One of my exes I left half a country away when I changed schools and started law school. And then I married the next guy I dated, so. . ."

"When you meet your ex," Amanda says, "you do *not* want to look bad. You want to look your best. You want to win."

"Win?" Abigail asks. "It's a competition?"

Amanda, Maren, and I all speak at the same time. "Yes."

Emery says, "Don't you feel like everything in life is a little bit of a competition?"

"Not really." Abigail blinks.

"That's just because you're always the one who's winning," Amanda says. "Trust me. The losers know it's all a contest."

"As if you lose things," Abigail says. "You're the most put-together person I know."

"Right," Amanda says. "I'm put-together, and that means that when I'm not prepared for something, I'm a total mess."

"It's true," Maren says. "Poor Eddy."

Amanda shoves Maren, but she deserves it, so I don't fuss at her.

"Okay, let's say that I agree with all that, which is a stretch, but even so, Tommy wasn't your ex," Abigail says. "So why would you need to lie to him?"

"She wanted to date him, but he didn't like her," Amanda says. "That's actually worse."

Abigail's shaking her head as she sits down. "But something happened at prom, right?"

"I don't think I should tell all of you anything else," I say.

"Why not?" Abigail asks.

"Because Tommy's coming soon, and the less you know, the less you can blunder through and destroy."

"Or the better we can cover your lies," Abigail says.

She *is* a lawyer. It's kind of her whole job. I drop into the chair on the end by the kitchen with a huff. "Only if you tell me that something like attorney client privilege applies." I look around the room. "With all of you. If I keep telling you about Tommy, you can't let any of this slip, not to him, and not to anyone else."

"Who would I tell?" Amanda asks.

"Who wouldn't she tell?" Maren glares.

"Eddy, for one," I say. "You can't tell your husbands. They know everyone in town, and their parents really know everyone I'm talking about."

Amanda's brow furrows. "But—"

"No buts." I shake my head. "Those are my terms."

Maren groans. "Just say fine, Mom. It's not like Eddy would even care."

"Why is Tommy coming into town now?" Abigail asks. "Because if it's legal stuff. . ."

"I'm buying his family's ranch," I say. "He's finally ready to sell their land."

"Oh," Abigail says. "Well, I guess you better tell me everything. As your lawyer, I'll need context." She's smiling.

"You better not send me a huge bill for all this," I say.

"You ruin all my fun." But she's still smiling.

"So a week before prom, no one had asked me to go."

Everyone's so quiet, so focused on what I'm saying that it's almost like I'm talking to myself.

"Manila isn't exactly New York City now," I say.

Maren snorts.

"But in the early 1960s, it was even worse. There was really nothing to do, so when I told Tommy that I wasn't going to the dance. . ."

❦

Tommy's jaw drops.

"Oh, don't act like it's really that big of a deal. Mom can't really afford to buy me a fancy dress, and she doesn't have time to try and make one for me now, thank goodness."

"You have to go," he says. "I can't believe that idiot hasn't asked you yet."

"By that idiot, you mean Jed." I'm not sure why I say it. We both knew who he meant.

"I keep waiting for him to finally get over himself, but he just can't do it."

"It all started with a dance," I say. "Maybe he's just too scarred to even think about—"

"No." Tommy shakes his head. "No, he doesn't get to play the wounded bird. It's been more than a year—almost two! How long is he really going to mope around, not talking to you?" He swings the saddle onto his horse, Ranger. "And you —if he's too stupid to ask you, you should go with someone else."

"Who are you taking?" I tighten the cinch on my horse Elvis, but I keep one eye on Tommy.

"Me?" He scoffs. "I'm not taking anyone, but I'm still going. See what I mean?"

"Whether I'm at the dance or sitting at home, why do you

care?" I yank the halter off Elvis and slide the headstall up, pausing so he can take the bit. "It's not like it matters."

Tommy bridles his horse in half a second and tightens the girth before swinging up on his back. "There's nothing to do around here. You can't miss out on things like junior prom. It's all there is."

"You talk like it's the end of the world if I don't go." I pull the girth two holes tighter and call it good. "I've got a pile of books to read that Dad brought back from that library that closed over in Salt Lake, remember?"

Tommy stops arguing with me for the moment, and just starts moving. I'm hard pressed to swing up on Elvis, because he's kind of a brat—he starts walking as soon as Ranger moves off. "Hey." I yank on his face, but he's not stopping. One of these days, I'm really going to have to make him listen, but part of me kind of likes having a cantankerous horse.

He breaks into a trot the second I'm fully on, eager to catch up to his best friend, but once we do, he drops into a slow and steady walk. I'm a little less eager to be near my buddy right now. He's being brattier than my horse. "And anyway," I say, deciding to needle him, "if you keep spending all your time with me, you'll never make a move on Patrice Delaney."

Tommy's head snaps back. "What did you just say?"

"I've seen you watching her lately. I can tell you were happy when she broke up with Lex."

"I'm not interested in her." His face flushes bright red.

"Okay, sure," I say. "But if I'm not at the dance, you'll have to talk to *someone*. May as well be her, right?" Once we reach the plowed arena at the edge of Tommy's horse pasture, I urge Elvis forward and he springs into an eager trot.

Tommy has barrels set up in the middle for me to work on my barrel pattern before our next rodeo in three weeks, but we've got to get warmed up before I can work on those.

"At some point, you'll have to actually bring in some calves," I say. "They don't give prizes for roping bales of hay."

Tommy rolls his eyes and keeps right on swinging his rope around and around until it snags the hay bale. I've seen him in action, and I know that he can rope most anything from Ranger's back. It's actually a little distracting for me, always having to practice out here with him. I should be worrying about my pattern and my times, but I keep finding myself watching him.

I know he's not interested in me. He made that really, really clear, but sometimes I forget, like right now, when he keeps glancing back at me, too.

And smiling.

I have caught him looking at Patrice a time or two, but sometimes I wonder whether he ever looks at *me* the same way.

It's stupid. I heard what he said. But people change sometimes. Their feelings change too, right? His feelings could have changed. Or he could like Patrice and just not want to talk to me about it.

Either way, right now, I have to focus on our run. Elvis has a tendency to clip barrels when I don't hold him away from them well enough. It's bad to knock one over, of course, but it also hurts like the devil sometimes, when my leg's caught between him and the barrel.

I've just put down a really, really good one when I notice someone coming down the lane on a bike. Even squinting, I can barely make out who it is.

Denise Crane, our class president, drops her bike by the house and starts waving, so she clearly sees me and Tommy out here. His mom probably told her we were out back. Tommy and I walk our horses toward his back yard to keep her from having to hoof it all the way to us.

"Denise?" I ask. "You okay?"

She's breathing heavily. "Girl, I have been riding all over town looking for you."

"You have?" I frown. "Why?"

"Well, I went to your house first, anyway, and your mom said you'd be here." She drops her hands on her knees. "Okay, so we tallied up the votes for prom prince and princess, and—"

I groan.

"What?" Tommy asks. "What's with the drama?"

"You rode all the way out to my place and then all the way here just to tell us something you could have told us tomorrow?" I really, really hope I didn't win. There are only seventeen girls in our grade in school, so it's not like a big prize. But if I won, then I *have to go,* and I've pretty much made up my mind to stay home.

"I guess you figured out that you won," Denise says.

My sigh's probably a little too pronounced. "You didn't need to ride all the way out here—"

"But I did," Denise says. "See, for the guys, it was a tie, and you're the only one who hasn't voted."

"You're kidding," I say.

She shakes her head, and then she says what I knew she was going to say from the start. "You have to pick which of them wins for prince: Jed or Tommy."

❧ 8 ❧

HELEN

The day after my horrible dinner with Oliver, I head straight home.

HOW'D IT GO? David texts while I'm en route.

But I can't stop thinking about David's face as he tells that little girl he wants a dozen children of his own, just like her. FINE, I finally respond.

WHAT'S WRONG?

Why does he assume there's something wrong? I often text him with short, even sometimes one-word replies. I'm not someone who gushes. I don't overdramatize things. I'm not effusive. I'm a baby hater who sends short texts. He should know that about me. I've been honest about who *I* am.

NOTHING, I finally reply.

See? Another very normal text from me. Only, I don't feel normal. I'm agitated. Which is why it's doubly important that I not see him right now.

MY PARENTS ARE STILL HERE.

I don't groan, because I'm not upset about that. They can stay as long as they want. I'm sure he's happy to see them. He must miss them a lot. SPEND ALL THE TIME YOU WANT WITH THEM. I'M BURIED WITH WORK RIGHT NOW.

Which is totally true. This morning I have an insurance physical. They make me do one every single year, because we carry a huge policy on me for the company. If I were to die, well. It would be bad for all the investors. I've taken all reasonable measures to mitigate the impact of my death, which is the best I can do, but with massive policies come lots of tests.

I MISS YOU.

Guilt claws at me when I read those three words. I miss him too, of course, but I also need some time to figure out how I feel about all this 'he wants a kid' stuff. If it's a deal breaker for him, what will I do?

I love David.

Admitting that is huge for me—I've changed to even be able to say that to him after all my Oliver damage. But how much more will I have to change in order to keep him? According to the law of parsimony, the simplest answer is usually true. Thinking about that keeps bringing me back to the same conclusion.

David told me that he was simply managing his parents expeditiously. If he let them think as they wished, they'd leave us alone. By the time they realized that we weren't doing what they wished, it would be too late for them to do anything about it.

But doesn't it make more sense that he's using the same plan with me? He did already compare me to a horse so stupid that it wouldn't get on a trailer.

He thinks I'm spooky.

He may even be right about that in some ways, but he's missing the point. There's a big difference between being spooky and knowing what you want and not budging. What I want is *not* a dozen babies. In fact, it's not even one baby. But

I also don't want to argue about it, and I don't want to lose him.

So what happens when what you want and what the person you love wants aren't the same? In my experience, that's when you break up. Only, I don't want to break up. I don't think he does, either. I'm worried that because of that, he's lying to me.

I find that this time, being at an impasse really bums me out.

SAME, I finally text back. MISS YOU TOO.

My phone dings again, but I ignore it, because the insurance people are finally here—one heavyset man and one very uptight woman who says 'hmm' in response to literally everything I ask and every test she runs.

They poke me repeatedly. They prod me with great energy. But finally, they gather up all their vials and swabs and start to pack things up. "We're done?" I scratch my wrist again, clearly irritated by something on it.

"What's that?" The woman peers at my wrist.

"Just a bug bite or something." I tug my shirt down.

"Can I take a look at it?" she asks.

I want to tell her no. "Does this have anything to do with the testing protocols?"

She shakes her head. "No, but I'm a nurse, and from the inch of your wrist that I can see, it looks like more than a simple mosquito bite." She doesn't mention that there aren't really any mosquitos in the fall in this area, but she doesn't have to. I already thought of that.

I frown, but she doesn't take the hint. "Fine." I roll my sleeve up, and I'm a little surprised by all the tiny red dots running across the back of my hand and up my wrist to my forearm. "I didn't really notice these before."

She peers at them for a moment, and then she says, "Can I check your bedroom?"

"Excuse me?"

"Where do you sleep?" She lifts her eyebrows.

"How is that relevant?"

"I believe those to be bedbug bites. They often don't cause a reaction until there are enough of them to bite you in some meaningful volume."

My jaw dangles open. "This house may not be that nice, but it's not dirty. I'm living here with my nephew because his mother just moved out, and I'm not here that often. It must be something else."

"Your file indicates that you travel a lot. The most at-risk individuals for bedbugs are those who travel. Hotels have an awful time trying to keep—"

"You must be kidding," I say. "I stay at the Ritz-Carlton —you're telling me they can't keep *bedbugs* under control? It must be a reaction to a new laundry detergent or something."

"Then you should be happy to show me your bedroom. With this many spots, one quick peel-back of the sheets should show some signs of them if they're the cause."

I want to refuse, but her logic is sound, so I find myself leading the woman back to my room. "I've barely been here two nights in the past week."

"Which would explain all the bites. They were probably hungry while you were gone."

I might be sick.

"Uh-oh." The woman's pointing at some kind of blotches on the sheets. "Yeah, you've got a problem with bedbugs."

"Did you say you're a nurse or that you work for Terminix?" The hair on my arms is all standing on end. I'm scratching my head, and then my arms, and then my entire body itches like mad. "This can't be happening."

But it is. Two hours later, I've bludgeoned the biggest bedbug company in Salt Lake into bringing everything they have down here. I've dumped all my clothing into a pile to be burned.

"You know, we don't have to burn everything," a man's telling me.

"Are you kidding?"

"Some of this stuff looks pretty nice." He's bumping my designer shoes with the toe of his black work boot. "If you put it into bags and left it in the attic for a few months—"

"I would rather die," I say. "Burn it."

He looks disappointed.

"Or take it home to your attic and sell it on Poshmark next year for all I care." There's a reason I never buy second-hand. I suppress my shudder.

He's gathering up my infested stuff so fast I can barely get out of the way.

"Where are you going to live while this is being treated?" the other tech asks.

I shrug. "It's not like there are great hotels here." I think about going to Abby's. I'm going to have to tell her—and Ethan—about the bedbugs, I guess. I hate the idea of telling *more* people, but Ethan can't live here either. He'll probably come home from Beth's with that poorly trained border collie puppy of his and stare, dumbfounded, at the house. I'm doing the full court press, of course. Heat treatment—we'll need new blinds—tenting with chemical treatment, and spraying around all the walls and furniture.

I want every single one of those bloody boogers and all their children and their children's children all deader than dead. Which the bug guys keep telling me isn't possible.

Actually, my preference would be to burn the house down, but the tech assured me repeatedly that it's not necessary. My bed was apparently, horrifyingly, ground zero. The Ritz-Carlton is going to be hearing from me, because this is just. . .

I shudder again.

I don't even have a bag packed, because I'm burning all my clothes. The obvious place for me to go is Abby's, but she has so many kids. Beth's place could be infested, with as much fraternization as she and Ethan have. I can't risk it. I could try Amanda's house, but Maren's worse than a baby, and Emery never stops talking.

Mandy Saddler.

She's a tough lady—she won't faint when I say bedbugs. She'll also let me take a hot shower and burn my current clothes. I can wear something of hers until my assistant gets my new stuff here. I told him it has to come quick. Quicker than quick.

I call Ethan on the way to her place, and I text David and tell him I'm in the middle of a nightmare, and I'll explain what's going on later. Ethan's way less worried than I expect, but then again, maybe he's just keen for any excuse to stay the night at Beth's place. Hopefully he won't be angry I had all his blankets and clothing burned along with mine.

Oh, well. By the time he figures it out, my assistant will have a whole new wardrobe of boring work boots and khaki overalls ready for him. He'll get over it.

There are a bunch of cars here when I reach Mandy's, and for a moment I worry that I'm interrupting a party or something, but then I realize that one of them is hers, one is Amanda's, and one is Abby's. Just the usual suspects.

Abby sent me a message earlier saying she had paperwork for me to sign—probably why she's here. We can get it all done at the same time. Plus, with everyone here, she can't really turn me away, right?

I march through the front door without knocking, and everyone turns toward me, their eyes wide, their breath almost bated.

"What's going on?" I ask. "Did I toss the invite for a Mary Kay party or something?"

"You have horrible timing," Abby says.

That's rude, but before I can respond, I notice the biggest, ugliest carved wooden giraffe I've ever seen. It's almost eclipsed by the tacky reproduction of a famous Eiffel tower that's way too big for this room. But none of that is as bad as the embarrassing elephants sitting on the coffee table and the weird tiger rug in front of the sofa. "What on earth happened to your house? Did you lose a bet?"

Mandy flops back against the sofa and groans.

"What's going on?" I ask. "Seriously."

"You are not going to believe us," Abby says.

"Oh, try me," I say. "I just found out that Ethan and I have bedbugs, and David apparently wants a dozen children."

Abby and Amanda stare.

Mandy swears loudly. "We need some wine."

"What about us?" Maren asks. "Can I have some too?"

"I think I have some of that sparkling cider," Mandy says.

Maren grumps. "So unfair."

"But you can't just stop the story there," Emery says. "Who did you pick?"

"What story?" I ask. "What's going on?"

"Did you just say you have bedbugs?" Abby asks. "Because—"

"Can I use your shower?" I point. "While I'm in there, you can burn these clothes. Throw the rug and elephants in with them and save yourself some time."

"Go ahead," Mandy says. "I'm assuming you want to stay here and that you'll need some of my clothes, since you don't have a suitcase with you."

"Just tell me who you picked," Emery says. "Tell me before you go get her some ugly clothes."

"Wait, you're saying my clothes are ugly?" Mandy's frowning.

"No, but it'll be funnier if you find some for her to borrow." Emery has a surprisingly mean streak tucked down in there.

Color me impressed.

"Wait," I say. "Who she picked for what?" I can't help narrowing my eyes. Mandy does strange things like this, and it would be just like her to invite Amanda and her kids, and have Abby draw it up, but not invite Ethan, Izzy, Whitney, and Gabe—not to mention Nathan—while she picks one of them for something big, like to inherit her estate or something. "What's going on?"

"Mandy has a boyfriend coming to visit," Emery says. "And she's telling us their tragic past."

"He's not my boyfriend, and we don't have a tragic past." Mandy stands.

"Well, wait." For the first time, something interesting enough to stop my itching has come along. "I want to hear about it, too."

"It's also why she has all the weird stuff in her place," Emery says.

"Okay, now I really want to hear," I say.

Mandy starts shooing me. "You're dripping with pests, apparently. Bugs that I do *not* want in my house. So first, off to the shower with you." She points at the doorway. "I'll bring you a trash bag and you can put the clothes in there so I can toss them in the burn pile."

"The pest control people wanted me to put everything in a bag in the attic for the winter." I shake my head. "Can you imagine?"

Mandy shudders. "Not at all." I can't help noticing that she's scratching her arms.

"Is there a chance you have bedbugs too?"

"I wasn't scratching before you got here, girl. Now, get."

"Okay, but." I lean a little closer. "Don't tell them the story until I'm back, alright?"

"They're likely to string you up," Mandy says. "I stopped at a bad spot."

I can't help my smile.

Mandy smiles back. "Yeah, we'll wait for you."

I'm laughing as I close the door, and I can hear her laughing, too. Part of the reason Mandy makes me so nuts is that she's a little bit like me, at least, deep down she is. If she'd been born to my parents and I'd been born to hers, who knows if we'd have made the same decisions or done the same things.

But maybe.

I take my time showering, intent on making sure there's no part of the disgusting nightmares that infested my house on my body or in my hair, but also because I love the idea of torturing everyone out there by making them wait. I can't help thinking about what kind of person would fall in love with Amanda Saddler. Someone like David, probably. Some sap who thinks he can fix her or change her or repair her.

Idiot.

I wonder whether he moved on, or whether, in his heart of hearts, he's still pining.

Is it bad I hope he's still pining?

Not because I want him to be miserable, but because it seems like maybe Mandy has been. When I heard about Jed, it really bummed me out. Two people living next door their entire lives and being in love and never doing a thing about it?

It's a depressing tragedy.

But a knight in a shining Lincoln Town Car, pulling into town now and sweeping her off her feet? Or, you know, up against his walker? That could be kind of. . .exciting.

It's still depressing it happened so late for her, but also inspirational—it's never too late to find the love of your life. Although, I don't really have some kind of tragic flame from the past who would show up and profess his love for me. No, that's not how my life goes. My ex was just supposed to apologize, but instead he basically took me to a nice place, told me how my current boyfriend wants kids, and ruined my present life.

Hopefully things don't go like that for Mandy.

While I'm drying off, my phone bings. I've apparently missed a flurry of text messages from David.

MY PARENTS ARE MAKING ME CRAZY. I'M COMING OVER.

WHOA. WHAT'S GOING ON WITH YOUR HOUSE??? THERE'S LIKE A TENT OVER IT AND PEOPLE IN WHITE JUMPSUITS MILLING AROUND OUTSIDE.

HOLD THE PHONE. YOU HAVE **BEDBUGS?**

I TRIED ABBY'S. YOU'RE NOT THERE. I CALLED ABBY, AMANDA, DONNA, AND BETH. ONLY BETH ANSWERED, AND SHE HAD NO IDEA WHERE YOU WERE, SO I'M HEADED TO AMANDA'S.

I hate that this town is so stinking small that everyone knows everyone's business. This is ridiculous.

I'm typing him a text to tell him that I'm staying with Mandy when another one comes through.

YOU'RE NOT AT AMANDA'S, SO I'M GUESSING YOU'RE AT MANDY'S. I'M HEADED OVER.

For the love—I erase my obsolete text and tell him to come over. I WAS SHOWERING, I explain. I JUST GOT OUT. NIGHTMARE.

YOU SHOULD HAVE TOLD ME.

DON'T TEXT AND DRIVE. Then I get dressed.

I'm just walking out of the bathroom when the doorbell rings. He got here fast. "It's David," I say. "Sorry. I had to tell him where I was—he's been driving all over looking for me."

But it's not David. It's Donna, her belly as big as a beachball, and a crying baby over her shoulder. "David came by. He said—" Her eyes widen. "What's going on in here?"

"Yes, by all means, *invite the whole town.*" Mandy's fuming. I'm not sure why she's so mad, but it must have something to do with this guy who's coming.

"I didn't even invite Donna." I spin around, but then I hear the sound of a car pulling up the drive behind me.

That car's not David's, either. It's Ethan. When the truck

doors start opening, Beth, Izzy, Whitney, and Gabe all pour out of his old truck with him.

I can't help laughing. "But apparently everyone's here, with or without an invite."

"No." Mandy hops to her feet and pelts toward the door. "No. You all have to go." She's making a shooing motion, but Donna ignores her, shoving past her and into the room. "I have got to feed the baby, and when anyone else is around watching her, she can't focus enough to eat. When David came by, she was already starving, but then I couldn't think until I knew where you were and what's going on, and on the way here, I saw some kind of insanity going on at Ethan's house. I need all the details, but I'll just be back to hear them in just a moment." Then she ducks into the first guest room on the left, where I'm planning to stay, and more people start plowing through the door like a herd of wildebeests.

Ethan and the other kids don't even pause before they just run through, as if Mandy's not even trying to stop them.

"I'm not sure what's going on," I whisper, "but I think you're going to have to tell your story again, starting from the beginning. Maybe try and come up with a short version of it. Or." I smile. "I know. You could write it all down and pass it out on fliers. That might be faster." Needling her is so fun. I'm not sure why, but it is.

"Why is that huge, ugly giraffe scowling at me?" Izzy asks.

"Whoa," Gabe says. "When you get tired of them, I want the elephants."

"Forget the elephants," Izzy says. "I want the Eiffel tower."

Ethan's stupid puppy came too, apparently, and he shoots right through the door, chasing Jed the pig through Emery's legs and toward the back door.

When David pulls up outside, I can't help laughing. I'm wearing Mandy's jumpsuit, which is much, much too short. She gave me slippers that had no shot of fitting my feet, so

I'm standing on her wooden floor, barefoot. My sopping wet hair's dripping on the jumpsuit, turning it bright purple instead of blue on the shoulders, and no one has even said a word about any of that.

They're all too busy trying to figure out why a circus threw up inside Mandy's house.

Where we've all shown up uninvited.

Only in Birch Creek would something like this happen, where all these people I'm not related to in any way act like we're family. As David walks up the steps of the porch, his eyes take in my ensemble slowly. "What on earth are you wearing?"

"I should have asked you to bring me some clothes from your place," I say. "And I would have, *if I knew you were coming.*"

"I've already sent my parents to the resort and called pest control to tell them to check out my place." David pauses. "I figured you'd want to stay there—at the resort. But you came here? Mandy's house?"

"That's because the people told me that hotels were the problem." I shake my head. "I'm not going to stay anywhere like a hotel until it's been checked."

"Wait," Amanda says. "Are you saying the resort might—"

"Already on it," I say. "They'll be by to check the rooms later tonight."

David looks around. "What on earth is going on in here? Why are so many people here, and who shot a tiger?"

There's a totem pole in the corner, a six-foot-tall wooden giraffe, a giant Eiffel Tower painting that's far too big for the room and also not well done, a giant blue and white vase that looks like a terrible Dutch knock-off, strange origami animals where there used to be glasses on a shelf, and David asks about the rug. Of course he does. "Mandy was about to explain all that, I think. But before we get sidetracked, is there any chance my overnight bag from our trip to New York is still in your trunk?"

David frowns. "Probably."

"Excellent."

He tosses me his keys, but before I can rush out to grab a change of clothes, I realize that the conversation has carried on around us.

"Oh, man," Emery's saying. "You're going to have to tell them all the reason why you redecorated your family room."

"And kitchen," Maren says. "This is going to be great."

"Get out," Mandy says. "All of you."

"Stop," Amanda says. "You know you're going to tell them —it's Donna and Beth and the kids."

Mandy's face flushes red, and she looks like she's about to cry. If I've ever seen someone who looks like they're dangling by a fraying rope, it's her. "Alright," I say. "We're all here right now because of me."

"What?" Beth asks. "Why?"

"I brought bedbugs back from New York, and now we have to treat the house and burn all our stuff. Just look at what I'm wearing. Why do you think I need that change of clothes?"

"But what about all the weird stuff?" Beth asks.

"None of it is weirder than me wearing this jumper." I laugh. "But the decor is all stuff I brought back with me," I say. "I picked it up in Los Angeles on this last trip, and I didn't want to leave it back at the house of pestilence, so I brought it here."

"*You* bought all this weird stuff?" David asks.

I widen my eyes and drop my hands to my hips. "Are you saying it's tacky?" I can't help it. Right as I ask, I notice a Ross Dress For Less tag on the top of the totem pole, and I cringe. "This stuff cost me an arm and a leg, and my interior designer has been collecting it for weeks."

No one's going to believe it. Mandy's still going to have to spill whatever secret is making her apoplectic, and they're all going to ask me why I'm making up stories.

Only, for some reason, they do appear to buy my far-fetched claim that all this kitschy, cheap crap is mine. Obviously Abigail, Amanda, Emery, and Maren know what's going on, but at least everyone else may not need to find out.

Mandy mouths, "Thank you," when no one else is looking, but then I grab my overnight bag and duck into the bathroom to change. I'll be stuck wearing a business suit, but anything is better than this far-too-small jumper.

I've barely emerged from the bathroom, feeling a little less insane, when my phone starts ringing with a call from an unknown number. Very few people even have this phone number, and I consider not answering, but I did share it with a handful of major stakeholders, so I can't ignore it entirely.

"I better take this," I say as I walk out the front door. The porch swing here is my favorite part of Mandy's house. When I sit down, that weird cardinal flies over and lands on the arm of the swing. I try to shoo it away as I answer. "Hello?"

It tilts its head at me, like it knows something, though what of value a little red bird could know, I haven't the foggiest.

"Helen Fisher?"

"That's me." I really hope this is one of the shareholders, ready to meet. A few more on my side, and my work's basically done.

"I'm calling because of your insurance physical this morning," the woman says.

"Oh, no," I say. "Please tell me they don't need to redo anything. I'm pretty busy right now, and—"

"No, no, nothing like that," the woman says. "But your test results showed that you were pregnant, and on the questionnaire you filled out *not pregnant*, so as a courtesy, we always call and notify people of the discrepancy."

A discrepancy.

Like the height I wrote down being off by half an inch or my weight being low by a few pounds. Or like, maybe my blood sugar's high. An anomaly. An inconsistency. That's what she's saying she's calling about. She's just calling to let me know there's a small discrepancy—nothing major.

I'm just growing a *human* inside my stomach. Carry on.

9

DONNA

My baby hates me.

That might be a bit of an exaggeration, but it's not entirely untrue either. When Aiden was born, he would curl up against me to nurse. He would wrap his tiny fist around my finger, and he would snuggle in, and when I finished, he'd usually go to sleep.

If he was upset, hungry, sad, scared, or tired, all he needed to calm down was his mother.

That's what mothers do, they soothe their upset children. It's our job.

It's tiring. It's exhausting. It's sometimes even demoralizing, but mothers change diapers, we feed, we burp, and we comfort those babies from birth, so we know *just* how to make them better.

Except with Althea, I don't have a clue.

I'm not sure whether it's because she's not my biological baby, or maybe it's because she's a girl? It could be that my husband is actually involved this time, so she splits her time with her dad. I've also been really sick with my pregnancy, and Beth stayed around and she keeps offering to help. Will's mother comes over quite a bit as well. With four different people who all lend a hand, maybe she hasn't really figured out who she can trust.

But she's just as likely to cry when I hold her as when anyone else does. She's just as likely to flail around, turn bright red, and slap at my face as she is to do it to anyone else. At six months old, it feels like my baby, my darling little Althea, doesn't really like *me* at all.

Once she's done eating, she shoves away from me rather forcefully, knocking the bottle to the floor. While I try to pick it up, she flails around trying to sit up. I twist and tug, trying to pull her against me, but with my huge belly, there's not much place for her to go, and she wants to get away. She kicks out hard, her small feet slamming into my belly, and I almost drop her.

I know every pregnancy is different. Every baby is different. Every child is their own person, and they all have ideas and interests that we have to discover. Abby talks all the time about how each child is unique. I get that.

Even so, it's not supposed to be like this.

I've thought that same thing over and over and over since we adopted her. Every single time I think it, I feel a little bit sick inside. What's wrong with me, that I'm feeling this way about my little girl? I know she's mine. I love her. I really, really do, and so do Will and Aiden.

Beth has been happy to see her grow and flourish. She's not upset or angry in the slightest about her decision to give her up.

But things still feel. . .not quite right.

I want to shake the feeling, but I can't quite rid myself of it. It might help if Althea would stop crying so much, but my pediatrician insists that it's "just a baby thing," so I muddle on. But today, today I realized that I'm only two weeks away from my due date with our surprise baby, and I'm about to have to spend a lot more time with the brand new infant, and Althea will probably stop loving me at all.

I might have had a little breakdown.

That's when I realized who I needed to ask for help. She always has all the answers. Her kids love her to the moon and back. She's the busiest person I know, so she must have some idea of how to make people love you even when they have limited time around you. Abby's probably the only one who can help me, if I can just get up the nerve to confess that I'm a bad mom whose baby doesn't even like her.

It took me most of the day, but I finally worked up the guts, drove to Abby's. . .and she wasn't there. I was on my way back home when Beth called and told me that Helen and Ethan's house had bedbugs, but she checked her place and it's fine.

I spared just a second to be happy that apparently Beth and Ethan aren't sleeping over. Or at least, I hope that's what that means. Surely she'll be smarter this time around. I love Althea, but I don't want round two.

That's about when I started to panic about our house.

Forty minutes of web-searching later, and a lot of scratching, and I'm convinced I'm dealing with bedbugs, too. I pack up the baby and leave right as Will arrives. He agrees to stay home, meet Aiden's bus, and summon some pest people to make sure we're safe. I decide to just drive around until I can find Abby.

She's basically my get out of jail free card, which is a little pathetic. I'm an adult for heaven's sake, but ever since my first marriage fell apart, she's basically solved every problem I've had. Ex husband? Toast. Custody battles? Destroyed. Not surrendering Aiden? Fixed. Problems with Will or in-laws, her advice was always spot on. She even handled the adoption.

With the new baby coming, with *bedbugs* threatening, I need my get out of jail card more than ever before.

It takes me several stops, but I do finally locate Abby, at Mandy's. By then the baby's squalling, which is pretty normal, and I need a moment to gather my thoughts. By the time I finally emerge from the family room, Abby and Amanda are talking to David, and Mandy's putting crackers and cheese sticks on plates for an army of kids, including Beth and Ethan.

"What's the vibe in here?" I ask. "It's really strange, like someone just made a racist joke and no one knows how to respond."

"Nothing racist," Mandy says, but even she's not meeting my eye.

This is beyond odd. "Okay, but—"

The door opens, and Helen strides inside like she owns the place. It's really the only way she enters any doorway. I swear, she was born to be queen of the world. "Well," she says. "I just found out that I have an urgent meeting, so I better—"

Only, my body chooses this moment of total chaos to cramp. . .and something about the intensity of this particular cramp makes my water break.

I swear loudly under my breath and grab the back of the sofa.

"Whoa," Gabe says. "Mom said if I ever say that word again, she's going to wash my mouth out with a bar of soap because it's really, really rude."

"I—" Another cramp rolls through me.

"I'll be sure to let Donna's mother know so she can decide how to deal with it," Abigail says with laughing eyes.

Gabe hisses. "Mom." His eyes are wide. "Her mom's *dead*. You're going to make her cry, and she already peed her pants."

All I can do is laugh. Isn't this just how things go around here? "I didn't wet my pants. I'm about to have a baby, Gabe, and I don't really feel ready, but I'm not about to cry, I promise."

"Wait." Gabe scrunches his nose. "When you have that baby, who's going to take care of the other baby? The one that cries all the time?"

"We're going to figure it out," I say through gritted teeth. "But I need to head for the hospital right away." There are some times when living so far from the nearest hospital is a real pain, and this is definitely one of them.

"I'll call Will," Abby says.

"And I'll call Dad," Ethan says. "I'm sure he'll get things all set up for you."

Will's only fifteen minutes away, but with my water broken and the contractions starting, I'm nervous to wait for him to get here.

"I'll take Althea," Beth says. "You should probably go now, don't you think?"

"I'll take the munchkins home," Ethan says. "Come on, guys."

"But I haven't even eaten my cheese stick," Gabe says. "Plus, I want to ask Aunt Helen about the elephants." His head swivels. "I know you said all this stuff is expensive, but I really want them." His eyes are wide. "And you have a lot of stuff already. Way more than me."

"Why would you want those?" Helen asks. "They're even worse than the giraffe."

"The giraffe is awesome too." Gabe's sigh is one of defeat after a long-fought battle. "But Mom said it's too big for my room."

"I'll think about it," Helen says.

Gabe shoves the entire cheese stick in his mouth, barely able to talk around it. "Fine." He nods. "You do that." He grabs a bag that looks pretty heavy and slings the straps up and over his shoulders.

"Dude, what's in that bag?" Whitney asks. "You left your school bag at home." She reaches for the top of the bag.

Gabe yanks it away. "Paws off, greedy. These are my old books. I brought them to read in case it gets boring again while the adults talk."

"Old books?" Izzy asks. "The last time you had something old—"

"I didn't take these. They were being thrown out. Leave me alone." Gabe's face is all scrunched up, like he's getting ready to bite her hand.

Abby hangs up the phone. "Alright, I told Will we'll meet him there. Why don't you come with me?" She points at my bag. "Is that for Althea? Or should I put it in my car?"

Helen bends over and grabs my purse before I can. "I'll drive. My car's way faster."

"You said you have a meeting." Abby frowns.

"This is more important," Helen says. "I'm coming."

Abby blinks, but doesn't argue, and if she can get me there faster. . .

I'm climbing into the front seat of Helen's sleek sports car when Will calls. "Baby time?" His voice is breathy, like he's out jogging.

"Are you alright?" I ask.

"I just met the bus—I have Aiden, and Mom's on her way. I'll go throw some things in a bag for you, and then once she's here, I'll head out."

"Don't forget to bring my toothbrush, my soft pajamas, and my slippers." But then a contraction hits, and I groan. "I'll text you with a list."

"You have that stuff in a bag already. Don't stress. I might even get there before you," Will says.

"Helen's driving," I say. "I doubt it."

I expect him to laugh, but he doesn't. "That's not a good idea. She's not a safe driver."

"Oh, stop," I say. "She's fast, but she's safe. German engineering and all that."

"I can't believe you just said that," Will says. "My Camaro—"

"Alright," Abby says from the back seat, her face leaned

forward near my ear. "Domestic cars are the best, and I swear I'll make sure Helen is as safe as anyone can be."

"You be safe too, Mister Domestic-Cars-Rule. Your son will want to meet you, and it'll help if you're still in one piece." I'm smiling when I hang up the phone. I wanted to ask Abby about Althea, but there's no way I'm doing that with Helen-the-baby-hater in the car.

I breathe through yet another quick contraction—they seem awfully fast—and then my phone rings again. "Hey," Beth says. "Do you have Thea's paci?"

I rummage around and find it in my purse. It's an effort not to swear again. "There's a spare in the bottom of that green bin," I say.

"But she doesn't like those as well, right?" Beth asks.

"I'm sorry," I say. "As soon as—" But another contraction hits, and I can't keep talking.

"It's totally fine," Beth says. "Really. I just thought I'd check and make sure we knew where it was. I think Will's mom has an extra one that she uses more. I'll check with her."

I'm a little defeated when I hang up.

"Are you alright?" Abby asks a few miles down the road. "You've seemed a little distracted the last few times we've talked. It could just be the new baby, but—"

"Thea hates me." As soon as I blurt it out, tears start to stream down my face. I'm not sure whether it's desperation or embarrassment that I spilled in front of Helen.

Helen's head whips toward me, her jaw dropping. "Isn't that your baby's name—Althea?"

"Helen," Abby says.

"What?" She sounds indignant. "I might be wrong, but I think it is. It sounds like she's saying her own baby hates her."

"You're an idiot sometimes." Abby turns and drops a hand on my shoulder. "She does *not* hate you. Some babies fuss more than others. Ethan was like that, actually, but he

88

was my first, so I thought all babies were constantly fussing."

Now I'm swiveling around, trying to get a good look at her. "Ethan hated you?"

Abby laughs, which isn't very reassuring. "Althea does not hate you, Donna."

I sigh.

"I'm sure of it. I've watched her with you. She watches you like you're an ice cream sundae."

Which makes me bawl like a big old baby myself.

"I'm not kidding. She loves you—but I'm guessing she's a hard baby, and the more help you bring in, the harder it is to see that she has a preference for you over anyone else."

Which is what I was wondering already, but somehow, hearing her say it makes it feel legitimate. "She likes Will and his mom and Beth as much as she likes me. Maybe more."

Abby's arms wrap around me from behind and pull me back against the chair. "First of all, being a mother isn't about being loved the most. But secondly, she *does* love you more than anyone else, and she always will. I can tell."

Now Helen's crying for some bizarre reason, but I can't focus on that. I'm too busy dealing with yet another contraction.

"And do you love our mother more than anyone?" Helen's swiping at her eyes as she careens down the road at seventy-five. "Really?"

Oh. This is about her baggage. I know Helen is Abby's sister, but I swear, sometimes I wish she'd just move away. Having a real sister hanging around her makes me feel like I'm a tagalong.

"In some ways, yes, I love Mom the most," Abby says. "But not many. I don't love her more than you, for instance, or more than Steve. I definitely don't love her more than the kids. She hasn't earned it." Abby's voice is soft. "But Donna has."

"How do you know that?" Helen asks. "Maybe she's like Mom."

I want to punch her, and I want to kiss her, because I have the same question, and I'm not sure I would have been brave enough to ask.

"Our mother cared about herself. Our mother cared about her career. Our mother cared about Dad. She cared about all those things more than she cared about us, and a really good mother cares about her children at least as much as those other things." Abby sighs. "Probably more." Abby pats my shoulder again. "You're a good mother, Donna. I've been busy with little Nathan, and with being a newlywed, and I haven't seen you around Althea as much as I might have otherwise, but I've seen you with Aiden, and I know you're a phenomenal mother to him. You're nothing like our mom was."

Abby hasn't told me anything or given me any advice, but strangely, it may be the one thing I really needed to hear— that I don't need it. I'm not doing something wrong. I'm not a bad mom. The next contraction isn't even that bad, not now that I feel a little better about my own competency.

"It's hard to parent a newborn." Abby sits back in her seat. "You're tired. They're tired. They're small, and they can't really communicate. They have stomach pain? A dirty diaper? They can't tell you. They just cry, and on top of all that normal stuff, this time you're pregnant, too. My kids are close together, but I was never pregnant while I tried to care for a newborn."

"With Aiden, he quieted around me. He snuggled with me."

"Some kids don't like being squeezed," Abby says. "Maren was like that, if I remember right. Amanda told me she'd always shove away. It wasn't until Emery was born, a tiny, grabby koala, that Amanda realized that some kids *like* to sit on their mothers' laps."

She's saying that if I don't feel like I'm connected to Althea. . . "It's not my fault?"

Abby laughs. "I've got five kids now, and the only thing I know for sure is that every single one is vastly different. They may share some qualities, but they're probably *different* in more ways than they're the same. When someone tells you that something is universally true with kids, be very, very dubious about whatever else they have to say."

I grab the armrest and try to remain calm through yet another miserable contraction.

"How fast are these supposed to be coming?" Helen asks. "Because it feels like she's contracting an awful lot."

"Maybe drive a little faster," Abbys says.

But of course, that's when it starts to snow.

❧ 10 ❧

MANDY

lmost as fast as everyone shows up, they all start to disperse. Ethan takes his siblings, little Althea, and Beth, and they load right back up in the car, leaving a huge mess on my counter.

David—noticeably not invited to the hospital either—blinks a few times and says, "I guess I'll head for the resort and make sure my parents got settled in. Maybe I should get dinner and take it to the hospital for everyone?"

"I'm sure they'd appreciate that," I say. What I don't say is, *Now get out of my house, because you weren't invited.* I'm a little proud of myself for exercising restraint.

"Well, I'm not leaving," Amanda says, the moment David walks out the door.

"Me either," Maren says. "You cannot end the story like that." She folds her arms.

"But Abby wants to know what happens, too," Emery says. "And she's with Donna."

"How did we wind up with a goody two shoes like you?" Maren asks.

"Just tell us what happened," Amanda says. "We'll fill Abby in later."

"Don't you need to get to the hospital too?" I ask. "Donna's your friend."

"Sure," Amanda says. "Grab your bag. You can talk while I drive."

I roll my eyes, but she's not totally wrong. We both ought to go.

"Me too," Maren says. "I'm coming."

"To the hospital?" Amanda asks. "You'll be stuck there—"

But Maren already has her bag in hand, and she's walking toward the door. "Let's go. Once we're in the car, she won't have a single thing to distract her from the story."

Unfortunately, she's right. Once we're in the car, there's no way to put them off. I feel Maren and Emery's eyes on the back of my head like a gun pressed there. Even Amanda keeps glancing my way as she puts the car in drive. "Spill," she finally says.

☙❧

"I'll make you a deal," I say.

"A deal?" Denise asks. "What are you talking about?"

"People only know who they voted for," I say. "They have no way of knowing who anyone else voted for, so how about this?"

Denise frowns.

"I'll vote for one of them, and you'll make one little change for me."

"No," Denise says. "That's not how this works."

I shrug. "Alright, then I'll continue to abstain."

"You have to pick one of them."

"I don't," I say. "You can't *make* someone vote."

Denise takes a step toward me, her pointer finger out and wagging. "But—"

"If you want me to vote, you'll have to do something for me."

"What?" She finally stops, one eyebrow arched.

I may have won the vote by our class, but Denise is the most qualified person at our school. There must be a lot of people who voted for her. "You tell everyone that the girl who got the *second*-most votes won."

"Whoa," Tommy says. "You can't do that."

I spin toward him. "Why not?"

"Because she didn't say it was tied for the girls, just for the boys."

Denise is shaking her head. "It's not tied for the girls. You won by a landslide."

"See?" Tommy asks.

"Who cares?" I ask. "Who got the second most?"

Denise blushes bright pink.

"Come on. Who is it?" It has to be her, right? It's got to be.

She shakes her head silently.

"Mandy, come on," Tommy says. "You can't ask her to do that."

"It was you," I say. "I'm sure it was. You can be the prom princess instead, and no one else needs to know."

"But they will know," Denise insists. "They will."

"Did anyone other than you even see the ballots?" I ask. "There's no way that they could possibly—"

"Five people voted for me," she practically shouts. "Five people, and they were all other girls. You got twenty-eight. It wasn't even remotely close."

My mouth snaps closed.

"See?" Tommy says. "No offense Denise, but it has to be Mandy."

"This is so dumb," I say. "And furthermore, if you won't be the prom princess, then I'm not voting to break the tie for the prince." I fold my arms over my chest.

"By your own logic," Tommy says, "you should vote for someone. No one will ever know you were the tiebreaker."

I spin around. "You and Denise will."

He splutters. "Like I'd tell anyone."

"What about her?" I point.

"If she tells a soul, I'll tell everyone she only got five votes to your twenty-nine." Tommy's smile is diabolical.

"It was twenty-eight, and who even cares how many votes she got?" I ask. "She won't care about people knowing that."

"You should have voted for yourself," he says. "Then it would have been twenty-nine. I'm quite sure Denise was one of those five votes for herself, and I think she does care."

It's clear from her face and the way all the blood has drained away that she will care, and possibly that she also voted for herself.

"Which guy do you choose?" Tommy asks.

"Why do you care?" I step closer to him, our faces inches apart. "It doesn't even matter, who wins prom prince."

"Then just pick someone," he says. "No big deal."

"I pick Jed," I say. "Because at the last dance I didn't pick him, and it was a disaster."

Tommy nods slowly, and then he turns. "See? Done."

Only, that wasn't the end. When they posted the prom prince and princess on the bulletin board the next morning, it was like some kind of explosion. Everyone was talking, whispering, hissing, laughing, and poking each other.

Everyone but Jed.

He kept ignoring me, and that meant that I hurt Tommy's feelings for no reason at all. It made me mad. Really mad. So when lunch came around, and Jedediah walked up to the front of the lunch line with a tray, shoving in front of poor little Nicholas Kensey, I took my chance.

"Hey," I say. "Stop being such a big bully. He was there first."

Jed spins around, not realizing it was me calling him out, probably, and then he freezes.

"Didn't know who caught you, huh?" I tilt my head. "Well, it's me. The ghost who used to be your best friend."

Jed's eyes widen, but he still doesn't speak. He just stares.

"We're also prom prince and princess." Tears start to well up in my eyes. I can't help thinking of all the times we swam in the creek. All the times we scrambled up on our horses' backs and raced through fields with a halter as our bridle. All the times we sat on the edge of his parents' lake and fished, leaning back and reading or joking around while we waited for something to bite.

All those years, thrown away because I paid just a little bit of attention to Clyde.

"Are you really never going to talk to me again?" I drop my hand on my hip. "I thought the prom prince and princess ought to go to the dance together at least." My heart's hammering in my chest. My throat is so tight that I'm worried it might close off.

And Jed's just staring.

People are starting to murmur.

Stupid Nicholas Kensey's snickering, his tray pressed to his chest, his eyes wider than the bottom of the plastic water glasses in front of him.

"You can't go together," a voice behind me says. "Because you said you'd be my date."

I spin around, unsure who in their right mind would poke their nose into the middle of this nightmare.

But it's Tommy. Of course it is.

"Technically I guess you never said you'd go with me, but I asked anyway." Tommy lifts his chin. "Or did Jed already ask you?"

He's knocking the volleyball up in the air and pushing Jed to hit it. If there's one thing the Brooks boys can do, it's play ball. I *will* Jed to see what Tommy's doing, to comprehend what his little bump is supposed to encourage.

But Jed's whole face turns bright red, and he throws his

brown tray against the wall. It shatters, and hard plastic chunks explode outward all over the cafeteria. I stumble backward, bumping into the person behind me, and then I rush out of the other door, desperate to get away.

I'm not even two steps out the back door when Tommy catches me. "Mandy." His hand wraps tightly around my wrist. "Wait."

I can't bring myself to turn back around. I'm crying. It's embarrassing enough for him to know, but if I slow down to talk to Tommy, who knows who else might see me? "I know what you were trying to do." I twist my hand and my fingers wrap around his wrist. I squeeze. "I know you were trying to help. I do appreciate it."

He tugs, his fingers lightening up, but not releasing me. "I wasn't trying to help."

I can't help spinning around when I realize he's angry. Tommy's almost never angry. "What?"

He drops my hand like it's on fire. "I wasn't trying to *help* him. I'm sick of helping Jed." There's a muscle working in his jaw, and I want to reach out and touch it.

Which is really stupid. Clearly he just wanted to keep me from being embarrassed. It's one of the things I like the most about him. Above all else, Tommy always protects things. He'll protect his mother. His pets and animals.

And his friends.

But in this case. . . "I wanted him to be forced to say *something*," I say. "I wanted him to face me." I sigh. "I'm starting to think that he never will."

"Go with me anyway," he says. "You can't let him ruin prom for you."

"It's just junior prom." I shrug. "Who cares, anyway?"

"You do," Tommy says. "You act like you don't, but this matters to you. You want to go, and you deserve to get a crown. All the guys want you and all the girls like you because you're nice and smart and funny. That's rare. It should be fun for you, and he's ruining it like a little baby. You ruined his year unintentionally when Clyde asked you out, and he wants to do the same to you."

"When will it ever be enough?"

"That's why I want to hit him. He's a real mush brain."

"Mush brain?" I laugh. "You sure know how to dish out the insults."

"If you want to deal out a major insult to him for being dumb, then come to prom with me and *enjoy* it."

"I don't think he'll even come." And I really don't think he will.

Not while I'm picking a big, floofy pink prom dress. Not while my mom's doing my hair. Not even when Tommy shows up in his dad's car to pick me up.

"Whoa, he's letting you drive?" I ask.

The long, black Chevy Classic—a V8, as I've heard over and over—is sparklingly clean, not a speck of dirt showing on its entire shiny, sleek length. Tommy's dad has had the nicest car in town for years, but I've never seen anyone behind the wheel other than Mr. Collins.

"I offered to weed Mom's entire front flowerbed," he says.

"That sounds terrible."

Tommy shrugs. "It was worth it."

To get behind the wheel, he means. He's always loved that car, and he's never had an excuse to really ask to drive it. When he opens the door for me, it almost feels like a real date. He's wearing a dark suit I didn't realize he even had, and on the seat, there's a little bundle of flowers.

"What's that?" I freeze, peering at it. There are tiny pink roses that just match my dress and a spray of delicate white flowers that look like lace bunched up below them.

"Everyone gets wildflowers for their hair and stuff. I asked your mom if you were, and she said no." He shrugs. "I thought you should have some flowers. You are the princess."

I can't help rolling my eyes. "I don't care about that."

"Still." He reaches over the center of the car and lifts the flowers. "This can go on your wrist." He shows me a rubber band. "Or I can pin it to your dress."

I think about his hands trying to reach underneath the small straps on the top of my dress and a tiny thrill runs up my spine. "My wrist is fine." Because I'm kind of stupid, and I'm worried I'll shiver while he tries to pin it, giving myself away.

But then he holds out his hands, like *he's* going to put it on me. My hand trembles embarrassingly as I extend it toward him. His hands are quick and deft—I've seen them do crazy things with ropes when calves are misbehaving—but I don't expect them to be quite so warm or anywhere near as large as they are when he captures my hand in his. His fingertips brush against the tender skin on the center of my palm, and he freezes, looking up at me slowly.

When his bright eyes meet mine, my heart catches somewhere in my throat. I forget to breathe. I'm just staring at him, my hand still trembling a little, but captured well and truly between his.

"Mandy?" He tilts his head. "Are you alright?"

"Fine." I yank my hand back and slide into the seat. Of course, my skirt doesn't exactly comply. It's all bunched up, and before I can figure out how to get it all subdued, Tommy has leapt to my side and he's gathering it up himself to tuck it carefully next to me.

When he closes the door, his face is just above mine, his eyes softer than usual. Now, in this moment, I'm not the one who's frozen. It's him. My heart isn't in my throat this time. It's hammering, like a frantic woodpecker, right where it's meant to be in my chest. It's so loud that I'm worried he can hear it.

But without a word, Tommy breaks away and circles around to the driver's seat. Maybe I imagined all of it, because it's gone as soon as it arrived, the strange awareness of him, the nervous energy at his closeness.

For years, the best-looking guy I'd ever seen in real life—the coolest, too—was Clyde Brooks. He was tall, handsome, and almost larger than life.

But my vision changes when Tommy shows up with flowers.

Thomas Collins, wearing a suit, his dark hair combed carefully back so he almost looks like Elvis, is stronger, more handsome, and more heart-racingly debonaire than Clyde ever was. I can't help noticing that my mom and dad are standing in the front window, even though they promised they wouldn't, watching. Mom's smiling and her hand is pressed against the window wistfully, like she's worried she won't see me again or something.

If she had come outside, I might have died of embarrassment. She'd have been sure to make some dumb comment about my *date*.

In that moment, I remind myself how stupid I'm being. Tommy's my friend, and he asked me out today from of a sense of loyalty. There's a reason I wouldn't let Mom and Dad come out and gush and take photos. There's a reason I'm keeping things low-key. I can still hear his voice echoing through my brain.

"I do not like Mandy!" He had been yelling it. And then he'd said, "She sings like an angel, and that's about all I care about."

He appreciates my singing voice, and that's that.

"Everything okay?" Tommy's dark brows draw together. "Should I slow down?"

Yes. I'll fob off my moment of idiocy on his unusual speed. "It's definitely faster than our bikes." I force a smile.

"That's true." He's smiling, and his hair's blowing softly because he cracked the windows, but moments later, we're stopping.

In the wrong place.

"The dance is—"

"I know where the dance is," he says. "But we have to eat something first, right? And you can't show up *right* on time. What kind of princess does that?"

"But you don't have to—"

He's already opening my door. "I do, though. The least I can do is get you some food at the Hub. It's hardly fine dining."

"Tommy."

He holds out his hand, lifting both his eyebrows and shrugging. "Mandy, stop arguing and get your cute, fluffy self out here."

Fluffy. I ignore his hand and climb out myself, shoving him to the side. He's calling me fluffy, which is a word reserved for cute, bouncy baby chicks and like, fuzzy little lambs, so clearly any romance I was hallucinating existed exclusively in my head. "Aye, aye, captain." I salute.

"Careful with that hand." He reaches for my wrist, and again, my heart stutters at his casual touch.

But he's just checking on the flowers. "They look just fine. I swear, that lady said she had used a whole spool of thread putting them together, but I didn't believe her."

"Wait, your mom didn't make this?" I take a closer look.

"Where would we get roses this early?" he asks. "I drove into Green River for it. That big yellow florist shop."

Why would he drive all that way? And pay so much?

"Let's go." Instead of releasing my hand, he slides his fingers down, lacing them between mine and drags me along behind him. The clicking of my heels just after the clomping of his dark dress shoes sounds. . .almost *right*, in a strange way.

I don't have long to obsess, though. Teri's waiting for us when we walk through the door. "Two prime rib dinners, ready to go." She bobs her head at Tommy, and I realize he must have talked to her in advance. They don't have anything but burgers, chicken fingers, french fries, and hot dogs on their menu, usually.

"Are you sure—"

But he tightens his fingers on mine and pulls me further along. "Stop kicking at all the pricks, and just come eat some nice food, prom princess."

I can't help rolling my eyes, but I'm also a little bit in awe. When we reach the booth in the corner, there's a tiny vase with little pink roses that just match my corsage. "Whoa," I say. "This is—did you get these, too?"

The lighting isn't that great in the corner, but it almost looks like Tommy's blushing. "They had some leftover roses when they finished, and the lady said I could have them." But that means he came by here earlier to drop them off. It was a lot of work.

He slides into one side of the booth and points at the other, but in the process, our hands separate.

My hand feels lonely, now.

I never realized how lonely my hand has been my entire life. Not until it was mourning the loss of Tommy's fingers did I fully comprehend it. It's strange, missing something you didn't even know you wanted until moments before.

"I—this is a lot," I say. "You didn't need to do all this."

"Jed should have done it." Tommy sounds bitter, but when he looks up, his smile's bright. "You really are a princess, Amanda. You deserve someone who treats you like one."

My heart darn near does a back flip. "Thanks."

A moment later, Teri brings out a basket of sliced bread and their famous cinnamon butter. As she walks off, she winks at me. I'm not sure why or what it means, but I'm beginning to. . .hope.

Tommy says Jed should be doing this, but Jed isn't. Tommy is. He's bringing me a corsage, and decorating our table, and when the prime rib comes, it's the best meat I've ever had. "Why is this so good?"

"Prime rib is slow roasted," Tommy says.

"Actually, that's not quite right." Teri's bringing out some kind of tray, but before she sets it down, she smiles. "You have to let the meat come down to room temperature, and then you cook it for just five minutes per pound at five hundred degrees. . .and *then* you turn the oven off and let it sit for two hours."

Tommy blinks.

"You can't open the oven in that time or you'll ruin it. Then you pull it out, and." She waves her hands. "Voila."

"I thought you were the waitress," Tommy says.

She shrugs. "Small place. I get to do a little bit of everything." She leans closer. "And believe me. If I let Chuck do the prime rib, you'd be sawing pieces off with a serrated knife."

I'm chuckling as she lowers the tray.

"Oh, I don't need dessert," I say.

"Should've told him that." Teri's smirking as she slides five different plates onto our table top. "He ordered them all." She's laughing as she saunters off.

"You ordered—" I look around more carefully. "A cheese-cake, a chocolate cake, some kind of fruit tart, a cobbler, and. . .what is that?" I lean closer.

"It's called Broken Glass Cake," Tommy says. "Teri said it's new, but I think it's basically different flavors of Jell-O, cut into squares and frozen in place with whipped cream." He shrugs. "It looks pretty, though, right?"

"How much did you really think I could eat?"

He sighs. "There aren't a lot of ways to make something special in Manila, but I'm trying, okay?"

I glance around. It's prom night, and not another single teenage couple is in here. Not that we're a couple. Now I'm the one blushing, and just because of my own errant thoughts.

"Are you alright?" Tommy's looking at me strangely. "Mandy?"

"Fine." I dig into the Broken Glass Cake, and thankfully, it's better than I expected it to be. Strawberry, Lime, and Lemon Jell-O all mix pretty well. But when we both reach for a bite of the cobbler at the same time and our hands collide, I can't help my gasp.

Tommy's mouth turns up on the edge.

I know what he said, but I can't help thinking that maybe he's changed his mind. Maybe he does like me after all. The way he's staring at me, the effort he's put into this, and the way his hand is still touching against mine. . .

"Alright, you two." Teri walks up, hands on her hips. "If you don't go soon, you'll be late for the announcement of prom court. Tommy made me promise to have you out of here in time." She tosses her head at the clock on the wall.

Tommy clears his throat and stands. "Right."

"I didn't bring money with me," I say. "But—"

"Your date already paid," Teri says. "He paid a few days ago, when he first came in here and dictated this crazy menu." She's smiling broadly now. "Pretty cute one you got there." She winks again, and this time, Tommy sees it.

I might die.

But Tommy acts like he didn't see a thing. He just walks me back to the car, opens the door, and helps me tuck my dress into the space before closing the door. Once he's walked round and climbed in himself, he smiles. "Ready?"

We only drive a few blocks, swinging around the corner to the school and then he slides into a space and cuts the growling engine just outside the gym. We're late and there are still plenty of parking spaces.

The walkway into the gymnasium is decorated with a bunch of huge paper flowers—Denise knows her stuff—and

I'm actually a little bit impressed with the enormous archway she made at the front entry. If I owned a camera of my own, it would be photo-worthy for sure.

"Wait," someone says.

We spin around right as Chip snaps a photo with a large black camera. "Yearbook."

Tommy blinks, probably trying to clear his vision, and then we turn to walk inside. At first, I'm worried it'll be awkward. Everyone saw the scene in the cafeteria, and everyone knows Jed's the prom prince and I'm the princess, but he yelled at me, and now I'm walking in with Tommy.

But before anyone can say a word, Tommy whirls me into the center of the room—the dance floor no one's even using. I'm not sure whether I'm excited or horrified that it's a slow song. That means he pulls me close to his body and we sway back and forth slowly. "So," he says. "Tell me your biggest fear."

"Fear?" I laugh. "Is that really a dance-floor conversation?"

He shrugs. "Why not?"

"How about you tell me your biggest dream? Let's start there."

"I want to see the world. The Taj Mahal. The Eiffel Tower. The Nile River."

"Wow," I say. "Really?"

He shrugs. "What about you?"

"That sounds pretty good," I say. "I didn't know enough to even know what things I'd want to see."

"I'm sure my list will grow," he says. "But for now, it's a start."

"Niagara Falls," I say.

"Oh yeah?"

"Mom and Dad heard about it when they were emigrating, but. . ." I almost tell him they couldn't travel up to see it, because they were busy dodging the paperwork trail that might have ended with Dad being drafted, but when they told me how sad they were to have missed it, I decided I'd like to go one day. A photo in front of the falls would have been nice, even if I was still in Mom's belly.

I remember to shut up just in time to avoid that disclosure.

"I'll add that one to my list, too. I hear it straddles the United States Canadian border, so that's kind of cool."

"Traveling is fine," I say. "As long as I have a safe, comfortable home to return to. My biggest fear is winding up all alone."

His eyes are sad, and he misses a beat on the song. "Why would you ever wind up alone?"

"Mom and Dad are all I have. They left their family on another continent, so if they die. . ." I shrug. "That's it."

"You'll never be alone, Amanda Saddler. Never."

It's not a promise he can really make. Unless. . .

He leaves when the song ends to grab us something to drink, and they announce the prom court. Of course, Jed doesn't show up. No shock there. I didn't think he would, but apparently other people are surprised.

I pose for some yearbook photos, and then I'm headed down the stairs when I hear my name. I freeze, and I realize it's coming from just around the corner. I can't see the speakers, but the person who said my name has a very distinctive voice. It's the poor kid whom Jed cut off in line that day, Nicholas Kensey.

"—Mandy's the fox in our class. C'mon man. There's no way you don't like her."

"I'm just helping a friend," Tommy says.

"But you stood up to Jed for her." Nicholas whistles. "He's straight scary, so you had to think you were gonna. . ."

There's some scuffling sound "Listen, I was doing a favor for a friend who needed someone by her side, and that's it. If I hear you so much as *breathe* anything about me liking her, I'll end you. Got it?"

Nicholas has always been a little blunt, but I'm the real idiot here. Tommy couldn't have been clearer that night after the play, and here I was, thinking maybe we could be more. Again.

When he comes back with my punch, I practically snatch it out of his hand. "Well, we got the photos. We can go home, now."

Tommy doesn't argue, and he doesn't even look shocked. "If that's what you want."

"It is."

He leads me out past the dumb old paper arch, helps me into the car, and drives me home. And that's the end of our junior prom *and* my relapse into idiocy all at once.

11

HELEN

When you're smarter than everyone else you meet, your life is often filled with all kinds of frustration. You explain your ideas, but no one gets them. Things you try to delegate take you longer to explain than to simply do yourself. You have to make your point in a half dozen different ways, or the people around you can't understand what you're saying. When you make what you feel are fairly basic statements, people can't keep up.

Simple things for me are often complicated for almost everyone else.

Maybe that's why one of my great joys in life is driving.

It's uncomplicated. It's something I can control. And it's usually a time when I can think. I release frustration, anger, and anxiety while the road flies past. I unwind from whatever deals I'm struggling with or problems I'm mulling over, and no one can badger me. "I can't talk now—driving." I love fast cars with great suspension, because they make an activity that already relaxes me even more fun.

But not when it snows.

If you're going to live somewhere that snows all the time,

even in October, that location should at least have a decent snow-removal system in place. Unfortunately, with a population density of one point three people per square mile, Daggett County simply can't afford any kind of effective snow control at all. Unless I decide to start plodding along behind the wheel of a snow plow—not likely—I'm sort of stuck slowing to a crawl when snow billows down from the sky to blanket the road.

I hate it.

But it's even worse when a pregnant woman's shouting in my ear.

"Those contractions sound worse," I say. "Or is that just me?"

"Not you," Abby says. "I think they're getting closer."

"So. . ." I clear my throat. "We're still twenty minutes away. If you could try *really* hard to keep that baby inside until we get there, that would be great."

"Yeah, thanks," Donna shouts. "Really helpful feedback."

She makes an effort not to scream, and no baby has popped out yet, but by the time we reach the emergency room, I'm worried that's only because something's wrong. Instead of panting and whimpering during contractions, she seems to be whimpering all the time. She's also sweating—profusely. During her next contraction, I whisper over my shoulder, hoping only Abby will hear. "Is she alright?"

"I texted Steve, and he called a friend over there. Labor and delivery is in the ER, waiting."

By the time I pull into the drive of the hospital in Rock Springs, Donna looks even worse.

"There," Abby points. "Pull over there."

"But it says Ambulance Bay," I say.

"Since when do you care about what's allowed?" she asks. "Go."

Everything about babies makes me nervous, and it's not helping that I apparently have one inside me right now, too.

Little parasites that wreck all the things that should work a certain way. "Fine," I say. "We're here."

Donna isn't moving, other than the panting and the moaning, and Abby's stuck in the back seat, so I hop out and run around to the passenger side, waving as I go. "Hey!" I shout at the top of my lungs. "Pregnant lady about to deliver out here."

No one seems to hear me, but when I open the door, Donna tries to get out. She's struggling, and I'm not strong enough to deadlift her when she's also growing a bowling ball in her belly, so I'm going to need a hand.

I shout louder. "Help us out here! Whoo-eee, whoo-ee! Pretend I'm an ambulance and come out already!"

A moment later, the door does open, and by that point, Abby has escaped through my side of the car. She's jogging around to lend a hand, too. "My friend here is very, very pregnant," Abby says. "She needs some help." Then she drops to a hiss that it's clear she's hoping only the hospital worker will hear. "We think there may be a complication."

Even at a hospital out in the boonies, within twenty seconds, several people have mobilized, and Donna's carefully transferred to her back on a stretcher. Less than a minute later, there's a tall doctor in dark blue scrubs at her side asking her questions.

"No," Donna's saying, "The last time I had a baby, it didn't hurt like this."

"Did you have an epidural?" The tall woman's pulling her hair back into a ponytail, which doesn't seem encouraging.

"Right before I had him, but that's not—" And now she's screaming again.

It's a bit of a blur, but in the next two minutes, the tall lady doctor starts putting stuff on her, and a man in a white coat shows up and checks her. . .lady parts. I try to look away, but I can't entirely. There's *definitely* a baby head that's visible when they're checking things out.

"She's crowning," the male doctor says.

"How long has the pressure been like this?" the tall doctor asks.

"I don't know," Donna groans. "Does it matter?"

"Its head's almost through," the shorter, male doctor says. "But then it kind of sucks back in."

"That could be a turtle sign. Donna, please listen to me. For right now, don't push, alright?" The tall woman looks completely calm. "I think you may be dealing with shoulder dystocia, and if you push. . ."

Then they're wheeling Donna through some doors and into a room off the ambulance bay, leaving Abby and me behind. Abby's phone is pressed to her ear, so I assume she's talking to Steve or Will.

"Yes, they're rushing her back to, well, to somewhere. No, I'm not sure exactly—when are you going to be here?"

Will it is. Steve's probably with their baby and can't leave.

"Alright, well, when you arrive, run inside. They won't let me follow, but it might be a different story with you. But Will, breathe. Do not get in an accident because you're worried about her. She's in capable hands. The head of the program happened to be here, and she really knows her stuff."

The second she hangs up, I grab her arm. "Is she going to die?" For some reason, panic grips me. That baby's going to kill her, and then Will's going to be all alone with that tiny little girl and the little boy who isn't even his. Actually, would that kid go to his awful father if Donna dies?

It's bad all around.

This is why people shouldn't have babies.

"Helen, it's fine, I swear. Shoulder dystocia's fairly common, and they know what to do about it. Trust me, she's going to be alright, and so is that baby."

And then, as if to mock Abby's words, there's screaming—so much screaming.

"What's going on in there?" I'm pacing, and I know I should stop, but I can't. Why's Donna screaming so much?

Then, abruptly, it stops.

"They probably had to do an episiotomy," Abby says. "When the shoulder gets caught, they have to make more space for them to get through."

I'm swearing under my breath, and now I'm sweating nearly as much as Donna was.

"Are you alright?" Abby asks.

I seriously *can't* stop pacing.

"Helen."

What if something like this happens to me? What if they had to do whatever they just did to Donna to me? What if I die? It's a no brainer. I have to terminate this thing. The sooner the better, really.

"Helen Fisher." Abby claps right in front of my face. "What on earth is going on in that brain of yours?"

"I'm—" I stop, swallow, and start pacing again.

"You're not even that close to Donna. Why are you freaking out? Is it making you think about my pregnancy? Because I'm done. That was my last one. You have nothing to worry about."

"Ma'am." A man in black scrubs is walking toward us. "Are you alright?"

Great. An orderly's worried about me now. "I'm fine," I snap.

"If you could just move your car, then there's a waiting room you can go to." He points.

My car.

Of course.

I'm nodding when the double doors fly open and Will comes shooting through, his eyes frantic and his breathing wild. "Where is she?"

Abby points, and then he's gone as fast as he appeared, consumed by the room where all the howling went to die, and now that orderly is gawking at me again. "Fine," I say. "Fine. I'll move my car."

Before I can put the key in the ignition, Abby's hand stops me. "Let me do it." She's calm, she's steady, and she's absolutely insistent. "I don't know what's wrong, but I'm sure you're not safe to drive."

I start bawling, then.

I'm not sure whether it's the stress of Donna's labor, or the miserably long drive to get here in lousy weather, or my worry for the obvious misery of a friend. Donna and I may not be that close, but I don't have many friends. I can't risk losing the ones I do have.

Or maybe it's something else entirely. It could be hormones. How embarrassing.

Whatever the cause, I'm suddenly sobbing *and* hyperventilating.

"Helen, what is going on?" Abby tucks my keys into her pocket and yanks me to my feet, and then her arms wrap around me. "Something is wrong, and I'm not moving until you tell me what it is."

"I'm pregnant," I say. "Or at least, some crazy woman who took a blood test earlier says I am."

Abby freezes. "Surely you've been using some kind of contraceptive."

"Of course," I say. "I mean, I'm almost forty-five. The OB told me I didn't likely even need one anymore, but I have a Mirena—that's an IUD they—"

"I know what it is," Abby says, but she doesn't look better. She looks even more concerned.

"What?"

"Let's get the car parked." She shoves me just a bit toward the passenger side, and I finally go.

She says nothing as she drives, slowly in light of the quickly accumulating snow, but once she reaches the parking lot, she pulls into a space and kills the engine. She doesn't turn toward me or interrogate me. She just sits there, staring at the steering wheel.

"Just say whatever you want to say." I'm not sure why I'm so upset. It's not like I'm keeping it. Surely Abigail knows that, too.

"I'm sorry," she says. "I know you don't want to be pregnant." She turns toward me slowly, then. "But you should get an ultrasound to confirm that test. It could be a chemical pregnancy, or worse, an ectopic one. I think they're common in people who have a Mirena. It blocks the fallopian tubes, if I remember it right. The doctors would need to do something quickly if it is ectopic, or your tube could burst and you could die."

She's finally talking to me, and I can't seem to do anything but stare at my hands. "Isn't this where you tell me that a baby is a life-in-being and that's a miracle?"

"Do you want me to tell you that I think abortion is wrong?" Abby asks.

I shake my head.

And my little sister, who in her entire life has never once kept her mouth shut, just shrugs. "All right, then."

"Come on. I'm ready for it. I didn't want to tell you, but now you know, so you may as well say it."

"Helen, we had the same parents, but you and I are very different people. In the gaping vacuum that was our family, I sought some kind of meaning and purpose and found God in my search. You found a different kind of peace. I'd never try to judge you for what you found or what you believe."

"But you think abortion is wrong."

"I love you, and I know this is hard, and I support *you*." She drops her hand over mine. "I always will. It's not my baby, and it's not my body, and I love you. I think that's the part that matters most."

That makes me bawl. Bawl, and bawl, and bawl some

more. "I was thinking about breaking up with David because he wants kids and I don't. And then this happened."

Still, she doesn't tell me it's some kind of sign. She doesn't tell me I'm wicked. She doesn't tell me that this baby is a miracle, and that I'd be a devil if I end its life. "I am worried about you, though," she says. "We're at a hospital. While we wait, at least get checked out."

"Fine."

So I let my little sister, the person I've always tried to look after, shepherd me into the waiting room, and then I sit while she goes and argues with some nurse until we're given a room.

"How's Donna?" I hear her asking the large, black nurse who just showed us into a small space and turned to leave. "Is she alright? Is the baby doing okay?"

"They think their baby boy may have a broken arm," the nurse says, "but Miss Earl's alright, and bones at that age heal quick."

"Thanks." Abby's smiling when she turns back.

"You're happy he has a broken arm?"

"I'm happy he was born, and other than that, that he's healthy. Babies recover in weeks at this age. They'll splint it or something, and he'll be alright." She nods. "Yes, I'm happy."

"I do not understand the joy you get from these babies. The world is full of babies. We don't all need to have our own."

Abby doesn't argue.

But a moment later, when the tall doctor in dark blue scrubs comes into the room, she stands up and takes charge. "My sister Helen is forty-four, and she's gotten a blood test that says she's pregnant, but she has a Mirena. We need an ultrasound to make sure it's not ectopic."

"Hey Abby," the doctor says. "Good to see you again. How's little Nate?"

"He's fine." Abby's face softens a little. "But I want to make sure Helen's alright."

When the doctor turns toward me, I recognize her. I met her several times while Abby was pregnant. I should have expected that she and Donna would have the same doctors. "I thought you were down in Vernal."

The doctor shrugs. "In this area, we have to take turns covering the hospitals with labor and delivery. I'm actually taking call for Doctor Fleemen right now, and right before your friend Donna came in, I delivered a set of twins. It's been a busy day over here."

"Can you do the ultrasound?" Abby's polite, but she doesn't let things go.

As it happens, a nurse is rolling a cart into the room at that very moment, and I recognize the machine it's carrying as an ultrasound. "The quickest way to check for pregnancy is a trans-vaginal ultrasound," the doctor says. "If we see the baby right where it should be, then we don't have to go hunting elsewhere. I'll also look around for that Mirena."

She's going to *look around* for it? Like you'd hunt for your keys if you misplaced them? That doesn't sound promising.

"How far along are you? Any guesses?" Her eyebrows rise, and I realize she's talking to me now.

"I didn't even know I was pregnant until a few hours ago."

"Alright, well, we'll see if we can get a decent guess on how far along you are as well." She hands me a gown. As I walk to the bathroom to change, she pulls out the disturbing looking wand and starts to put a plastic sleeve over it.

Peachy.

As I change clothes, it occurs to me, and I feel a little bad about thinking this, but if it *is* ectopic, I won't have to feel guilty for terminating the pregnancy.

Trans-vaginal ultrasounds are just exactly what they sound like they'd be. They stick the ultrasound probe up into places it should not be, and they take photos of what it finds with buttons on their little machine. As it happens, this particular cart at least has heated gel, and the doctor seems to know what she's doing. Definite perks if you're ever subjected to this particular form of abuse.

After a moment of shifting and making small squeaky sounds, the doc says, "Oh, there you are."

"The Mirena?" I crane my neck to try and see the machine's monitor.

"No," Abby says. "And if you don't want to see your baby, you should keep your eyes down."

"Down?" I turn again, and this time, I can see the corner of it. I shift a little more and it comes clear. The image on the monitor looks like a little otter stuffy, all rounded and bulbous. "Should it look like that? Why's its head so big?"

The doctor turns the machine, and suddenly I can see it almost perfectly.

"How old is it? That's not a tiny bean. It looks huge."

"It's measuring between 10 and 12 weeks," the doctor says. "And it looks just fine to me. The head starts out much larger than the body and slowly grows into it, but even when babies are born, their heads are much larger than an adult's would be. Babies can't even touch their hands together above the top of their heads, for instance."

I exhale for some reason, like I'm relieved that it's healthy, which is ridiculous. We're only doing an ultrasound to rule out an ectopic pregnancy. My hands are shaking, and my heart's racing, and the baby keeps kicking on the screen, and it's all too much. I have to look away. I know it's still small, but I didn't expect it to look like anything yet. What's ten weeks? Two and a half months?

"How could I not have known?" I ask. "Isn't that weird?"

"You had a Mirena to prevent this from happening," the doctor says, removing the probe and then clicking away on a lot of buttons on the keyboard. "That particular device is also known to eliminate periods, the lack of which is usually the first indicator of pregnancy."

"That's kind of a stupid side effect for a contraceptive, now that I think about it."

"It's a huge bonus for many women," the OB says. "But it can also make it hard to know when you're pregnant. You haven't gained much size or mass yet." She shrugs. "It's not uncommon not to notice. I've had people come in who were in their third trimester who had no idea."

She must be kidding. "Don't they feel the baby moving?"

"It's actually pretty common with a first pregnancy that people mistake any movement they feel for acid reflux or indigestion, and even seasoned mothers usually don't feel the baby before about sixteen weeks, so it's not at all strange you wouldn't know."

"Indigestion?" I can't help flattening my hands against my stomach. "They think it's indigestion?" It seems nuts.

She clicks a few more buttons and a little paper prints off. She hands it to me. "Congratulations. It looks like a very healthy baby, and you're out of the scariest miscarriage risk window in the next week or so." She leans a little closer. "At this age, your odds of getting pregnant hover right around five percent each month, and there appear to be no signs of abnormalities so far. Of course, you'd want to get a full ultrasound read by a radiologist to confirm all that, and you'll need to start taking a prenatal vitamin right away if you want to keep it. If not, you can make an appointment for that too."

"I—I'm not sure—"

"I have to go back and check on Donna, but I'll swing back by in an hour or so to answer any additional questions you may have."

"Should I be worried that you didn't see the Mirena?" I ask.

"If you do a complete ultrasound, they can search for it,

but I didn't see it in the uterus or anywhere obvious." She stands and then shrugs. "Sometimes they just fall out."

"*Fall out*?" I ask. "Are you kidding?"

She shakes her head. "Nope. That's the one percent they talk about when they say it's ninety-nine percent effective."

I'm doing the math in my head as she walks out. One percent of the time, Mirena fails. Five percent of women my age can get pregnant. So that's like one percent times five percent. . .My chances of having this baby are five one-hundredths of a percent. "I did everything that anyone reasonable would do," I say. "I tried to prevent this from happening."

"I know you did," Abigail says. "No one could accuse you of being careless."

I flop back against the pillow. "I can't believe it." But I keep thinking of that little otter, over and over. "I just can't believe it."

"I'll call Steve and let him know I need to stay overnight," Abby says. "I can keep an eye on you and Donna both."

"Why?" I sit up. "Why do you need to keep an eye on me?" I narrow my eyes.

"I looked it up, Helen. Abortion's legal in Wyoming, but only until 24 weeks. Since we're already here. . ." Abby inhales and exhales slowly, and then she forces a smile.

"What if I said I might keep it?" I don't even understand the words coming out of my mouth, but something about Abby being so supportive, for her, and seeing that little otter.
. .

I don't want a baby.

I don't.

I never have.

I don't even understand why Donna and Abby and, to a certain extent, even Amanda seem to love babies. Kids are fine, I guess, but the babies just take over and ruin everything. My board would lose their minds. My body would be wrecked. My life would be desecrated.

But that little otter.

"Excuse me?" Abby asks. "I feel like I misunderstood you."

"What if I kept it?" I ask again.

Abby's face comes alive in a way I've never before seen. Her eyes light up. Her lips tremble, and suddenly, tears begin rolling down her face. Her voice is wobbly and her brow is furrowed when she says, "Are you really thinking about that?" Her hands are shaking.

"Maybe," I say.

"Oh my gosh!" Her voice is high and stringy and her hands are flapping around like she's trying to swim through a riptide, and she keeps repeating the same phrase over and over. "Oh my gosh! Oh my gosh! Ohmygosh, ohmygosh!" Then she hugs me.

Not like a good-to-see-you hug. Not like a thank-goodness-you're-alright hug, either.

No, this is a pop-the-bones-in-my-back kind of hug.

She shakes the bed I'm lying on.

And then she keeps right on hugging me. When she finally releases me, she's still crying. Her voice is ragged and stringy. "Oh my gosh, Helen! You could have a *baby!*"

I hate that I like her excitement, but I can't help it. In all my life, I doubt I've ever made my sister that happy. I've probably never made *anyone* this happy. Her excitement isn't enough to ruin my life, but knowing she was holding all this inside of her, reining it all in to try and make sure I knew she loved and supported me, well.

It's significant.

"Okay, okay. That's enough excitement for now. I think it's pushing me the wrong way," I lie. Because if I don't, I might do something stupid just to make Abby happy. Which would be the worst reason ever to have a baby I don't want.

Abby drags in a huge breath, and then she drags in another. "Right. Right. Of course it is. Yes." She swipes at her cheeks, and she wipes her nose, and she dries her face on her shirt. "And who knows what you'll decide to do. I support you either way."

That makes me laugh—great, big, gulping peals of laughter that fill the entire room. "Sure you do."

Now my sister looks entirely sober. Utterly serious. "I do, Helen. I'm really, really trying."

And she is. It's probably the truest thing she's ever said. In this moment, I love her more than I knew I could. The idea of terminating a pregnancy fills her with the worst kind of dread, I know. Her children are her whole life.

I've spent a little bit of time hating them for it. I'm a jealous person. But is it really a stretch to guess that she wants the same thing for me that she prizes for herself? Only, it won't be like that with me. They won't fill me with boundless joy. I'll be much closer to Amanda's constant low-key irritation. If I'm lucky.

"When I was pregnant with Whitney. . ." Abby sits next to me and looks down at her hands. "It was miserable. I was tired. I. . . Nate and I decided it was a smart move for him to get a vasectomy. I couldn't handle any more pregnancies."

"Spoiler alert," I say. "You were going to have *two* more."

"Yeah, so apparently less than a half a percent of vasectomies don't actually work. The man's tubes, like, repair themselves."

"You're kidding."

She shakes her head.

"And Nate was among them?" I sit up straighter. "Wait, was Gabe an oops?"

She shakes her head again. "No, we had Nate tested six months after the procedure as they recommended, and we discovered that it hadn't worked." She sighs. "We prayed about it then, and I know that's not your thing either, but we both felt like we were supposed to have just one more baby, and that's why it didn't work."

"Yeah, yeah." I flop back against the pillows. "Every baby is a miracle."

"No." Abby laughs. "Most babies are tired, grumpy, miserable little brats."

"What?" My head whips sideways, but she seems serious.

"Babies are demanding little tyrants who make you wish you could just die so you could sleep without being interrupted." She sounds sincere, but her eyes are also sparkling. "You've actually been around a little bit for Nathan, so you might realize that I'm serious."

"And you think I should have this one?" I splay my hand over my stomach again.

"I do hope you'll choose the adventure." Abby smiles. "It's horrible and scary and awful and also beautiful, exciting, and brilliant. But what matters isn't what *I* want. It's what *you* think." She pats my hand. "The one piece of advice I'll give is this. It took two people to make that little baby."

David. She thinks I ought to tell David.

We sit there like that for half an hour or so before Abby decides it's time to go check on Donna. I stand up and tuck the photo into my purse. "I'll come too. Maybe it'll be good for me."

"Not all deliveries are as hard as Donna's," Abby says. "In fact, most aren't. You should know that."

"But some are worse."

Abby shrugs. "True."

"If I tell him and then I decide not to have it," I say.

"I know."

"Nothing could hurt him more than that."

"But most of the time," Abby says, "babies bring people together. Keep that in mind, too."

I'm thinking about it as we walk out of the door and into the waiting room, and it's right then that David Park walks through the sliding doors of the parking lot, his arms straining to carry four very full bags of food. "Hey!" He lifts his arms a few inches. "I thought people might be hungry!"

His face is so bright, so animated, and so beautiful.

Until I decide what I want to do, he can't know. Losing this baby would break us, and losing him might break me. I just want to come out of this whole thing unscathed.

I'm starting to worry that my wish isn't even possible.

🎈 12 🎈

DONNA

My baby's in the NICU, and I'm stuck in this hot, muggy room.

It's not ideal, but they said I'll likely be discharged sometime tomorrow, and then I can spend all my time in the NICU, keeping an eye on little Andrew.

"Are you sure about the name?" I'm filling out the form, but. . . "It's not too late to name him after you."

"He is named after me," Will says. "Andrew William Earl."

"We could make him a junior."

"Aiden, Althea, and Andrew," Will says. "They all start with a. I like it. We've talked about it."

"I guess," I say.

"And the more I thought about the junior thing, the more I felt like it might make Aiden feel bad."

I blink.

"Think about it. If anyone ever asked, 'why's your second son the junior?' we'd have to say, 'well, Aiden's not really my son.' And how do you think that would make Aiden feel?"

His unassailable logic, even when making decisions about names, makes me cry again. It's the hormones, I'm sure, but it's also this man. He's always putting everyone else in front of himself. He might want a junior, but he'd never admit it, not if it might make Aiden feel bad.

I feel sorry for some kids who have stepparents, but I never feel that way about Aiden. No one has a better dad than he does. And no one has a better husband than I do, either.

Some woman in black scrubs drops off a tray for me just as I'm finishing the paperwork. I'm nearly done with it, taking a break to poke at the dry and burned lasagna in a little foil pan with my fork, when Helen, David, and Abby walk into my room.

"How are you?" Abby's face is full of concern, her eyes wide and scanning.

"I'm fine," I say. "Just fine."

"You didn't sound fine," Helen mutters. "It sounded like they were amputating your leg."

"Have you ever had an episiotomy?" I ask.

For some reason, that question makes her entire face blanch.

"It's not fun," I say. "And without an epidural, it's uncomfortable."

"I'll remember that," Helen says. "Epidurals good. Episiotomy bad."

"Luckily, we won't need to remember that," David says with a chuckle.

"Right." Helen's nodding, but she still looks pale.

"I thought you might want some real food," David says. "But if you just got dinner, we can wait outside and let you eat."

I shove the tray to the side. "No way. Bring over the real food."

"Our chef has been working on the menu by country," David says. "He's not very good with Mexican food, which is hardly surprising out here, but he's mastered Italian and French."

"I love spaghetti and meatballs," Will says.

David cringes. "The thing is, he was working on Mexican today, and he said the tacos and enchiladas were both a bust, and he can't sell them." He sets the bags on the counter by the window. "I said we'd take it all—free food, right!"

I'd curl up my lip and snarl at him, but I can already smell the garlic and tomato sauce, so I know he's kidding.

"Olé," Helen says.

But when David opens the bags and starts passing containers around, I notice that Helen visibly shies away from several of them.

"Is there Mexican in there after all?" I joke.

"No." David frowns. "Why?"

"No reason," I say. "But pass me some of that fettuccine alfredo, would you?"

A few moments later, Amanda, Mandy, Maren, and Emery show up. They all grab some food as well, and it's nice to know my friends care enough to drive all the way out here with no notice.

After we've all eaten, Mandy and Amanda grab some flowers from the gift shop, head to the NICU to take a peek through the glass, and head home. I sort of expect Helen to take Abby and David home double quick as well. Helen's not much for extended hospital stays. In fact, the only time I've seen her spend more than five minutes inside a hospital room was when her sister was basically shackled to the bed. She bought an ultrasound machine so her sister could come home, for heaven's sake.

"You guys can go," I finally say. "You don't have to stick around for me. Will's here, and I'm fine."

But they don't leave. Eventually David kisses Helen on the cheek and takes off, but Abby and Helen stay.

"I mean it," I say. "You don't have to be here all night."

"I need to leave soon to pump," Abby says. "I'm trying to wean Nate, but it's been harder than I thought it would be."

"Ah, the joys," I say. "I'm actually looking forward to it. It's made me sad not to nurse Althea."

I don't confess that I plan to try once my milk comes in for Andrew. I have no idea whether she'll latch after six months of using a bottle, but I can at least give it a shot. I might be holding out hope that it'll make her love me.

Which is stupid, I know, but the feeling won't quite go away. When they wheel in the pump, I assume Helen will finally leave.

"What's that for?" she asks.

"It's a pump," I say. "I'm not cleared to move around much, so I've only been to see him in the NICU once so far."

"And?" Helen's eyeing the pump strangely, but she knows Abby uses one. Maybe it's the hospital grade variety that's throwing her off.

"I have to try and make sure my milk comes in alright without him to stimulate it." I point. "So I have to pump every two hours until he can nurse."

"Oh." Her eyes widen. "I thought your milk hadn't come in yet so. . .you could just wait. But maybe I should take Abby home."

"Good plan."

Abby looks terribly tired.

"Can I ask you something, though?" Helen's still eyeing the pump.

"Sure." I start assembling the pumping equipment, sticking the plastic flanges together and poking the little rubber gasket in place. There are just so many tubes.

"You have a six-month-old baby," she says. "And now you have another one."

I can't help my smile. "Yes."

"Do you worry that there won't be enough love to go around?"

That makes me laugh. "No."

"Really?"

I shake my head. "That's the funny thing about families." I sigh. "When I was growing up, there never seemed to be enough love to go around. But now that I'm with Will, and now that I've watched Abby and your family, I've learned better. With a family that works the right way, the more people in the family, the more love there is for everyone."

A few hours later, they discharge me and I'm free to visit the NICU cubicle thing that Andrew's in. I'm able to nurse him for the first time at seven a.m. It's magical—he latches right away. It's uncomfortable, but I'm still happy.

Around eight, Will's mother brings Althea and Aiden to visit. I'm tired, so tired, but Aiden's smiling face brightens me up immediately. And when Althea sees me, she lunges forward, her arms outstretched, her eyes wide.

"Ma-ma!"

She's probably babbling, but I'm counting it for her first word.

Most babies' first sound isn't 'ma.' It's harder to say than 'da.' But Althea's first word, if you can call a repeating sound a word, is to call for *me*. I'm taking the win.

I pass Andrew off to Will and take my other baby in my arms. She snuggles up to my neck and sighs softly. It only lasts ten seconds, but it's exactly what I need. I'm shaking just a bit when Althea and Andrew meet for the first time, and then Will's sweetheart of a mother takes some photos of the five of us, together for the first time. Moments later, Althea's wiggling again like an unhappy spaghetti noodle, but I had a brief interval of time, and it was enough.

This is not at all the family I thought I'd have a year ago, not with two babies under seven months old. It's not the family I thought I'd have six months ago, either. My daughter's growing into a real handful, and I struggle to parent her properly. Even so, it's much more than I ever hoped for, mostly in the best ways.

And that's enough.

MANDY

I'm too old for babies.

Don't get me wrong. I like them just fine—they're cute and bubbly and squishy in all the right ways. But they don't sleep very well, and I barely sleep as it is these days. The combination's not good, starting with all the visits you have to make when someone has a baby. From the reports we're hearing, Donna had a rough delivery, but that doesn't stop us from at least going by with flowers.

Poor Will looks like someone beat him.

After we visit with Helen, David, and Abby while eating, walk by and check in on the baby, who is blessedly okay, and pick up flowers for Donna, there's not really much for us to do. I forgot to bring all the cute baby things I ordered in advance online—I found the cutest stuffed llama, of all things. They're making so many cute stuffed animals these days that it's almost criminal—but maybe that's for the best. It would just be one more thing for her to haul home when she does leave. We all sort of stumble over the same idea at the same time after dropping off the flowers.

We have to step out for Donna to pump anyway, so we're

just loitering in the hall when I whisper, "We should probably go home."

It happens to be the very same time that Amanda asks, "There's not much more we can do here, is there?"

And that Maren says, "I think we've stayed long enough."

We all laugh.

Except for Emery, our conscience. "Donna's labor was a mess and her baby has a broken arm."

"But now it's all under control," Amanda says. "If we hang around for very long, we'll just get in the way when she wants a nap or something."

"Besides, I have more questions," Maren says. "You told us what happened that night—a big bunch of nothing—but you had a whole other year of school after that." She levels an impressive glare at me. "So what happened during that last year?"

"Nothing, really," I say.

"No plays?" she asks. "Or what about homecoming? Senior Prom?"

"Jed kept being a pain—angry with anyone who looked my way, but not willing to actually ask me out or even talk to me. Stubborn as a mule. And Tommy had already shown me two different times how he felt, or you know, didn't feel."

"Let's head home." Amanda pulls out her keys. "We can grill her on the way."

"Grill who?" Eddy's huffing a little. "Sorry I'm so late. I had animals to feed, and then the Gibson's draft colicked." He grabs Amanda by the side of her face and kisses her.

And then he keeps right on kissing her.

In the middle of the hospital, they kiss like he's returning from war. I swear, I thought it would wear off, but it has not. Not even a little bit. Those two act like teenagers who don't have a bedroom with a door.

I clear my throat.

"Seriously," Maren says. "It's so gross."

Eddy's smiling when he finally comes up for air. "I love your mother. You can't hate me for that."

"I guess not." But Maren's lip is curled. "But I can be disgusted about watching it on Prime Time."

Emery giggles. "What's that even mean, prime time?"

Maren shrugs. "Who knows? Some old television thing or something."

"Hey, do you have your work truck?" I ask.

Eddy nods. "Fed the animals and then came straight here."

I can tell—he's in his work clothes. It's hard to make Eddy look bad, but vets do not dress for success. They dress for abscesses and eye ulcers and hoof trims. "How about I take your truck home and you can ride with your wife and girls?" I hold out my hand for the keys. "Tomorrow morning, you can drop Amanda off at the retreat and pick up your truck."

Eddy's smile's almost blinding. "You're a genius and a saint." He drops the keys in my hands.

And I escape.

No more explanations. No more grilling. No more pointed questions and interrogations. I'm free.

Amanda tries, feebly, to stop me, but I shoot out of the hospital and beeline for the old blue truck like an oil-slicked pig headed for its trough. I'm *ready* to stop talking about Tommy.

Even so, the whole way home, I can't help thinking about my senior year. It was a whole extra year, and we did not one, but two plays together—both musicals. But Tommy didn't act in those, and neither did Jed. I was the lead in both, and I sang quite a few songs, but there wasn't so much as a *moment* between me and either guy.

The only time I struggled that entire year was actually when that photo was taken, the one Emery found in the box. The one where both the boys are staring at me. But if I get lucky, life will distract the bloodhounds again and I'll be home free. Tommy's coming into town in a few days to sign some papers, and then I'll purchase his family land, and he'll have no reason to come back here, ever.

Not that it would be hard if it came to that. He hasn't come back since his senior year, so I worried it might be painful when I saw him again, but it wasn't. It was as easy as a Sunday morning brunch. As easy as a walk to Birch Creek, the stream that runs across the back of my property. As easy as a drive home from Rock Springs in the summer. By the time I turn down the driveway to my house, I've calmed down.

Tommy will come by, he'll see that my house is just as he thought it would be, and he'll sign those papers. Then he'll leave, and all this painful past-dredging and all the questions will go away. I can live in peace again.

Only, when I pull up in front of my house, someone's car is parked out front. It's a dark blue sedan of some kind, and the plates say Hertz Rental Car. Who would be sitting outside my house at eleven at night? Did Helen's fancy import break down? Or maybe she didn't feel like it was safe to drive in the snow. Either way, she must have been flying to beat me home, because I thought we left first. There's not much hope she's already asleep. I assume she's still planning to stay with me, even with all the baby drama we didn't anticipate.

I brace myself for an interaction with Helen—her new business deal has kept her from being quite as involved with the retreat, and I won't lie and say I've missed having her full attention directed our way. Every interchange with her feels like a game of tug-of-war. In her family, Abigail got all the chill, that's for sure.

Which is really saying something. Abby's not exactly relaxed.

As I walk up the steps, I expect the light in the family room to be on. Helen knows where my spare keys are kept, and I'm sure she grabbed one before she left. But the house is dark.

I hear Jed, rifling around inside as he hears my approach, but there are no other sounds.

So when a dark figure stands up in front of my porch swing, my heart nearly gives out. "Oh!" I swing my purse around like it's some kind of baton and clock the dark man on his side as hard as I can.

"Mandy," he says. "It's me! Don't shoot."

Shoot? As if. . . It's a familiar voice, though. "Tommy?"

I rummage around for my key and open the front door, and then I flip on the lights. Jed comes shooting out, grunting and sniffing and squealing.

"Whoa." Tommy backs up a step. "What's that thing?"

"It's my pig," I say. "Jed."

He laughs then, and I see my dear friend in the old man in front of me. He has the same bright eyes, the same ready smile, and the same unruly hair. In the dark, I couldn't quite connect the boy I knew so well with the man I haven't seen in months. His once dark hair is nearly white, but it's still thick and shiny. Where his eyes were once unlined, the skin framing them is now crinkled with age.

I saw him less than a year ago, and he looks about the same tonight as he did then, but it's different somehow, seeing him here. Seeing him on my porch, the porch I stood on, waving, after he biked me back to my house. The swing we sometimes sat on, reviewing homework. The porch where I sat, dreaming about him for years and years and years.

By now, the boards in the deck have all been replaced. Actually, the hardware on the swing's all new too. But it all looked just the same when he lived here. "This place hasn't changed at all," Tommy says. "But why do you live here? I figured you'd be down at Jed's house."

I frown. "Ethan Brooks owns that ranch now, and did you notice the signs for the retreat?" I can't help my laugh. "We decided to make my family land into a resort, and the entrance for it is about fifty yards down the road. It has made the rest of my family's property *pretty* different, and living close made those renovations much simpler."

"Well, yes, I did hear about that, and I saw the signs. They somehow look both elegant and rustic at the same time."

"That's Amanda's input." I can't help smiling with pride. "You can't really stop change," I say. "So I've been working on learning how to roll with it."

"You look like you've been rolling well, Mrs. Brooks."

"Saddler," I say. "I never changed my name."

"Why not?" He frowns.

Time to change the subject. "Why are you three days early?" I ask. "And why are you here, sitting in the dark?"

"I should have asked whether I could come earlier, I suppose," he says. "And whether I could stay with you."

I splutter.

"You stayed with me when you came out." His voice is matter-of-fact.

"You had a guest wing," I say. "It had its own entrance."

He shrugs.

"I already have a guest," I say. "My business partner just found out her house has bedbugs." I pause so that horror can sink in. It should send him running. Any normal person would shudder in uncontrollable repulsion at the very least.

"And?"

I swallow. "She's staying with me while they clean up her house."

"Okay." He frowns. "Do you only have one extra bedroom?"

"Well, no," I say, "but—"

"You've at least got to let me come in and use the restroom, right? I've been waiting for nearly an hour."

I sigh in defeat and widen the door.

"After you." He gestures for me to go in first.

134

I'm grumbling about faux chivalry as I walk through the door.

"Wait." He picks up my purse and holds it out to me. "Don't forget your baseball bat, officer." His eyes are sparkling.

"It's called a baton, thankyouverymuch." I snatch it out of his hands and shove past him.

No one cleaned up the mess from all the kids and there are cheese sticks that have dried out and look like contortionists. Fabulous. Just the type of image I wanted to present.

"You've totally redone this place," he says, looking around. Then he takes off his shoes and lines them up beside the front door, like he's one of those people who walks around barefoot inside his own house. "It looks great, really great."

"Did you expect it to have the same brown linoleum sixty years later?" I laugh like I changed it more than five years ago. Like my life has been exciting instead of exactly the same since he left.

When really, it's been basically the same for decades.

How pathetic.

"Look at all the cool things you've collected over the years." He runs his hand down the back of the elephant as he walks around the family room. "It really makes everything feel. . .fun."

I'm such an idiot. Why did I buy all that junk? "Well, the bathroom's just through here." I walk toward the hall and gesture.

Tommy follows my direction and walks past me, but he stops just a step away and turns back. "And Mandy?"

I raise my eyebrows.

He whispers, "I'm not afraid of bugs—bed or any other variety." Then he ducks into the bathroom.

Who does he think he is? Fred Astaire? What's he even saying? Because if he thinks an innuendo about *bedbugs* is going to interest me, he has completely lost touch with reality.

I'm not even one inch into figuring out what he's saying when the door swings open. "Oh, man. I've been up since early this morning, and I cannot wait to go to bed." Helen dances through the front door and promptly trips on Tommy's neatly discarded shoes.

I step toward her and catch her windmilling hands, stopping her from falling face-first, but her purse is collateral damage. It hits the floor and sprays things out in all directions. I bend over and start gathering things up and handing them to her until my fingers close around a small photograph. A very unique type of photograph.

"Helen Fisher, what on earth is this?" I wave the ultrasound in front of her. "I may not be an obstetrician, but that looks like a *baby*."

Helen straightens, shoving a handful of something into the bottom of her very expensive, very fancy designer bag, and then she extends her hand imperiously. "It's nothing."

I yank my hand back. "It doesn't look like nothing."

She rolls her eyes. "It fell out of Abby's bag in my car last week, I think from her purse. She's been working on Nate's baby book, and I didn't want her to lose it." She snatches her hand back. "But by all means, you keep up with it instead."

"Oh." I take three steps into the kitchen and drop it on the counter. "Speaking of keeping up with things, I have a friend who was supposed to be coming out in a few days."

"Is that why you bought all this ugly, bizarre stuff?" Helen spins in a circle. "Because the idiots you call friends bought my lie, but if you don't at least take the tacky Ross Dress for Less tags off everything. . ." She shakes her head. "No one's going to believe that my decorator who costs me several hundred thousand a year actually bought a knock-off totem pole and a terrible reprint of Seurat's Eiffel Tower—that's not even the right color palette." She's frowning.

"Helen," I say, glancing back at the bathroom. "You're talking really loud, and that friend I was talking about—"

"Wait, is it a guy?" She bites her lip. "So that's why you got all this weird, new stuff. You want to impress him. I hate to be the bearer of bad news, but you went the wrong way. Trust me. Even the cabin-chic you had going on before this was better than. . ." She waves her hand through the air. "Whatever this is."

I'm going to kill her, but I'm still holding onto hope that perhaps Tommy can't hear any of what she's saying through the door. "It *is* a guy, but I don't want to impress him. And I didn't buy all this stuff recently—"

Helen leans over and yanks a tag off the top of the totem pole that I was too short to see. "Nice try, but *this* tells me otherwise." She tosses it at me, and it bounces off the end of my nose and spins round and round, fluttering down to the ground like an oak pod buffeted by the wind.

The bathroom door opens, and Helen's eyes widen as Tommy emerges.

"Did you really want to impress me?" Tommy's smiling as he exits the bathroom. "Because if so. . ." His grin widens. "Even if all your stuff burned in that fire, you didn't need to buy replacements."

Yes. The fire. I should have thought of that. It would have been a great excuse for why I didn't have anything from my trips. "It's just that—"

"Whoa." Helen's clutched her purse to her chest like it's a shield. "Who are you, and what were you doing in that bathroom?"

"Well, I don't usually talk to people I've barely met about my bladder control and bowel movements, but if you insist." He's smiling.

The usually unflappable Helen looks well and truly horrified.

"This is my friend," I say. "The one I was trying to tell you about. He was coming to visit in a few days, but he surprised me and came early."

Helen lowers her purse, slowly, but she still looks unimpressed. "You're not staying here, are you?" Her nose is scrunched up more than Jed the pig's is, and that's saying something. He's been captivated by something on Helen's pants.

"Who's having a baby?" Tommy picks up Abby's ultrasound photo and peers at it. "What a cute little gummy bear."

"I thought it looked more like an otter," Helen says. "But gummy bear works."

"No one's having a baby," I explain. "That's an old image from Abby—she's making a baby book for her little guy, who's almost nine months old now."

Tommy's eyebrow arches. "Plenty of things in life confuse me. It happens often enough that it's almost a state of being for me at this age. But after forty years in medical equipment sales, I do know that this photo was taken by a Phillips Epiq 5, and with that model, the date's always stamped right here." He taps the top of the image. "Unless I've completely lost my mind, this photo was taken today, so it's not the ultrasound photo for a nine-month-old baby."

I turn slowly toward Helen. "You don't say."

She crosses the room and snatches the photo out of Tommy's hand. "How wonderful that you came early." Then she stomps to her room and closes the door.

"She's a lot scarier than bedbugs," he says. But then he walks past me and slowly turns right in front of the door. "And it's still not enough to scare me away, Amanda. I'll come back to see you in the morning."

❧ 14 ❧

HELEN

I can move like a cat when I want to—not making a single sound.

I'm not sure I've ever wanted to leave without being noticed quite so badly in my life. With her friend there, Mandy was too uncomfortable to drill me about the ultrasound, and I reciprocated by not asking her more questions about said friend.

But this morning, all bets are off.

I've nearly made it out the door, no coffee, because the smell might wake the old bird, when I stupidly step on the slightly-lighter-than-the-others floorboard that squeaks.

I cringe, but I don't hear anything. Maybe it wasn't loud enough. I'm just closing the front door when I hear the bellow.

"Helen Fisher, you stop right there."

I close my eyes and exhale, wondering whether I might be able to sprint to my car and close the door without her catching me. Heart condition or not, she's in good shape. I'm not confident I can make it in these heels, and they're all I have until I meet my assistant later today.

And if I try and fail, it'll be worse, because she'll know I ran.

I inhale and exhale once, channeling all my breezy, no-stress vibes, and then I step back inside. "Good morning, Mandy." I force a smile. "I didn't realize you were awake. I'm in a bit of a rush, since I've got a meeting with—"

"I don't care if your meeting is with God himself." She points at the sofa. "You've got a meeting with me first, and God's patient. He'll wait." She drops her hands on her hips. "I won't."

So much for breezy. "The thing is—"

She steps toward me, one bushy grey eyebrow arching imperiously. "The *thing* is that you're pregnant, and you got an ultrasound when you could've just gotten an abortion, and you had the proof in your purse instead of tossing it in the trash, and so you're going to tell me whatever kind of rubbish is rolling around in your misguided brain, and then I'm going to tell you what to do about it." She points again. "Now, *sit*."

The best defense has always been a good offense. I drop my briefcase and put my hands on my hips. "I'll sit as soon as you tell me why you filled your house with bizarre, tacky, disjointed decor and then tried sneaking some hottie with a smolder in here right under everyone's nose." I can arch my eyebrow and glare with the best of them. "God probably also wants to know what you're doing, but he'll have to wait in line."

She glares at me for about ten seconds.

And then she bursts out laughing. She drops onto the edge of the sofa she was pointing at. "Fine." She huffs. "I'll show you mine if you show me yours."

I exhale gustily and step around the edge of the sofa. "You already saw mine."

"But you lied and said it was Abby's baby. Please tell me you're not going to hide and dispose of that child like you could do with an ultrasound photo."

I roll my eyes. "It's not even a *child* yet. It's a gummy bear."

"Helen."

"Don't *Helen* me," I say. "I know that you and Abby and—"

Mandy leans forward, startling me. "This isn't about religion and it's not about any other nonsense like that."

I blink.

"I'm *old*," she says. "And because I'm old, I can tell you that regret is a pretty constant companion. Do you want to take a guess what my biggest regret is?"

I shrug. "Something to do with Jed?"

She laughs. "No. Try again."

"How about we skip the part where I take a half dozen more stabs in the dark and you just tell me?"

Her smirk is annoying. "You're so smart, and you can't guess my regret?"

"Not having a baby?" I roll my eyes. "Because if you tell me you had an abortion before they were easy or safe, and then you say it was the biggest regret of your life, so help me. . ."

Her hand slams down on the end table, harder than I'd expect from a lady her age. "You're such a brat, Helen. No, I never did that, because I never even got pregnant. But you're engaged to a man who adores you—a *hot* man—and he's willing to put up with all your crap. You may not be *old*, but you ain't young either, and you have a chance to bring a child into this world with that man." She shakes her head. "If you throw that chance away, that'll be your biggest regret until the day you die. Mark my words."

"So what will you do to make sure I don't screw up?" I ask. "Fake a pregnancy of your own, pretend to get an abortion, and then skip town until I see the error of my ways?"

Mandy's frown deepens. "Why are the smartest women also the most universally irritating?" She sighs, collapsing back against the sofa. "Until your brilliant sister and her sister-in-law Amanda showed up in town, I was all alone." She reaches down and scratches Jed's head. "You think that'll be fine. You're happy alone. You have work, and you have enough money to keep yourself comfortable, and you haven't got a clue. In fact, you're probably even dumber than I was."

"I'm not like you," I say. "You had no one. I have Abby and her kids."

She shrugs. "That's true. It's different for you. You'll always be the crazy aunt. But why settle for that when you could be the mother?"

"I don't want to be a mother," I say. "Because if I was, I'd profoundly screw up my child. I'd wreck that kid, because I'm too selfish to be a proper mother."

"As someone who profoundly screwed a few things up, I will just say that you never think you're doing it when you are. The people who are the most afraid of screwing up are usually the ones who do the best job."

I'm too upset to interrogate her. I'm too upset to do much of anything except throw one more glare over my shoulder as I finally march through the front door for a meeting I don't even have. As if running away from the old broad wasn't irritating enough already, I realize she still hasn't told me anything about her visitor or all those tacky rugs and carved figures. Luckily, right as I reach my car, my phone dings, which distracts me from my spectacular retreat.

It's not David, like I expect.

It's not Abigail, which would also be normal.

It's not even my amazing assistant, who's almost always the first person to text me, thanks to the time difference between here and New York City.

No, it's Oliver, my jerk of an ex.

I HAVE ANOTHER SHAREHOLDER FOR YOU. CAN YOU FLY TO BOSTON?

It *is* my favorite time of year to visit the east coast, with the leaves changing and the crisp fall air. And this feels like a good time to break away from all the people here and their provincial sensibilities. Maybe once I'm surrounded by people who haven't been brainwashed by the pro-life movement, I'll be able to make a smart decision.

I call my pilot, waking him up, and ask whether we can get clearance to take off after the recent snowstorm. It was only three or four inches, and it's been hours since it stopped snowing, so about twenty minutes later, he confirms that we can.

I'LL BE THERE BY TWO P.M.

Oliver texts back almost immediately. DINNER AT 6? CAPITAL GRILLE.

Capital Grille opened in Boston not long before he and I graduated from business school, and it was our favorite place to go back then. It's not a strange place to suggest. In fact, it's one of my favorite chain restaurants, but it's weird that *he's* suggesting it.

Up through now, there has been no reason to really have a conversation with David about Oliver. Yes, he's my ex. Yes, he broke my heart almost twenty years ago, but I haven't had much interaction with him since, and I have no plans to in the future.

Or, you know, I *had* no plans.

Now I do.

I'm nearly to the tiny hangar we use while I'm here, just off East Airport Road. I used to drive into Rock Springs to take off, but that's way too big a hassle, and my pilot's actually dating someone who works at the True Value now, so he doesn't mind staying in Manila, thankfully. I have just enough time to call David before leaving.

My adorable boyfriend picks up before the first ring has even finished. "Hey, I was just thinking about you."

"That's not good," I say.

"Well, usually it is," he says, "but in this case, I was contemplating a suicide pact."

"Enjoying time with the parents, are you?"

"They really, really want to take you to dinner. Any chance you love me enough to endure one tonight?"

I cringe. "I definitely love you enough, but we may have to do tomorrow. I just told Oliver I'd meet him in Boston for dinner so he can introduce me to a new shareholder with Vitality Plus."

"Oliver?" David sounds like he's wracking his brain.

"Oliver Lawrence," I say, hoping maybe he won't connect that it's my ex.

"Oliver *Lawrence*, from business school?" He sounds like he's choking. "The guy who stole your senior project and had his daddy bankroll it for him?"

"That's the one," I say. "He was the shareholder at the last meeting—the guy's name, McFarland, was some kind of weird cover."

"Fantastic," David says. "Well, I'm sure it's just delightful for you to be working with that guy again."

"He apologized," I say. "But like everything with him, it was underwhelming and unconvincing."

"And you're flying to Boston to have dinner with him?" One of David's best qualities is that he's almost never jealous. He never throws fits over my time or my interactions, which are predominantly with other men, thanks to their complete entrenched domination in the business world. In fact, no matter who I've been in contact with for the past year, he's never so much as grumped. He doesn't sound jealous now, or at least, not precisely. "Do you need me to come along?"

"And what? Punch him for me?" I laugh.

"Actually, I'd do that for free," he says. "That guy may have stolen your senior project, but I saw him cheating on tests at least twice. Even before he screwed you over, I had no respect for him at all."

"Trust me," I say. "Neither do I, and he knows I feel that way. But if Elon called me himself to offer to introduce me to some shareholders, I'd go."

"After what he said about your dress last year?" David whistles.

"I know, and I hate leaving you alone with your parents too." That's actually a lie, but I care enough to make it sound almost believable.

"Look," David says. "If you need reinforcements, let me know. I would be willing to forgo the pleasure of my parents' company and come to your rescue."

I'm sure he would. His wry humor has me smiling as I board the plane. I'm even in a good mood as I land in Boston. I have a few hours to kill before dinner, so I wander down Newbury Street. It's been a while since I tried on any clothes. Usually my personal shopper takes care of bringing things to me, but it feels like a good time to shop, what with the chaos in my life ranging from bedbugs to internal parasites.

When I wander into the Ralph Lauren store, it's because of a gorgeous black dress in the window. The bodice is simple, but looks almost whalebone in its severity. The skirt is asymmetrical and yet somehow, still full. It looks like the skirt of a wedding gown, but tucked and ruched and rucked up in various places.

And black, of course.

I'm debating trying it on when something just to my right catches my eye. Socks. Tiny, pastel socks. They have a little bear swinging a golf club on the pair in the front, and there are two polo symbols on the other two pairs in the set.

They're clearly socks made for babies.

I pick them up without thinking. I should be examining them for Nate, but they're far too small for that. I bought him the cutest moose socks last month, or rather, my assistant picked them out. He spent half an hour staring at and wiggling his own feet when Abby put them on. Even to someone with a heart of stone, it was pretty cute.

But these are newborn size. They'd be far too small for Nate.

Children grow quickly.

I'm sure it feels like an eternity of long, sleepless nights at the beginning, but as a bystander, Nate has more than doubled in size already and he's not even a year old.

I could buy them for Andrew. He's small enough, but I don't need to get him a package of socks. It's stupid. I should put the socks down. I'd have far more use for a black dress. I decide to try it on, but I take the socks with me to the dressing room, tossing them in the corner of the bench when I try on the dress. The dress is everything I hoped it would be. It's everything I won't be able to wear in another month or two, if I'm stupid enough to keep this baby.

Which I'm obviously not.

Now that I'm away from Abby and Mandy and all the other little goodie goodie moms in Utah trying to force their hopes and dreams on me, I know it would be the ruination of my entire life to have this child.

But when I look at those socks, lying at a strange angle in the corner, alone and neglected, my heart turns over. I plan to walk out of this dressing room with just the dress, march to the register, and buy it. I'll never so much as look back.

As I walk out though, I bend down and grab the socks, and in that moment, I realize that I may be more conflicted than I realized. It may not be Mandy and Abby who are confusing me. I may not know what I want myself.

I march to the front and I buy both the black dress and the tiny socks.

They're diametrically opposed in my mind. I should only be able to have one or the other. I should pick the path I want to follow and stick to it, tenaciously, doggedly. That's what Helen Fisher does.

She never deviates from the path. She plows ahead like a snow plow.

A sleek, beautiful, sparkly snow plow.

Before dinner, I change into the black dress. It looks even better than it did in the dressing room, and when I pair it with an intricately designed onyx necklace, tiny flecks of black stone glittering like dark lace around my neck, and large, crystal cut onyx on my hand and at my wrist as well, I'm ready for dinner. When I glance in the mirror on my way out the door, a black widow stares back.

The woman in that mirror eats men and destroys companies for fun.

She's not nurturing.

She's not kind.

She'd make a terrible mother, and she knows that. She doesn't care. That's Helen Fisher, at her most basic. No matter how much I want the socks, I know what I am.

As I walk through the doors of The Capital Grille, I'm prepared to make my pitch and either buy or convince another shareholder to help me take over Vitality Plus, because this is what I do. Only, when I reach the table, the only person waiting for me is Oliver.

"I lied." He's smiling. "There's not another shareholder."

"What?"

"I thought about telling you they couldn't make it," he says. "But lying got me into trouble with you last time. I thought you might value my early confession." He's dressed impeccably, as always. He's wearing a dark blue shirt—Brioni, I think—open at the top. Not many men hit the gym harder as they get older, but Oliver has. I can see it in the four inches of skin that he's left bare. His smile broadens. "You clearly put some thought into how you wanted to look when you saw me again."

But the only reaction I have to his attempted smolder is revulsion. "You lied to get me out here, and you think that'll be endearing?" I step closer. "Please tell me you're kidding and there will be another Vitality shareholder here any moment."

He bites his lip, eyes me up and down, and then doubles down on the smirk. "You can't fool me, Helen. You didn't dress in *that* to meet a shareholder. You wanted to see me again."

"You have got to be kidding me."

"I'm not." He reaches for my wrist.

I step back, managing to bump into our waiter as he approaches. "Welcome to the Capital Grille. I have menus." He acts like I didn't just crush his foot, so he should get bonus points for having a high pain tolerance.

But I'm not about to order stone crab and reminisce over old times with someone who lied *again* to get me here. "I won't be joining Mr. Lawrence," I say. "In fact, if I were you, I'd kick him out." I pause. "He stinks." I spin on my gorgeous, strappy, Valentino heels and head for the door.

"Wait." Oliver, shockingly, is following me out. "Clearly this was a misstep. I did try to reach out to some of the shareholders I know, but none of them were free on such short notice. I should've waited, but Helen, I couldn't." His voice cracks. "I think I'm still in love with you."

That makes me laugh. Loudly. People around us turn and stare, and the waiter who handled being stepped on so well looks like he might have a heart attack. He's not sure how to usher us out fast enough, clearly.

"I didn't chase you last time, and I didn't apologize, but this time, I will. I'll do anything."

"It's been twenty years, Oliver. We were done a long, long time ago." I start walking again, but he keeps coming.

"He could be cheating on you, you know. Guys like him are always high risk, but with as much as you both travel, how do you know he's even faithful to you?"

We've reached the foyer, at least. Even with the dark

lighting that's a hallmark in places like this, I can see his face. He looks. . .desperate. I have no idea what he wants from me —money? A recommendation? A job?

I don't care what his endgame is. I have no patience for it. "If someone had said that to me while we were dating, or really, while I was dating anyone in the past two decades," I say, "I might have been worried. Or maybe not. Maybe that's why I never dated anyone I cared about. But for the first time, I am dating someone I trust." I smile. "And it's glorious. You should try it sometime."

As I walk out, I realize that it's the first time I've ever dated someone like David. That's the real reason I said yes when he proposed. It's not that I wanted to get married. The very thought almost gives me hives. But with David, it wouldn't be so bad. He'd never have another woman on the side. He'd never be unreasonable and demanding. He'd never betray me in business, either.

He's the kind of guy who gives money to kids with cancer.

He offers to fly out and punch my ex, who clearly deserves a shiner.

He lives in Manila half the year, because I have family there.

He'd be a wonderful dad.

The thought, as I'm climbing into a car that will take me back to the airport, shocks me. It's true, but it shouldn't matter. Those stupid socks are in my bag, the one that's already in the trunk of my car, headed for the airport. The socks I don't need. The socks I don't want.

By the time I reach Utah, it'll be late. Past midnight. Way too late for me to try to talk to anyone. But I want to, anyway. So I text David and tell him that I need to see him. I tell him the meeting didn't go well, but that I'll be back late, and I know his family's there, and I know it's bad timing.

I'LL WAIT UP FOR YOU. COME BY MY PLACE?

I knew he'd say that. I knew it. His place is a small house

he bought from a retired couple and renovated with leftover stuff from the resort. It's far, far too nice for the area, and I'm sure he'll sell it before too long. But there's space for his parents in his guest room, and he doesn't have a dog, so showing up shouldn't wake them.

On the flight, I plan to review my leads for the last few shareholders. I'm only about three percent away from a controlling vote, but that three percent can make or break any attempt to take over. I need to lock the last few votes down, fast.

Instead of working the leads, though, I find myself opening a Word document and making two columns.

Keep. Terminate.

The reasons on the terminate column fill up fast. Health. Time. Sleep. Freedom. Financial success. My happiness. Health and business risks. Baby's happiness. Baby's health. Possibility of health issues for child, increased because of my age.

The more I think about it, the more obvious it becomes that the cost of my having a baby would be catastrophic. If it just means I do one less deal a year, my board members would be justified in losing their ever-loving minds.

The keep column, on the other hand, has nothing listed beneath it. It's still blank. I finally type, 'Make Abby and Mandy happy.' I reluctantly type 'Make David happy.' That is a big one, and I know that. I want to make him happy. I do. I finally write two more words. Otter and then socks.

But looking at those columns, it's clear.

I was confused by bear socks and rhetoric. The only smart move is to tell David—so my conscience is clear—and either tell him that I have an ectopic pregnancy or that I'm termi nating the pregnancy. The white lie about the ectopic would be easier, but I'm not sure whether I can say it out loud.

I'm not sure whether I can survive *not* saying it.

When I finally drive out to his house, my hands are shaking. I'm still wearing the black dress. I feel less like a black widow and more like a widow in mourning. Will David hate me? Will Abby?

Will I hate myself?

Why do women have to go through all this while men get off scot free? I've wondered that a dozen times during my life, nearly every time myself or a friend has had a pregnancy or STD scare.

Until now.

I pull out my phone to text him, but David's already walking toward me. He's wearing plaid flannel pajama pants and a dark blue shirt, which I can barely make out from the backlight of the porch. He opens my door and pulls me up and into his arms.

His mouth presses against my temple. "I've missed you so much." He sighs. "Are you alright? What happened?"

I've never once shown up here late at night like this. Never.

I practiced my speech the entire way over. I know exactly what I should say, and I need to be sitting across from him, in a chair, calm and collected.

But my speech falls apart. The columns blur. My heart is pounding, and I feel sick, and I'm scared, so I just blurt out the words, "I'm pregnant," like they're a grenade I'm lobbing.

David freezes for a split second, and then he pulls me even tighter against his chest. "Oh, Helen, I'm so sorry."

He's *sorry*?

"I know that's been hard for you, but it's alright. I know how you feel about it." He shifts me until he can see my face. "I know what it means to you, and I'll support you however I can."

He's assuming I'll terminate it.

Of course he is.

I've been really, really clear. I've been vocal. He knows me.

And he loves me anyway.

"I made a list," I say. "I didn't just drive over to tell you the second I found out."

His half smile just makes him even more handsome. "I wouldn't expect anything else. Actually, I'm a little surprised you're telling me at all." His hand slides down my arm and his fingers lace through mine. "I'm proud of you for that. Let's go inside. We can talk."

"But you're not going to fight with me?" I blink. "Argue for the future of our baby?"

He sighs. "Would it make a difference if I did?"

I'm not sure. I don't tell him about the socks.

"Your sister Abby would already have done that, I'm sure."

I can't help my wry smile. He knows me well enough to know that Abby already found out, and that she would have made a case for keeping it. "Abby was pretty good about it, actually."

"It's not like you've been close-mouthed," he says. "We all know where you stand."

It hurts, in that moment. Being pro-choice doesn't mean I want to kill babies. It means I value *choices*. It means I think women should be able to choose.

"But that's not what I'm doing," I say. "I bought something." I reach through the open door of my car and rummage around, shoving things down and back until my fingers brush against the soft, fleecy fabric. I pull the socks out and hold them up, triumphant. "I made a list, and there was nothing on the 'keep' side." I clear my throat. "Except making you happy, and making Abby happy." There's no way he would understand otter and sock as logical reasons in that column. But I realize what he will understand.

"And making *me* happy." I hold out the socks. "I thought maybe we should have the baby. If you want that, too, I mean."

I worry he might whoop loudly enough to wake his parents or the neighbors. I worry he might stop breathing.

But I didn't expect him to start sobbing. My big, strong, tough man starts to cry then, his hands reaching slowly toward the socks, as tears roll down his face. "Do you mean that?"

I didn't. Not until this very moment.

But the way he was willing to support me without recriminations, without manipulation, without making me feel less. . . It was just what I needed to know. If he can act like that when I know he wants kids, if he can do what I need instead of what he wants, and if he can do it without making me feel bad, then maybe he and I can do this, together.

The world needs more families with fathers like him.

"I'm worried," I whisper. "I don't think I'll be a very good mother."

"Only the best mothers worry about that," he says. "Trust me."

"That's almost exactly what Mandy said." I'm crying now, too. I hate it. And I love it.

He slowly brushes my tears away with his thumbs. "How many people did you tell before me, exactly?" But he's smiling. He's smiling, and he's crying, and he's happier than I've ever seen him. "Just so I know what to expect."

"The stupid Salt Lake Tribune said they can't run the full-page article on it until tomorrow," I say. "So there are lots of people around who don't know yet." I'm smiling too.

"It was the socks, wasn't it?" David takes them from me. "You saw these adorable little socks, and you decided you had to have the baby."

How does he know me so well?

"I'll have some research to do," he says.

"About what?"

"I want us to buy Ralph Lauren," he says. "As a thank you, I mean." He sighs. "Or maybe we can just name the baby Ralph."

"What if it's a girl?"

He shrugs. "People give girls guy's names all the time. I had this roommate in college named Whitney—cool guy—and he always insisted it used to be a boy's name, you know, before Whitney Houston ruined it."

Now I'm laughing. "You have no naming rights. None at all."

"Oh, come on," he says, tugging on my wrist to try and pull me toward the house. "You know I'll be doing almost all the diapers. I should at least be able to name the little pooper."

"It's not a pooper," I say. "It's a he or a she."

"We should talk about that, too," he says. "I don't think we should force it into a gender box. We should let it choose its own gender when it's old enough."

"You're kidding," I say.

He can't help his grin. "I'm kidding."

Thank goodness. "I need to paint the nursery."

"Oh, no." He groans. "You realize. . ."

"What?"

He takes my hand carefully and strokes the back of it, his fingers coming to rest on the top of my shackle ring. "My parents are going to lose their minds if we aren't married before this baby comes."

"Married?" I lift my eyebrows.

He shrugs. "They're old school."

I lean closer. "Well, as it happens, about that, so am I."

He laughs. "Not even close."

"And I was thinking. . . If we do it soon, I could wear this dress."

He steps back. "That *black* dress?" He raises both eyebrows.

"What?" I spin around. "I like it. Not that many blondes can wear black, and it's flattering. I can still squeeze into it, and I was wearing this dress when I decided to keep our baby."

"I'm sold," he says, "but prepare yourself for all the comments about whether it's a wedding or a funeral."

"My wedding," I say. "Your funeral." I'm smiling even broader, now. "I like it."

He sweeps me up into his arms and carries me across the doorway into his house. "You would. You're a disturbing woman, Mrs. David Park."

"So," a woman's voice says from down the hall. "Does this mean you will be getting married after all?" David's mother is glowering as she steps into view. Not a night person. I make a mental note.

"We don't have much choice now," I say with a grin. "Your son knocked me up."

The look on her face is priceless. It almost makes everything else worth it.

❦ 15 ❦

MANDY

O nce, when I was a teenager, my dad brought home a
horse who had clearly been abused. She shied away
every time anyone had anything in their hands—a
crop, a stick, a bag, a jacket. Anything. If I lifted my hand to
pet her, she'd flinch. Dad wanted to get her under saddle right
away. Nothing gets better while sitting on a shelf, he said.

I had known it was the wrong move, but he's my dad.

He was an expert craftsman of horse tack, hence our
name, Saddler. He knew more about horses than anyone I
had met. But in this instance, he was dead wrong. When we
approached Spooks to saddle her, a nickname that stuck, she
darn near impaled herself by leaping through a wooden fence.
If she hadn't been in a breakaway halter, she might have
snapped her neck, too.

I knew that Spooks needed us to go slow. Slower than
slow, really.

Sometimes I've wondered why on earth my dad thought
that pushing her was a good idea. All it did was scare her
more, causing more damage and trauma at the hands of
humans. But as an adult, I've done some dumb things too

from time to time. As I'm showering, I can't help wondering whether pushing Helen was one of them.

I'm not sure I've seen a human as spooky as her. Amanda was close, but not quite as bad.

The knock at the door when I've barely stepped out of the shower sends my heart racing. I did finally pack Tommy off to the Earls' little motel late last night, but only because Helen's arrival threw him. I'm not sure why he came out several days early, and I'm not sure why he thought he would be staying with me, but I'm not looking forward to seeing him.

I mean, I am.

But I'm also not.

Even thinking about him makes my old heart race, and I'm sure all my doctors would agree that's a very bad thing. I don't have the strongest heart, and even with the rotor-rooter job they did, I'm not sure it's really ever going to be back up to full speed.

Whoever is banging on my door has gotten impatient.

"Coming," I holler. Then I jam my feet into some pants, lament the horrible state of my hair in the mirror, and pull my head through a bright purple blouse that makes me look less yellow and white. Then I'm jogging toward the door, where Tommy's probably the one knocking.

Does he think I'm deaf?

"I said I'm coming!" I swing the door open with a huff, ready to slice him open for just barging over like that.

Only, it's not Tommy.

"What on earth are you doing here at this hour?"

It's Amanda, Emery, and Maren, their arms full of muffins and coffee. "We're coming in," Amanda says.

And then they do, nearly trampling me in the process. "Don't even think about trying to kick us out," Maren says. "I'm missing cheer practice for this."

"For what?" I ask. "You already missed the fireworks with Helen." I clamp my mouth shut a little too late.

"What fireworks?" Amanda asks. "I thought things were going alright—she hardly ever barges in and bosses us around now that the retreat's up and running. I thought she'd moved on to terrorize new people on other projects."

'Running' might be a strong word for our little retreat. According to Helen, it's barely hobbling along so far, but for a retreat in the literal middle of *nowhere*, I think it's off to a good start. Now if she'd share her rolodex or better yet, start making some calls herself, I'm sure we could fill it up double quick. "Never mind that. She's a difficult houseguest." Hopefully they'll think we got into a fight over wet towels or dirty socks.

Amanda frowns. "You're just trying to distract us, aren't you?"

"From what?" I sigh. "You're here at—" I glance at the clock. "Ten till seven in the morning? School doesn't even start until eight-thirty, and—"

"Precisely," Emery says. "That's how we convinced Mom to drag us over. Aunt Helen texted Aunt Abby last night and said she ran into *Tommy*, and then Aunt Abby texted Mom. I thought you said he wasn't coming for a few days."

"We don't even know the whole story yet," Maren practically wails. "And where's this photo Emery saw?"

"What photo?" I sink onto the end of the sofa in defeat.

Amanda shoves a banana nut muffin in my hand, and then she offers me a coffee. "It's decaf," she says.

I stand back up. "Ah, ah, ah. I'm not eating the crappiest muffin and drinking decaf, not if you want the rest of the story." I shove them back at her.

Amanda begrudgingly takes them.

"Why'd you even get banana nut?"

"The Grill only had one chocolate muffin and two blueberry." Maren snatches the chocolate one out of the bag and licks the top. "Mine."

"You are so gross," Emery says.

"Give me a blueberry." I hold out my hand until Amanda gives me one.

"Now pay up," Emery says. "We're wasting time. What happened your senior year?"

"I already told you." I sit down again, this time, eyeing the blueberry muffin. "His dad died, and he moved to live with his uncle."

They all light on seats all around me, reminding me of birds in a flock, settling in on electric wires to chatter.

"Come on," Emery asks. "That photo I saw—with both of them looking at you. When was that taken?"

I sigh.

"Just tell us," Amanda says. "We may as well know it all before we meet him and pretend that you aren't in love with him and that you didn't lie about traveling the world and *marrying* Jed."

"Wait, she lied about marrying Jed?" Maren asks. "I thought she just lied about—oh, wait. I guess I did hear that. It's hard to keep all the nonsense straight."

Amanda laughs. "It is. Speaking of, how did you keep it all straight when you went to stay with him?"

"It was easy," I say. "We didn't talk about when I was supposedly married. We didn't talk about my traveling much either. We just. . .watched television. We went to dinner. We laughed about the old days." I shrug. "No big deal."

"But every single person in town knows you never married Jed," Emery says. "Aren't you worried he'll find out?"

"I am," I admit. "A little, but he hasn't been here in sixty years. No one will even recognize him, and if they do, it's unlikely they'll say anything that would set off red flags. My biggest liabilities are the three of you, and you know the lie."

I take a bite and chew it. "But that's why I want him to sign his papers and go right back home."

"Wait," Amanda asks. "What papers?"

"He's not here for a visit," I say, "even if Emery invited him. He came out to sell me his family property. Once he does that, there will be no reason for Thomas Collins to ever return."

"That's so depressing," Maren says.

"No." I shake my head. "It's exactly as it should be. That piece of my past will stay where it belongs."

"Tell us the end, and we'll decide whether we agree with you," Amanda says. "Stop delaying already." She looks at the clock. "Don't think we don't know what you're doing, putting us off."

"Our senior year was just like any other year. I did two plays with Tommy, and he didn't act with me. He directed."

"Okay, but what about homecoming?" Maren asks. "It seems like the dances are when things really start to happen."

"I had a big horse show," I say. "I didn't go."

"Prom, then," Maren says. "What about prom?"

I sigh. And then I dive in.

Pep rallies when your school's as small as Manila High School are kind of a joke. I mean, I shouldn't really be thinking that, since I'm a fill-in cheerleader. But I'm only doing it because Mrs. Lyons begged and Simone sprained her ankle. Once we're done with the obligatory cheers to get us going, Principal Lyons stands up and claps himself. "Thank you, ladies. Appreciate the enthusiasm." He smiles.

So do we, because his mustache has a piece of corn stuck in it.

Tommy elbows me. "What's strange is that it's ten in the morning. Did he have corn for breakfast?"

I don't even try to suppress my grin. Clearly the principal is clueless. "Or has that corn been in there since last night?"

"Isn't he married?" Tommy asks. "Why didn't his wife notice?"

"Ooh, maybe they're fighting," I say. "Maybe he was on the couch."

"Hush," Denise hisses. "You're being rude."

"I'm sure you're all wondering why we're here." The principal's now grinning even bigger. "We have a suggestion for how to handle prom this year that the faculty thinks is a good one. You know our focus this year has been on growing our school pride—our spirit."

Boy do I know it, but bigger pom poms and extra pep rallies can only do so much.

"Instead of having our classic vote on students to fill our prom court, we've decided this year to do something a little different."

At least we're all listening, even if it's because none of us can seem to stop watching that little yellow piece of corn bob up and down.

"Each club will be able to nominate someone to be a part of the court, and then those members will compete in a series of events on the Saturday before prom. The winners will be the prom king and queen!"

"Events?" Denise asks. "What kind of events?"

"Oh, don't you worry about that," he says. "We have something big in mind, and it'll double as a fundraiser. People can buy tickets to come watch the competitions."

"Are you kidding right now?" Frank's the biggest jock at our school. Not the best athlete, but the literal largest jock. He must be six foot four and two hundred and twenty pounds. "That's a stupid idea."

"It was my wife's idea," Principal Lyons says. "Care to change your position?"

"My what?" Frank frowns.

"I'm not here to ask for your opinions," Principal Lyons says. "I'm informing you of a change. Your clubs will vote in their nominees today, and then at the end of the week, we'll be ready for the competition."

By the end of the day, I've been selected for choir, theater, and 4H. I told them to choose someone else, but with a small school, there aren't that many options. There are only two other girls who have been chosen by the other eight clubs. That means me, Denise (who was chosen for honor society and debate), and Janet (who picked up all the sports) will be competing for the prom queen spot. Principal Lyons has summoned us all to his office to review more details of the rules.

"I'd be happy to concede," I say. "I'm sure that either Denise or Janet will win anyway."

"That's stupid," Tommy says. "You're usually really competitive."

But I'm staring at what looks an awful lot like my past repeating all over again, because for the boys, Tommy was chosen for theater and 4H, and Jed was picked for all the athletics. There are two other boys—Gregory, chosen for honor society and debate like Denise, and Jerry, chosen for choir. I would really, really like to ensure that I don't plunge headfirst down the same path.

"If you want more competitors, why don't you invite the juniors to—"

"No," the principal says. I'm relieved to notice the corn is finally gone. I can't help wondering whether he ate it inadvertently or it just fell off. "Adding the juniors would give us too many people. And you can't back out, either. We've already sold dozens of tickets for the event, many of them marking down that they'll be cheering for you." He smiles at me, and I want to puke. "We're seating them in sections based on who they're cheering for."

"That sounds mean," I say. "How will we feel if we have the smaller section?"

"You won't," Principal Lyons says. "So you don't need to worry about that."

"I can't believe you're selling tickets." I roll my eyes. "Trying to finance a new rolling chair?"

"We need to raise money to pay for the refreshments and decorations for prom, so the more people who come to watch, the nicer your event will be," Principal Lyons says. "You should be thanking me. We might actually have decent food and more than a few flowers made of paper this year."

"Assuming any of us are still talking to each other and want to go," Gregory says.

"Oh, please. My Manila High Mustangs won't get upset about a little healthy competition," Principal Lyons says.

"What are the things we'll be doing?" Jed asks, looking askance at Tommy. "Tug of war? Or perhaps a weightlifting competition?"

"You wish," Tommy says. "Not everything in the world is solved with muscle."

That reminds me of his pronounced chest muscles during *The King and I*, and I shake my head to clear it.

"There will be five different competitions for both the boys and the girls, and they will reflect the following qualities, which we like to encourage. First, academics, to show a developed and inquiring mind." Principal Lyons smiles. "We are proud of the intelligence of our students."

"But what's the contest for that?" Tommy asks. "Is it like a sheet of math problems we have to work?"

"That wouldn't be any fun to watch," Principal Lyons says. "But we aren't telling you what the contest will be until you're about to start, so none of you need to worry about that."

I'm not the only one who groans.

"The second test will determine who has the strongest body."

"Nice," Jed says.

"And the third will test the competitor's artistic talent."

Jed groans this time, which makes me laugh. For a split second, it feels like we're still friends.

"The fourth is a test of animal husbandry, since we live in a predominantly ranch-based community. The last will be a test of your ability to work with others and build a group."

Tommy looks like he wants to drop out too, but he doesn't ask. As soon as we're dismissed, we all head outside. Jed has a work truck, so he disappears almost right away in a growl of the diesel engine. Neither Tommy nor I have families with enough income to afford more than one vehicle, so we're still stuck riding bikes.

Like always, he keeps riding beyond the turn off for his house, riding me home to keep me company. "This whole thing is so dumb," I grumble.

"I don't know," he says. "I've been hanging back so Jed could try to get himself together. Maybe that was the wrong plan. He's been sulking for two years. It may be time to push him a little." I don't like the look on Tommy's face as he waves goodbye.

And I can't help trying to work out what exactly these contests are going to look like over the next two days. Nothing prepares me for what Principal Lyon's wife had in mind.

When I arrive on Saturday morning, barely convincing my parents not to come with me, I've chosen to wear jeans and a t-shirt with sneakers. I have a pair of boots in my backpack. I have no idea what the athletic contest will entail, but if I wind up riding a horse at any point, I want jeans. My boots chafe the sides of my legs, otherwise. I'm not that keen on winning, but I'd rather not embarrass myself entirely either.

When I reach the school, there's no one there. There are signs directing us to continue to the fairgrounds. It's only a block away, just past the sheriff's office and the DMV, but now I'm going to be late. As I hop back on my bike, I notice there are more people arriving and rerouting behind me. In fact, as I head down the road I see waves of people meandering over. I'm not sure whether to be annoyed or excited.

I settle for both.

I don't want to create any more issues with Jed than I already have, and I certainly don't want to be an idiot who thinks Tommy likes her *again,* so things like this are irritating, shoving us all together and shaking us into a tizzy. But in another way, we've never done anything like this, so it feels a little exciting.

Last year Manila High had its first yearbook—a book that Denise spearheaded, showing all our individual photos for students and faculty, as well as pictures of all the club events and meetings, dances and parties. It was pretty fun, even if it was a little pricey. I thought Mom was going to pass out when she found out it cost ten dollars, but she insisted I had to have one.

Memories. That was her reason.

This will certainly make for some interesting memories, but the people gathering around me aren't just students. Most of their parents have come along too. It's probably a commentary on just how pathetic Manila's social scene is, but Mom's going to be mad I didn't get her a two-dollar ticket once she hears that everyone else brought their parents along. The parking lot behind the arena is nearly full. There weren't even this many people at the last rodeo.

Tommy's parents climb out of the car at the end, and Tommy jogs over to meet me where I'm parking my bike. "You look ready."

Like me, he opted for jeans, but unlike me, his boots are on his feet, not in a bag.

"We could be doing races or soccer or something," I say. "You're going to do those in boots?"

Tommy shrugs. "If we're playing soccer or basketball or

doing a footrace, Jed's going to beat me whether I'm wearing boots or sneakers."

"Do you really care?" I ask. "I mean, who cares who wins prom king?"

Tommy shrugs. "I do hate losing, though."

The idea of Denise being prom queen doesn't faze me, but I hate the idea of her beating me. While everyone else is walking to the bleachers, Tommy and I keep moving around and head for the entrance, near the judges' stand. That's where Principal Lyons is standing, along with Jed, Denise, Jerry, and Gregory.

"You made it." Principal Lyons smiles. "Excellent. Now, once Janet arrives, we can get started."

While we wait, the high school yearbook coordinator snaps photos of most of us. I force a smile for mine, but then Tommy shoves me a little to the right, in Jed's direction. "How about a photo of Mandy and Jed?" he asks.

"That's fine," I say at the same time Jed surprises me by saying, "Sure."

"Great idea," the coordinator says. "But you should be in it too. Aren't the three of you good friends?" She's smiling blithely, clearly oblivious to the actual relationships of all of the students.

"Uh, sure." Tommy steps toward us, and I force another smile at the camera. I can feel the guys' eyes turned inward, but I ignore it. They're either looking at me or they're glaring at each other. Either way, it's not my problem. I'm grateful when the photos are all done.

Over the next five minutes, people slowly trickle over, but there's still no sign of Janet. I can't help, along with the other participants and the audience, looking at the center of the arena where there are several large tents in bright colors set up. "What's underneath those tent flaps?" I whisper.

"A clown, a face-painter, and a juggler," Tommy says.

"You're such an idiot," Jed mutters.

"What was that?" Tommy asks. "I thought you didn't know how to speak."

Instead of scowling, or fuming, or muttering a swear word, Jed half-smiles. It's a breakthrough of shocking proportions, and I begin to wonder whether Tommy might be right.

It makes me think about the one time I really made him mad when we were kids. At an end of the year party for school, we went to Libbert's Pond—a pond on the Libbert family's property with this cool rope swing. Jed had pulled my hair while we were eating lunch, and I had squawked. Everyone laughed, so to get back at him, I shoved him into the lake. It seemed equal and opposite to a ten-year-old. Only, instead of falling in the lake, he slipped and landed face-first in the mud. Every kid in my class had howled with laughter when he stood up.

He was mad at me all day—right up until another kid, Kyle, started trying to convince me to get a ride home with him instead of Jed. That's when Jed finally stopped being mad and dragged me to his mom's car.

When pushed, he got over it.

We've tried pushing a little. The play was a bit of a push, but he got sick. The dance was too, sort of, but not really. But now he has to fight for a spot to be prom king, and Tommy and I are right here beside him.

Maybe what he needed all along was a little pressure.

Just then, Janet comes jogging up, wearing shorts, even in this chilly morning air, and a t-shirt and sneakers. Her hair's pulled into a high ponytail, and her eyes are bright. She looks like she could be jaunting over for a photoshoot for some fitness magazine.

"Alright, everyone," Principal Lyons says. "Thank you so much for your patience while we collect tickets and provide ballots to all the attendees. We're so excited that this Crown Challenge has been so well received and attended. I'm delighted to announce that we've raised almost twice as much money as we needed to fund the prom, and not only will the tickets now be free, but we'll have a full dinner at the prom instead of simply bowls of chips and dip."

"Probably soggy ham sandwiches," Jed says.

It wasn't directed at me specifically, but he did speak in my direction. I can't help the lightness that rises up inside of me. Maybe Tommy was right. Maybe by prom, Jed and I will finally be fine again.

"Better than those stale potato chips last year," Tommy says.

That seems to remind Jed that he didn't go the last year, and he frowns. I bump Tommy, and he shoots me a chagrined look, at least.

"And now, it's my honor to announce the contest for today. But first, I'm going to welcome my wife, who's going to share her favorite fairy tale, which inspired our competition today. You may have heard of it before—Hansel and Gretel."

There isn't a lot of applause as Mrs. Lyons stands up. I think people are a little confused. I know I am. The story I know is about kids eating a candy house and getting thrown into an oven or something, so I'm not sure how that might have inspired a competition for teenagers. . . Unless they're planning to bake us?

"Hello, everyone. For years now, I've stayed home with our three children while my husband has gone out into the world to bring home some bacon for our family."

There's some scattered, lackluster applause and hooting.

"But a few weeks ago, as I was telling little Ricky his bedtime story, he asked again for Hansel and Gretel, his favorite tale too, and my husband had been talking about ways to raise funds to pay for prom, and also about the process for selecting the prom court, and we had an idea."

The gathered audience of nearly a hundred people—students and parents—seems to be as lost as I am.

"The story of Hansel and Gretel is about two siblings

whose mother dies. When their father remarries, it's to an awful woman who sends them to chop wood in the cold all day while she eats all the food, leaving them nothing but scraps. The children are starving slowly, as you might imagine."

Connect the dots quick, lady. "We're not little Ricky," I mutter, "and this is really weird."

Jed laughs, looking sideways at me.

I smile back, and he doesn't recoil. My heart lifts, and I can see that Tommy sees it, too.

"Well, those children finally decided they should run away instead of starving at the home that's no longer their home, so they gather their meager belongings and leave." She drops her voice a bit, but luckily she's still talking into the mic. "Hansel asks his sister Gretel how they'll find their way back if they can't find food in the forest. She tells him they can take their scraps of bread and break them into tiny pieces and leave a trail of bread crumbs the whole time they walk into the forest, and then if they have to, they can follow them back."

"They're starving and she uses their tiny bits of food. . .as a trail?" Jed arches one eyebrow. "That's pretty smart."

Now we're all laughing.

"They do search far and wide in the forest, but they find nothing that they can eat. In defeat, they finally decide to go back home." Mrs. Lyons sighs dramatically. "When they try to turn around, they discover—"

That hilarious little Dolores kid from the play shouts, "The bird ate it all!"

Mrs. Lyons smiles. "Yes, you're right. A naughty bird had eaten all their bread crumbs, and they were very lost."

"That's what you get for making the worst plan ever," Tommy says.

Jed and I both laugh.

"Starving, scared, Hansel and Gretel wander around

without much hope, assuming they'll die in the forest. But that's when they find—"

"The candy house!" Dolores shouts. "And they eat it."

Mrs. Lyons is starting to look irritated. "Yes, that's also correct. They find a candy house and start to eat it, but then an old woman catches them and scolds them for eating her house. Luckily, she offers them real food if they come in, and those naughty little children follow her right inside and eat up the soup she offers them. They notice piles of messy bones in the corners of the home, but they're so tired from their ordeal, they curl up and fall asleep right away."

"So they stole food off her house, and then they fell asleep on the floor?" Jed shakes his head. "They kind of deserve to be eaten."

"When they wake up," Mrs. Lyons says, intentionally ignoring us, "Hansel, the boy, is stuck in a cage. Gretel is told that she must cook and clean for the witch until her brother is fattened up."

"Ew," Jed says. "Who wants fatty meat?"

Mrs. Lyons powers through. "But when it comes time to cook him, the witch prepares the oven and asks Gretel to check it. Gretel, being quite the little—"

"Miscreant," Jed says.

Everyone laughs.

"Yes, I suppose that, too, but being an opportunist, shoves the witch into the oven, and closes the door. Then she saves her brother and they escape. But before they do, they find a big barrel of jewels, and they fill their pockets with them, as many as they can carry. They wind up using a few of the gems to secure a ride home on the back of a horse ridden by a passerby. When they get home, their stepmother is dead, and their father is quite happy to see them. They live happily ever after with the jewels they stole."

"Great. It's a story about how grand theft and murder pays," Tommy says.

"And candy houses," I say. "Don't forget that part."

"We haven't forgotten any of those parts," Mrs. Lyons says. "In fact, we have several tasks you'll have to complete today, and we have a panel of judges who will be scoring you on how you do. If the audience can look at their ballots, they'll see an area where they can vote for their favorite candidate in each category. Their combined votes will be equal to one of the appointed judges. The male and female candidate with the highest scores will win."

"But what are the activities?" I ask.

Mrs. Lyons nods at her husband. "Almost time to find out."

He walks toward the big blue tent closest to us. "In the story, Gretel has to save Hansel. So we have asked a Hansel to be with us today, a brother of one of the candidates, but we also understand he's someone who's precious to quite a few of you. All our activities today will have as their goal, saving our handsome Hansel from being eaten by the witch."

Mrs. Lyons nods at her husband. "Go ahead and reveal Hansel, who is home from college and agreed to help us out."

Principal Lyons yanks the blue fabric down and underneath, in a very strange cage made of what appears to be scrap lumber, is Clyde Brooks. Instinctively, I whip my head sideways. All traces of the smiles and lighthearted behavior from Jed earlier is gone.

Clyde smiles his winning smile and winks at me. "Hey, Mandy. Be a doll and win prom queen. That'll get me out of this thing, right?"

16

MANDY

Two years' worth of work, undone with one cocky smile.

Normally, I don't blame Clyde for what happened with me and Jed. It was Jed's stubbornness and my misguided decision-making that broke us, but in this moment, it's hard not to blame Clyde at least a little. He's clearly needling his younger brother on purpose.

No matter the reason, watching Jed's face return to being open and expressive. . .only to close off again hurts. It also makes me want to win, just so I can kick Clyde—hard. He has to know that Jed and I haven't been speaking, and to come back and pose and smile and wink in front of most of the town. . .it feels low, even for him.

"Our first exercise will be one that will test your physical strength and the dexterity of your fingers." Principal Lyons points at a large green tent, not far from where Clyde's preening. "If you would all accompany me over here, we can begin." He starts to walk.

"Dexterity of our fingers?" Tommy's expression is hilarious. "What's next? The strength of our sinews?" I'm chuckling as we walk closer, and that makes both Clyde and Jed frown.

Why are all men such babies? Is it reasonable to want a woman to like *only* them? To laugh for *only* them?

Please.

Principal Lyons has a real flair for the dramatic I didn't notice until recently. He's smiling broadly at first, and then his face becomes serious as he slowly whips the blue tarp away to reveal. . .

A pile of logs.

Or to be more precise, it's a large tree that someone has split into seven round sections.

"What are we supposed to with that?" Tommy asks. "And how in the world is it going to show that we have dexterous fingers?" His eyes are wide and this time, because he's louder, the entire audience laughs.

Principal Lyons is frowning, which is bad for Tommy, since he's one of the main judges. "Over on the other side you'll find axes. Each of you has ten minutes to chop these hunks of tree into blocks of firewood, and the person who has the most usable pieces at the end *wins*." He glances at his watch. "Now, *go*."

We're splitting wood?

It must be from the story—they had to split wood at the beginning, right? But this is really stupid. It takes me a minute just to get an axe, with everyone rushing over and snatching one like the Big Bad Wolf is coming. In my entire life, I have never once split firewood. I suppose that means I'm spoiled, but this isn't my task at home.

Plus, we have a furnace that my dad sprang for three years ago, so even he hasn't had to cut much wood since then.

When I finally do manage to drag a large, round block of wood away from the others and heft my axe, then bring it down, the end of it sticks in the surface and it takes me a good minute and a half to free it again.

Meanwhile, Jed and Tommy have both split their rounds and then split them again into nice fat quarters. They're well on their way to having eight or ten pieces of wood each. It's a little reassuring to notice that Denise is just as bad as me. She's staring at her wood, and eyeing it strangely, as if she might cow it with a good, strong glare.

But then she walks back to the woodpile and grabs a smallish piece. It doesn't look like it'll make much for her. Until she stacks it on top of her big round chunk and splits it in half.

I'm swearing under my breath as I bring my axe around again.

But I either have a faulty axe, or I'm just really, really bad at this, because when the ten minutes is up, I've managed to chunk off a few strange pieces of bark, but my main hunk of wood is mostly intact, whereas everyone else has managed to split at least one big round hunk into smaller pieces.

"Well, it was neck and neck, but it appears that our winner is Jedediah Brooks." When I glance over, they're actually *weighing* the wood that was split.

What a stupid game.

"And the clear loser for this game today is Amanda Saddler." That's not fun to hear, and neither are all the giggles and chuckles and jokes coming from both the audience and my co-competitors. "But let's talk about why this task matters." Principal Lyons points at his wife, which is really strange.

She starts talking right after, so I'm thinking they've been watching too many television programs. "What a great idea," she says with a smile. "The next portion of our competition is about to begin, so the placing you held in this first portion will determine the position into which you enter the second part of our contest."

Great.

Mrs. Lyons pulls a bowl out from behind the cage where

Clyde's still smiling, and holds it up. "This bowl holds the assignment for the next portion of our game. In the story, there was Hansel, Gretel, the bird who ate the bread crumbs, the witch, the stepmother, the father, and a bystander with a horse who saved the children at the end. As you all remember, we already have our Hansel." She points at Clyde who waves and takes a bow. "But this bowl contains papers that will give each competitor information about their role in the story. You come and draw your papers one at a time in the proper order." She holds out the bowl. "You can draw in the order you earned with the last game."

"But how do we know what to draw?" Denise asks. "Even if I was first place, my draw would still just be luck, right?"

"You weren't first, though." Janet's smiling.

"I haven't even told you what the goal is," Mrs. Lyons says. "So let me explain that now, before you all draw." She smiles. "If you're the witch or the stepmother, your goal is to kill all the other competitors."

The crowd murmurs, and a few of them boo.

"If you're Gretel, your goal is to save Hansel before he can be eaten."

Clyde flexes and half bows over in his poorly made cage.

"If you're the father, the horse, the bystander, or the bird, your goal is to survive by helping identify and eliminate the witch and stepmother. The witch will eventually have to kill everyone other than the stepmother to win."

"How would we kill someone?" Jed asks.

The audience laughs.

"Just because you're a loser doesn't mean you'll be the witch," Clyde says. "Have a little more faith in yourself."

Jed scowls.

"It's a good question," Mrs. Lyons says. "Should you draw the witch, you'll be the only one in the game who can murder the others. The stepmother will help you, because she only wins if the witch wins, and if the witch inadvertently kills the stepmother, the witch will lose, so she must be careful to defend her ally. And here's the real catch. The paper with the stepmother on it will tell whoever draws it which color paper is the witch. The Gretel card, on the other hand, will identify who the stepmother is. That means that the stepmother will be known to Gretel, and the witch will be known to the stepmother. The witch won't know who's on her side and who's against her, just as the witch in the story was blind."

"Lemme get this straight," Jed says. "If we draw the witch, we know nothing, but we're supposed to kill everyone *but* the stepmother?"

"Right," Mrs. Lyons says. "So it would be wise for the stepmother to reveal herself in some way. Of course, the others will also be watching."

Tommy's frowning now, too.

"But," Jed says, "if we're Gretel, we have to. . .what? How can we win?"

"Great question," Mrs. Lyons says. "The witch wins by killing everyone except the stepmother, but Gretel only wins if she can retrieve the necessary objects and slay the witch before dying herself."

"So other than Gretel, the witch, and the stepmother, we're all pawns?" Tommy asks.

Mrs. Lyons shrugs. "Sort of," she says. "Except you'll be doing activities that require you to be graded, and so anyone could conceivably still win for prom queen or king based on their overall scores."

"What are the objects?" I ask.

"You'll hear about them once we've drawn," she says. "Be patient."

Presumably those things are hidden beneath the additional tents. None of us look very excited, and the audience looks almost as irritated as I do. I think the Lyons let this get a little too complicated.

"Well, let's get going," Mrs. Lyons says, probably more

worried about the half-confused, half-bored audience than I am. "Jed, you draw first. Then Tommy. After that, Janet, then Jerry, Greg, Denise, and finally Mandy."

I'm dead last. Of course I am. Stupid wood-cutting chore.

I watch as Jed draws a blue card, Tommy, a green one. Then Janet draws black, Jerry draws white, Greg grabs purple, Denise grabs yellow, and all that's left for me is bright red.

I read my card.

CONGRATS. YOU ARE GRETEL, YOUR STEP-MOTHER'S CARD IS GREEN.

I scan around the circle, trying to remember who drew green. My eyes stop on Tommy, where he's eyeing me curiously.

Great.

My best friend is the stepmother, one of two characters bent on destroying me. How typical for my life. My one real ally is my enemy. Now I just need to watch him to see whether he sends the witch a signal of some kind, but I can't make it obvious that I'm watching him, or I'll give myself away.

"Wait," I ask. "How does the witch kill people? You never said."

Mrs. Lyons says, "The witch's paper comes with small stickers, and if he or she manages to put one on you, you're dead."

"I guess that means she's not the witch," Jed says. "Or she'd already know that, right?"

"Or she's really smart and realized that no one would know what a sticker meant without her drawing attention to it." Tommy shrugs.

Jed rolls his eyes.

We all shove our papers into our pockets.

"Now, our first task is one of art. You're all going to make candy houses, and the audience is going to vote for which one is the best." She points, and Principal Lyons yanks the cover off the largest tent-structure. It also happens the be the farthest from us. It's nearly all the way across the arena by the stands. I'm sure that's by design, so the paying spectators can see us fail miserably to stick a cookie house together with frosting.

"But that's not all," Principal Lyons says. Could he be any more corny? "Each seat here has the cookie parts necessary to build a house, and the individual sheets are equipped with frosting as well. But, each seat has only one type of candy decoration. In order to make the most beautiful house possible, you'll have to negotiate with the others for a trade."

Of all the ridiculous. . .

"Now, the fastest of you will get the best seats. Go."

Oh, good grief. I wasn't chosen for my athletic ability, but I hoped I'd at least beat Denise, Gregory and Jerry. When I come in dead last, it's a little depressing. It also leaves me with the last seat of all, which has a huge bowl of. . .Bit-O-Honey? Really? How exactly am I supposed to do to decorate my house with a bowl full of sticky brown taffy?

Jed snagged Good and Plenty, which are bright pink and white pill-shaped treats. They'd make a great boundary on the rooftop, and a wonderful pavement item. He could also use them as bricks, I suppose. Tommy got Boston Baked beans, which are bright red peanuts covered with sugar. He could do basically the same things with those, but they're more homogenous.

Denise pulled Lifesavers, Janet has Lemon Heads—little yellow balls. Jerry nabbed sugar babies—little, sticky brown balls, and Greg, who ran surprisingly fast, managed to get chiclets. Those may actually be the best choice of all.

Other than Tommy, no one will trade with me, leaving me with a pile of toffee and a handful of Boston Baked Beans to decorate my entire house once I've assembled it. Janet's having trouble using the icing to hold things together, however, and I realize pretty quickly that I can lick either side of a Bit-O-Honey and it'll hold even better than glue.

"How about now?" I ask Janet, eyeing her red, irritated face. "Want to trade for some Lemonheads now?"

She's scowling, but she offers me a handful.

And now I'm ahead of her, and I have Boston Baked Beans and Lemonheads with which to decorate. I also realize that Bit-O-Honey is pretty decent to use for a paved walkway, and with my knife, I can even make it look like there are paving stones.

Pretty soon, little wrappers have nearly filled my trash bucket, and my house looks pretty decent, if I do say so myself.

"What happens to the first and last place houses?" Jed asks.

I glance at his, and I'm absolutely disgusted for thinking mine looked good. Jed's looks like it was made by some kind of famous artist. His house looks like a Barbie mansion. He used every single piece of gingerbread they provided and it's at least twice as big as mine.

"Four minutes left," Principal Lyons says.

Jed swaps Greg for some chiclets, and hastily mashes down a driveway made of rainbow squares, and when they call time, it's clear he's going to be the winner.

I don't even give other people's houses much notice, because none of them can even compare. Until I glance over at Tommy.

Instead of making a house, he made what looks like a supermarket.

"What is that?" I hiss.

Tommy shrugs. "I had all these baked beans. I thought I'd make something that would be all brick, like a bank."

A bank? When I turn to look it over directly, I recognize the building he copied. There's even a sign that says 'Vernal National Bank' on the front in a combination of white Good and Plentys and Boston Baked Beans, outlined with the taffy he swapped me for. I can't help shaking my head and smiling.

They have us carry our houses over to where the audience can see, and then we wait as they vote, but of course, Jed wins. Surprisingly, Tommy comes in second place. I manage to get dead last, *again*. Even with the chiclets, people kept saying mine was boring. This whole thing is turning out to be a little embarrassing, honestly.

"The next prize is one that all our competitors should be pretty good at," Principal Lyons says.

"Wait," Greg says. "What's that?" He points at Janet's arm.

There's a tiny red sticker on her elbow.

"How exciting. We have our first murder." Principal Lyon's eyes are lit up like he's announcing an ice cream party. He actually claps.

"That means," Mrs. Lyons says, "that we need the other competitors to take a vote!"

"A. . .what?" I frown. "What are we voting on?"

"I forgot to mention that with every vote, you have the chance to out the stepmother." Principal Lyons nods. "Or the witch, of course, but you don't have the tools you need to vanquish her yet, so I'd recommend you only try to identify the stepmother. If you can find her, then the witch will lose her largest ally, because if you correctly identify her, you can cast her out."

"Of course, she's also the witch's biggest liability," I mutter.

"But Gretel already knows who the stepmother is," Tommy complains, rather obviously, I think. "So that hardly seems fair."

"It takes a vote to cast her out, though," Principal Lyons says. "If Gretel comes right out and says he or she knows who the stepmother is, then she'll die next and the witch will win."

"The sticker's red," Jed says, "and Mandy had a red paper. I think Mandy's the witch."

"But the stickers could be multicolored," Janet says, "for all we know. It could still be anyone. Plus, we don't even want to find the witch yet."

"Can Janet really be talking?" I ask. "She's dead."

"Oh, on the contrary, the deceased can guess," Principal Lyons says.

I want to ask him what part of that is contrary to what I said. I asked a question.

"But," he continues, "they can only talk about the circumstances surrounding their own death and any guesses they have. Then once this vote is finished, they're out of play."

"Let's hope the witch was surreptitious with their murder, or Janet will be able to name him or her," Principal Lyons says. "Janet, tell us what you think."

"It was Jed," she says. "I think he stuck it on me when he traded for those Lemonheads."

"She's just mad that I beat her," Jed says. "She should've built a bigger house."

"I traded you for Lemonheads too," Tommy says. "And Jerry did, and Denise."

Tommy's defending Jed, which makes me suspicious of Jed, to be honest. Janet rolls her eyes, but I find it interesting she doesn't actually know, which means whoever did stick something on her was sly about it.

"It doesn't really matter who the witch is yet," I say. "We can't kill her anyway."

"Or him," Jerry says.

"I vote for Tommy as the stepmother," I say, figuring I may as well accuse him.

"No, it's definitely Jed who's the stepmother," Janet says.

"You just said he was the witch," I say.

"Fine, then I think it was Greg," Tommy says.

For the love.

Thanks to Janet's inability to keep anything straight—not impressive, even if she prides herself on athleticism—and Tommy's intentional tomfoolery, we bicker back and forth for another few moments, and then everyone votes for Greg. He was sitting right next to Janet, and he's so innocuous that no one was really paying attention to anything he did.

"Greg is not the stepmother." Principal Lyons sounds gleeful. "He was the bystander, so unfortunately, he's now dead as well."

"Wait," I say. "Janet's dead, and so is the bystander?"

"Just five of you left," Mrs. Lyons says. "One of you is Gretel, and the stepmother and witch are both still in play."

Fabulous.

"Our next task will be an obstacle course you must complete in the shortest time," Principal Lyons says.

"But you said," I say, "that not everything would be athletic."

"You'll be placed on teams," Principal Lyons says, ignoring me. "The winning team will receive the broom."

"The what?" I ask. "Why do we even want a broom?"

"The broom is the one thing that will slay the witch, and Gretel needs to obtain it or she loses." Principal Lyons is smiling right at me. I'm worried he's so obvious that everyone knows I'm Gretel, but no one seems to be picking up on that.

"But there are five of us," Denise says. "How will we make teams?"

"Jed and Tommy have placed first and second in each event," Principal Lyons says. "Jed can choose first, meaning he'll have two people on his team, and Tommy will have just one."

I'm almost surely going to be picked dead last. I think Tommy saw me glance at him, knowingly, and I wonder whether he's figured out that I'm Gretel. He knows I accused him, at the very least.

I sigh.

Jed picks Jerry, which is probably smart, since we have no idea what the obstacle course will involve yet, and then I wait for Tommy to pick Denise. She's the smart one, and if he knows I'm Gretel. . .

"Mandy," Tommy says. "You're on my team."

I can't help smiling, if only because I wasn't chosen last. Then it hits me—he's the stepmother, and now we're partners in our attempt to recover the dumb broom. "Oh, great."

When I reach his side, Tommy whispers, "You know I'm the stepmother, so that makes you Gretel."

I want to swear. Loudly. Am I really that obvious?

"Jed's the witch."

My eyes fly up to his face. The stepmother knows who the witch is. . .and he just told me. Also, Janet was right, bless her heart.

Tommy's smiling broadly. "Let's take him down together."

"But you'll lose," I say.

"Sure, but if you win, did I really lose?" Tommy smirks. "I said I like to win. I didn't say I care about *their* version of what that means."

✽ 17 ✾

MANDY

"I'm tired of placing second to Jed," Tommy says. "Aren't you?"

I blink. "I'd love to be second. So far, I've been dead last each time." I can't help chuckling. "Guess you're realizing that you chose poorly."

"I like a dark horse."

But then they're telling us the obstacle course—which involves riding and roping—and it looks hard. Mr. Wallace is leading a pair of horses up to the entrance by the squeeze chute, and they've uncovered the contents of two more tents. One covered two sets of poles we'll have to run—easy—but the other was hiding a pile of old bags and crinkly tree branches we'll have to ride across. . .on unknown horses.

We'll be lucky not to break our necks.

"You take the poles," Tommy says, "and I'll—"

"And for the final part," Principal Lyons says, "you'll need to rope one of these sheep." He gestures to the sheep they're leading to a pen in the far corner.

"Never mind." Tommy's smiling. "We only have two of us, and both of us can ride. "You do the poles and the spooky crinkle run, and I'll take over for the roping."

I don't even bother arguing, because there's no way Jed can beat Tommy once we get to the roping part. No one in the entire county can beat Tommy at roping and tying. And hopefully they gave us horses who won't try to kill us when walking over a few tarps and feed bags.

A girl can dream.

I'm climbing up on the little buckskin Mr. Wallace hands me the reins for, while Jerry's mounting the leggy sorrel. "Do we know what these horses are used to doing?" I ask.

"They've both run the course," Mr. Wallace says. "We're not trying to break anyone's neck."

"But I can't ride," Denise wails. "We don't even have horses." Her family owns the auto repair shop, and her dad has famously said anyone who rides horses is an idiot.

"Looks like Mandy's found some luck finally," Tommy says.

And then they wave us forward. I fly through the poles course—my buckskin gelding is a champ, and very willing. We come out at least a horse length ahead of stupid Jerry and his sorrel, and I shoot toward the crinkle pile.

"Wait," Jed says. "If they had a third member, they'd have to mount and dismount before they could go to the next part."

"You'll have to get off and back on," Mr. Wallace says. "It's the only way to keep things fair."

I roll my eyes, because what parts have been fair up until now? But I swing off.

Just as some kind of noise from the audience spooks my buckskin, who darts ahead. I barely keep my hands on the reins, popping the poor guy in the mouth to stop him. He swings around, dancing backward, his eyes rolling, his sides heaving, but I manage to calm him down and tug him back to my side.

Meanwhile, I've lost my lead. Denise is being helped up

onto the skittish sorrel, which is clearly looking around for whatever spooked my buckskin, when I see it.

A small blue sticker flutters down from Denise's elbow.

"Wait," I shout. "Denise is dead."

"What?" Jed asks.

Everyone in the arena has frozen.

I point at the tiny sticker. "That fell off her elbow."

"What do we do now?" Tommy asks.

"Jerry will have to take over," Principal Lyons says. "But we'll postpone the vote until the end of the obstacle course."

That's a stroke of luck for Jed—but then I realize, it's not. Jed killed his own teammate because she was a liability. I'm annoyed, but also a little impressed. Too bad it didn't really help him much.

I swing back up and manage to get the jump on Jerry. My buckskin doesn't mind the tarps, but he hates the tree branches, whereas Jerry's sorrel just tromps right across all of it.

They're ahead of *us* when I finally charge through and toward where Jed and Tommy are waiting. They're arguing when I pull up, but they both shut up as we approach.

I don't wait for a complete stop before I swing off, and I practically throw the reins at Tommy. "Go, go, go! We need that broom!"

But Jed's smiling at Tommy. He doesn't care whether Tommy gets the broom. Because he knows Tommy's the stepmother. I close my eyes and exhale. I'm pretty sure I've just been played.

I watch as Tommy ropes the sheep in half the time it takes Jed, and Principal Lyons awards him a broomstick with a flourish. Then Tommy wheels our cute little buckskin around, rides over to my side, dirt clods spraying, and tosses me the broom.

His horse, predictably, freaks out. You really shouldn't ever throw things around a horse, even one you know. But

Tommy calms him down, and I catch the broom. Before they can push for another stupid vote, I shout, "Jedediah Brooks, I know you're the witch." I start running across the arena. "And as Gretel, I'm here to slay you and save my brother."

Jed looks utterly floored.

I jab him with the end of the broom, and even though he's sitting on a horse, I manage to strike his stomach.

"Wow," Principal Lyons says. "That was even more exciting than we had hoped it might be."

Mrs. Lyons nods. "I suppose we have a winner. Gretel has saved her brother Hansel, and she has vanquished both the stepmother and the witch."

The audience cheers.

Even more surprisingly, they all vote, and the audience, Principal and Mrs. Lyons all vote me in as prom queen. It happens so fast that it feels like I'm reeling. "But I got dead last in everything." I blink.

"But you managed to convince Tommy to betray his own best interests," Mrs. Lyons says. "That shows an impressive amount of team building. Your showing in the horse was admirable, too. But, because Jed beat Tommy each time, and because Tommy turned on his own teammate, he loses. For the second year in a row, Amanda Saddler and Jedediah Brooks are our prom king and queen," Mrs. Lyons says. "Congratulations to them both!"

Technically last year, we were just the prince and princess, and Jed skipped out on prom, so I think he should forfeit his title. I don't point any of that out, and when I look around to joke about it with Tommy, I'm alarmed to realize that he's gone.

But they've released Clyde from his cage, and he's now strolling across the arena toward me and Jed. "Nice work, little brother. You didn't embarrass the Brooks family name."

Jed looks like he might snatch the broomstick away from me and impale his brother with the very blunt end. I grab

Jed's hand and wave with my free hand as I tug him toward the edge of the arena. "We need to talk."

He's resisting, but not nearly as much as he would have been a few months—heck, even a week ago. We do manage to jog nearly to the opposite end of where the audience is now spreading across the arena dirt.

"You are going to talk to me for once," I say. "Because if we're supposed to be prom queen and king together, you're going to have to." I drop my hands to my hips, releasing him.

"What would I even say?" Jed asks.

"You could tell me how you're feeling, having Clyde here."

He shrugs.

"Or you could tell me that you've been an idiot for the past two years."

His scowl deepens.

"You could congratulate me on winning," I say.

"You only won because Tommy threw you the win." He crosses his arms.

"So what?" I ask. "He's my friend, and—"

"You have a lot of friends," Jed mutters. "That's the problem."

"Only because my best friend stopped talking to me," I say. "Who would you say is to blame for that?" I arch one eyebrow.

"I've always been your friend." Jed's still scowling.

"Oh, yes," I say. "I can see that. Most people's friends never talk to them, and they scowl all the time, and they refuse to do anything with them."

"Who do you think has cut all your wood for the last two years?"

"What?" I blink. "What are you talking about?"

"Or what about your fences?" he asks. "You think they've been mending themselves?"

"Jed, are you saying—"

"Don't tell me you didn't notice."

I shake my head. "I don't do that stuff. My dad does."

His mouth opens, but he doesn't speak.

"Have you really been coming to my house and chopping firewood?"

He sighs. "Not that it matters, apparently."

"But why would you—"

"Hey, gorgeous." Clyde has finally reached us, and he waves. "They want a photo of Hansel and Gretel for the school yearbook."

"They—what?" I shake my head. "Don't be stupid."

But Principal Lyons is actually waving us over.

"They'll get photos of the prom king and queen later," Clyde says. "Don't be sore. Just come on over and smile."

Only Clyde Brooks would somehow figure out how to be featured in the school's yearbook two full years after he'd already graduated. "I'll be over in a second."

"Just go," Jed says. "It's not like we have anything else to talk about." He's scowling as much as he ever was.

"I'll be there in a minute." I shove Clyde's arm. "Stop being such a nuisance and give me a second."

Clyde's eyes dart between Jed and me. "Is there something going on—"

Jed kicks the ground, spraying dirt all over his brother. "Just go for once, will you?"

Clyde, covered in a spray of dirt, finally walks away, his eyes wide. "Calm down. Geez."

"It's a waste of time," Jed says. "You and I are doomed, and we always have been. The timing's always wrong. The universe is stacked against us."

"That's a little dramatic," I say. "If you'd been willing to talk to me—"

"I *couldn't*," Jed says. "I've tried, believe me, but I keep thinking. . ." He sighs. "Just go, get your photo, and then go home."

I realize that we're not going to get anywhere big right

now, not with a dozen people watching us, but at least he's talking to me. It's progress, right? It has to be.

After my photo with Clyde, I look around for Tommy, but both he and Jed are gone. I can't find them anywhere. I try riding my bike to Jed's house to talk to him more, but his family isn't home. They must have gone out to get food or something.

I should go home. I should tell my mom and dad what happened before they hear about it from, well, from most anyone. But instead, I find myself pedaling over to Tommy's place. "Just to tell him thank you," I tell myself.

But in the moment they announced that I had won, and that Jed and I would be prom king and queen, and in the second that Jed actually spoke to me, I wasn't as elated as I thought I'd be.

I was confused.

Over the past two years, I've thought a few times that maybe, just maybe, Tommy and I. . .but each time, I've been wrong. Tommy has always inadvertently shown me just how wrong I was.

I told myself I'd never find myself here again.

But I can't help it.

I pedal to Tommy's house with the flimsy excuse that I need to thank him, but really, I want to tell him that I *like* him. It's not the same as I felt about Clyde, or even about Jed, either. No, when I think about Tommy, I'm not elated or excited or fizzy.

I'm nervous.

I want to crawl out of my own skin and dance around. I feel far too small for my own body, and I want to touch his hand, and the thought of that makes me want to die somehow, too.

It's confusing and stressful and I can't *not* see him.

Even if I'm about to look like an idiot yet again.

Only, when I get to Tommy's house, he and his mom are

loading his dad up in the car, and his mom's crying, and I watch stupidly as they drive away, bound for the hospital in Vernal.

The next morning, I hear that his dad died.

A few days later, Tommy and his mother are both gone, never to return.

❧ 18 ❧
AMANDA

When I was in high school, my most epic love story was when my boyfriend kissed me in front of the lockers for the whole school to see. He was tall, and he had facial hair, and I practically swooned, right up until he mouth-mauled me, anyway.

Meanwhile, Mandy's high school love triangle could easily be turned into a full-length movie. Maybe it would be a tragedy, à la Romeo and Juliet, but still.

"You really never saw him again?" Maren looks incredulous. "How can that be?"

"Obviously I saw him again," Mandy says. "Don't be ridiculous."

"She lived with him when she was. . ." Emery looks at her shoes. She hates when I get all angry with Mandy over it. "Anyway, she's seen him."

"Yeah, but was that the first time you saw him since high school?" Maren presses. "When you went out there last year?"

Mandy sighs. "We've been in contact this whole time. Letters. The occasional phone call."

"I think it's romantic," I say.

"But it's nothing but lies," Maren says. "He finally sees her after sixty years, and he thinks she's a widow, mourning the death of her beloved husband." Maren snorts. "I mean, come on."

"I'm too old for epic romance," Mandy says. "I have a bad knee and a heart that barely works."

"Maybe it's just been broken." Emery's smile is shy. "I wonder if you know anyone who might heal it."

I swat her shoulder.

And someone knocks at the door.

"You really need a dog." I bump Jed where he's snoozing at the base of the coffee table. "Your pig sucks at telling you when people are here."

"I'm sure it's Tommy," Mandy says. "He said he'd be by this morning." She starts brushing at nonexistent lint on her pants.

"Well, get it already," Maren says. "Can't keep someone that old waiting."

"You can't be here," Mandy hisses. "You guys have to leave."

"We do?" I lift my eyebrows. "Because you said last night, you were nervous when he wanted to stay."

Mandy splutters. "When did I say that?"

"Last night, on the phone."

She frowns. "Fine, then you answer the door." She drops her voice to a whisper. "But remember that I was married to Jed. We traveled the world."

Maren and Emery are rolling their eyes, but I'm smiling as I open the front door. At least, I'm smiling until I see some guy in a white button-down shirt and a blue tie holding a big brown envelope.

"Are you Amanda Brooks?"

That is *not* what I expect him to say, but then I'm not expecting a nondescript man with thinning brown hair to be at the door at all. I was expecting a very debonair man in his eighties. "Um. Yes. I'm Amanda Brooks."

The man grins, and I can't help thinking his parents really should have sprung for braces. "Excellent." He thrusts the thick envelope at me.

I take it without thinking. "What's this?"

"You've been served." He snaps a photo with his phone, pivots on his heel, and jogs back to his car.

"Oh, man," Maren says. "We're going to be late for school. We better go. You can read whatever that is later."

"Later?" Mandy asks. "Have you lost your mind, girl? 'Served' means she's been *sued*. Open it. Find out who's suing us!"

"Us?" Maren asks.

"We're in business together," Mandy says. "It's got to be something to do with the retreat, and being sued is never good."

I'm groaning as I slide my finger under the flap of the envelope.

"Seriously, Mom," Maren says. "Emery and I should go. Maybe I can take your car, and then—"

"In a second, Maren." I pull out the papers, and I start to scan, but it's so much legal mumbo jumbo that I can't tell. . .until my eyes light on a name I know. "Why does this say the petitioner's name is Maren Brooks?" I lower my hand and stare right at my little girl. She's not even eighteen yet, not for nine more months.

And in that moment, I know. No wonder she was desperate to get out of here. She wanted me to have time to cool down before we talked.

"I'm petitioning the court for the right to be emancipated." She lifts her chin. "Then I can make my own decisions."

"And who's paying for this?" I drop one hand to my hip. "On what grounds would you possibly get emancipated? How would you even pay your own bills on your own?"

"It's that label, isn't it?" Mandy asks. "The persistent one. They're paying for this?"

"The lawyer's working on a contingent fee, sort of," Maren says.

"What does that mean?" I ask. "*Sort of?*"

"When the motion's granted, he'll become my new agent," Maren says. "Did you know that a lot of the industry's top agents are also entertainment lawyers?"

"Go to the car, right now." I point.

"Good luck with that," Mandy says.

"At least it's not about the retreat," I say. "I can handle Maren."

Mandy's grim smile tells me that she's not so sure. But what she's forgetting is that I have a secret weapon.

Abigail.

There's no way that I'm going to lose control of my own kid in the last nine months of her first eighteen years. No. Way. Not with Abigail by my side.

Maren doesn't say a single word to me on the way to school. She doesn't remind me that her stupid YouTube video got six million views before we pulled it down. She doesn't tell me that her TikTok recording has been used for over twenty million reels. She doesn't argue with me about how much I'm ruining her life.

She doesn't have to, not anymore.

Because now she's got someone with a much bigger stick to do her arguing for her. How desperate must that stupid record label be to offer a minor a deal and then help her find an agent who will help her emancipate herself? And if they're that eager to sign her, how bad must their business be doing?

Yes, based on her past single, she's probably close to a sure thing. In this environment, they must feel like they need it. And beyond that, the story's making news already. Something like this—tyrannical parents from whom she must be freed, and famous parents to boot—would guarantee them good publicity. But it's the worst thing that can happen for Maren.

Whether she believes it or not, part of the reason she's

gotten so much attention is that her stepfather has had a successful career. The fact that I was somewhat well known before I disappeared doesn't hurt, either. People are clearly curious. They want to know more about Eddy and me, and it doesn't hurt that she's beautiful and that she can sing pretty well.

I've just dropped the girls off at school when my phone rings. As if she's clairvoyant on top of everything else, it's Abby.

"Hello?" I say.

"I have some bad news," Abby says.

"How did you know?" I ask.

"Izzy showed me," Abby says. "Wait. Why do you think I'm calling?"

"Just tell me what you need to tell me," I say.

"Maren has another single up online, and this one has already hit five million views within just two days of being posted."

"You're kidding." I'm going to strangle her.

"She did it under another account—some girl on her cheer team back in New York City—but it has taken off as well as the last one did. Probably because of what it's about. . ."

"What does that mean?"

"I'll give her this," Abby says. "The tune *is* catchy. I even found myself humming it earlier, and that was after hearing it once."

"What?" I ask.

"It's a song about two kids who are in love, and their parents won't let them see one another, but they find ways. The thing is, the chorus says, 'Mom don't know, and Dad ain't dad, and they think they're right, but they're so wrong it hurts.'"

"I am going to strangle her." I'm clutching the steering

wheel so hard that my knuckles have gone white. "Abby, she sued me this morning. She's asking to be emancipated."

Abby laughs.

She actually laughs.

"Oh, good." I sigh. "So you think she doesn't have a case?"

"Of course she has no case," Abby says. "If every kid who threw a temper tantrum was emancipated, think what our world would look like. She's well-cared for by well-educated parents who love her and meet all of her physical, emotional, and mental needs. No judge in his right mind would emancipate her. I'm assuming they've filed in California, where there are judges who are certifiably nuts, but we'll object first to the venue and get it moved to her current locus."

My sigh's bigger than any that have come before. "Thank heavens."

"I personally think you should let her make the album, though."

"What?" I'm coughing again. "Why would you say that?"

"She's suing you because she doesn't respect you and your decisions. She thinks you're holding her back. You can beat her in court, but you'll just make an angry girl even madder, and I think you could really damage her ability to trust you in the future."

"Well, thank you for your advice, Dr. Phil, but I think the only thing I need from you is the legal help right now." I snort. "Oh, and get that YouTube account pulled down immediately."

"If you're sure."

"I am." I hang up. I'm practically shaking when I walk through the doors to our house. Eddy must have a light morning planned, because he hasn't even left yet. "You are not going to believe what just happened." I wave the manila envelope at him.

"Maren has more record deal offers?" He lifts both eyebrows and swivels the laptop around, showing me that someone else sent him the newest song already. "I'm not surprised."

I fill him in on her stupid lawsuit.

He looks like he might be sick. "But what if the court—"

"Abby says they won't." But now that she's not on the phone with me, insisting it'll be fine, I'm nervous again. "She seemed pretty sure."

"If she's sure, then it's fine. The one time she lost, she told you she might lose."

That's true. I wasn't listening at the time, but she wasn't saying it was a slam dunk. "She also said. . ." I can't actually bring myself to say it.

"What?" Eddy straightens. "Abby said something, you mean? Or Maren?"

"I should watch the video." I sit down and hit play on the YouTube channel. The song is good, and I worry about how many people will see it in the days it takes Abby to get it pulled down. The last thing we need is more people clamoring to sign her.

I do have to begrudgingly admit that Maren's dancing has improved, and she's even recruited some of her friends as backup dancers. The girl has an eye for choreography. I'll give her that, too. Even their outfits are pretty cute. . . "Do you think she has been in touch with the stupid label this whole time?"

"I'd be shocked if she wasn't," Eddy says. "They don't relinquish gold mines easily, especially these days. They're all hurting for money right now."

Great.

I hate to admit it, but the tune really is catchy—Abby was right. The lyrics are even pretty good. "Did she make this up herself, do you think?"

"That might be my fault." Eddy's broad shoulders fall a bit. "Two or three weeks ago, she was playing around on the piano."

"What?" I can't help arching my eyebrow. "Your piano?"

He scrunches his nose. "It was that one, my practice one." He points at the corner. "She was going over and over this melody, but it was missing a consistent theme."

"You helped her." I should have known.

"I didn't realize she was planning any of this." He sounds sheepish. "I thought we were bonding, and we didn't say she couldn't learn, just that she was too young to sign a deal."

"Maren's always been someone who's willing to use any angle to get what she wants. She gets that from her father."

"Or she's a typical teenager," Eddy says. "They all do that. It may be from her dad, or maybe she's just itching to have control she's just not ready for yet."

"Abby thinks we should let her record the album." I finally blurt it out. "Can you believe that?"

Eddy swallows, but he doesn't look outraged. At all.

"Don't tell me you agree."

He shakes his head slowly. "I'm not saying that. Not at all. But I have wondered how much of our vehement denial was because of what *I* did and not because of her situation."

"All of it is because of what happened to you," I say. "Think about it. Because of your past, you're uniquely qualified to know exactly how hard this would be on a teenager."

"But my parents knew nothing about the music industry, about contracts, or even about traveling more than twenty miles from home." He sighs. "They didn't get in over their heads, they basically chucked me into the ocean. Without a raft or a paddle or even a life preserver. That's not what it would be like for Maren. We could guide her."

"Or we could tell her *no*, because that's not the kind of life she needs."

"We know that because we had it and we walked away," he says.

"Right, that's *why* we have to say no for her. She's too naive to do it for herself."

"When you were a kid, did you ever just stick a lemon wedge in your mouth?" He tilts his head. "Or kick an anthill just to see them come pouring out?"

I roll my eyes. "Just say what you want to say, Eddy. You're not Abigail. Your analogies suck."

He's smiling. "Takes one to know one, Abby-wannabe."

I kick his steel-toed boot. I know it won't hurt him, but at least he can tell I'm mad. "Just say it."

"For the record, I don't want to be Abby. Steve maybe, but not Abby. I like my man-parts right where they are, thank you very much."

I laugh.

"The thing is, I think that when you're young, you can't really learn some lessons by being told that it's a bad idea. Sometimes you have to touch that stovetop for yourself."

"But she'll get burned." A tear wells up in the corner of my eye. "I can't let her. She's been through too much already —don't ask me to watch that, too."

"What's worse than her being burned?" Eddy looks a little sad.

I shrug.

"Being burned when we aren't there to bandage her up."

I *hate* that he might be right.

19

HELEN

When Abby was eight, she left my art kit out on the front porch, and the neighbor's cat puked on it. The pencils, the eraser, and even the sheet paper, it was all ruined. Soaked clean through.

We had to just throw it all away.

The look on her face that morning, when she came to confess that she'd left it out. . . She looked just like she does right now.

"What?" I ask.

"Do you remember when you hated Steve and thought he was ruining my life?" Her eyes brighten up, and her whole face shifts. I hate how she can do that. Hide her guilt and beam in a believable way. If I didn't know her so well, I'd think I had imagined the whole guilt part entirely.

"What did you do?" I narrow my eyes. "Don't act all chipper and put a spin on it."

"Mom called," she says. "She does that an annoying amount lately, probably because she and Dad have discovered Face Time and now they want to see Nate, like, biweekly."

I groan. "Mom?"

"I hadn't told the kids they couldn't say anything about the wedding, and Izzy—"

I drop my face in my hands. "You must be kidding me," I mumble into my palms. "Abbbbby!"

"She's flying in tonight, and she's really, really excited to come dress shopping with us." She grimaces.

"I'm going to kill her." I straighten.

"Wait, you're going to kill me?" Abby asks. "Or her?"

"Both of you, probably." My sister has now gone full-wedding-planner on me, bringing me bridal magazines—which I didn't know still existed—and texting me with flower arrangements and bridesmaid dresses. "While we're on the subject, I will have exactly one bridesmaid." I glare. "You."

She shakes her head. "It doesn't work that way. David actually *has* friends, so you have to come up with a bridesmaid for every one of his groomsmen."

"Absolutely not."

She's nodding. "And you need to pick colors that will fit the season. Since you're in a hurry, I'd suggest you choose fall tones. That's why I've been sending you mums and marigolds and—"

"I will *not* have marigolds in any part of my wedding."

Abby laughs.

I wish I could bottle up her laughter for a hard day. It's like the bubbles in champagne. It's like the glimmer on the top of snow after a blizzard. It's that little drop when your plane is descending that you didn't expect.

"Why can't you be my only bridesmaid? You're the only person I really like."

"Other than David," Abby says. "And there's about to be one more." Her eyes well up with tears *again*. It was cute the first time, but does she really have to cry every single time she thinks about my baby?

"He might be a total brat."

"She might be an absolute angel."

"Or a devil," I say.

"You're right. He'll probably take after his mother and be practically demonic." Abby's smiling again, swiping at the errant tears. "I just can't wait to find out. I hope she's a total Helen, ordering people around and turning her teachers on their heads."

"I never did that," I say. "I was a delight to instruct."

"Tell that to the five teachers you got fired."

"I only did that to incompetent ones," I mutter. "And of course they'd complain. Their attitude was the problem."

"Here's what we're going to do. I hired you the best wedding planner in America, and she quit. I hired the second best, and you fired her."

"I've never settled for second best."

"You're going to offer that first one double what we were paying her, and then you're going to listen to everything she tells you to do. Because if you don't do that, we'll never make this happen in the next two weeks, even though you own two resorts in the area. And we can't delay this if you're still insisting on wearing that black monstrosity."

"It's not a monstros—" I sigh. "Do you really think it's a bad gown for a wedding?"

"I think you should wear whatever makes you feel beautiful for your wedding," Abby says. "I may not understand it, but we'll make it work. It will be visually *stunning*, and if your in-laws and the world all think it's going to spell the doom of your marriage, well, you'll prove them wrong."

"I've been proving people wrong my entire life. What's one more round of it?"

"I did have an idea for a way to kind of. . ." Abby pauses. "Jazz it up."

"Jazz?"

She rolls her eyes. "I'm not sure what word to use. Bling?"

That's not promising, but before I can let her tell me her strange plan and shut it down, a car pulls down her drive.

With rental car plates. "When did you say Mom was coming?" I ask.

She glances at her watch. "She said eight o'clock. I just assumed. . ." But it's almost eleven in the morning, and it looks like Mom meant that she would land in Salt Lake at eight a.m. Because she's now climbing out of the beige sedan and striding toward us with her best "that guy isn't getting tenure" expression.

Abby puts Nathan down and hands him a toy before she opens the door, gesturing Mom through. As if she doesn't even see Abby, Mom marches straight up to me. "Well, I heard you had bugs in your house, and that man finally convinced you to marry him, and it was not a good time, what with fall midterms, but I had to get on a plane." She drops her hands on her hips. "I can't believe that we came out here to save your sister, and she managed to drag you down instead."

I hardly need my mother's approval, but I'm a little surprised. Didn't Abby say she was excited?

"Mom," Abby says. "What on earth are you saying?"

"Your sister was the top of her field. She was *remarkable*." She sighs. "And now you're telling me that she's being well and truly shackled. That stupid ring David gave you was prophetic."

"I mean, it was an engagement ring," Abby says. "You can't really be that shocked that she's actually getting married."

Mom leans over and runs her hand down the side of the black gown that's hanging from the fireplace mantle. "Please tell me this is the wedding dress." Mom's smirk irritates me.

"Yes," Abby says.

"No," I say. It was going to be, until Mom looked at it like it was the perfect gown—a symbol of how our marriage is doomed.

"No?" Abby and Mom say in tandem.

"We're going shopping for the most beautiful white wedding dress you've ever seen. And I'm going to be the most stunning, classic, savagely happy bride you have ever seen." I cross my arms. "David isn't shackling me. He's made me happier than I've ever been. The ring was a joke, because he gets me." I can't help muttering, "Unlike you."

"The next thing I hear, you'll be telling me you're having a petri dish set of triplets or something equally ridiculous," Mom says. "Mark my words. If you go through with this, you'll regret it, and then the divorce will just waste even more time and resources."

"I actually am pregnant, Mom, and it took that to wake me up. You and I can think whatever we want, but being the top of my field never made me as happy as Abby is when she holds her little baby or when she cheers for her daughters on horses."

Mom steps closer. "But you're not like Abby, are you? You're like me, and holding a baby never made me happy."

Her words lodge in my chest like a sword through the heart. Is she right? What if she's right? What if I have this baby and I resent it? What if it ruins my life, and I spend the next few years slogging my way through a horrible divorce? Great people become harpies in divorces, and I'm not that great to begin with.

Abby's usually the kind one. She's usually the sister who smooths things over, who bakes cookies, and who holds and calms a distressed child.

But not right now.

No, right now, she's holding a rolled-up fashion magazine and brandishing it like it's an iron spike-studded club. "Get out, or I swear I will beat you to death with this oversized special edition of The Knot, and there's no judge on earth that will convict me, because you're the worst kind of mother." She steps toward Mom.

Mom backs up, eyeing the magazine as if she's not sure whether Abby's serious.

"I mean it." Abby takes another step. "You said yourself that you've been a terrible mom, and it's true. We don't mind you coming around sometimes, because it's not like you left us in a box on the steps of an orphanage or something, but you will *not* fill Helen's beautiful brain with your toxic filth. So if you can't keep your garbage mouth shut, then get out and don't come back."

Mom blinks.

"And I won't call you so you can talk to Nathan or send you more videos, either." Abby's eyes are flashing. She looks like that scene when Maleficent transforms into the dragon, ready to strike with righteous indignation and razor sharp. . .magazine pages.

"She can stay," I say, fighting back tears.

Abby turns her stony glare on me. "And you." She shakes her head. "Not a single word of that was true. You took care of me when she didn't, and you always made me feel loved. You're not broken like that." She shakes the magazine at me. "Delete all that crap from your brain right now."

That's it. Now I'm crying.

The stupid baby has already broken me.

"Oh, no." Abby drops the magazine and falls to her knees to hug me.

"I should go," Mom says.

Abby doesn't turn to stop her. She doesn't say a word.

"Wait," I say. "It's fine."

Abby shoots to her feet. "No, it's not fine." She has relinquished her grasp on the club, its brightly colored pages now fanned out across the floor, but she still looks more than ready for a fight. "You can stay. . .if you apologize."

My sister is delusional if she thinks—

"I'm sorry." Mom doesn't look very contrite, with the muscle pumping in her jaw, but she did say the words.

"For what?" Abby asks.

Mom's eyes dart sideways.

"You're sorry for telling Helen that it wasn't a great idea to marry the kind, generous, and hard-working man who loves her." Abby arches an eyebrow.

"Sure," Mom says.

"And you're sorry that you didn't squeal with joy that your smartest, richest, most successful daughter is going to have a baby." Abby narrows her eyes. "Say it this time."

"I'm sorry I didn't congratulate you." It may sound like she's biting down on every single word, unwilling to let them fly out into the world, but she does say it. "It's wonderful you're having a baby."

"Try it without looking like you're sucking on a lemon," Abby says.

I stand up. "It's fine. That was pretty good progress."

Abby's suppressing a smile, which is good. Mom has come further than I'd have thought possible, but if we start laughing at her, I can tell she'd storm out. "I guess," Abby concedes.

"Also, it's good to know that if your daughter ever loses her law license, she can probably find a job as a bouncer." I arch one eyebrow.

"A bouncer?" Abby pulls a face. "I thought I was putting off more of an, 'I'm Inigo Montoya. You killed my father. Prepare to die,' vibe. No?" Abby sighs. "I'm grabbing a fire-place poker next time. The magazine was closer, but that was a mistake."

"Eh, it was close. The poker would have helped." Thanks to her, I'm smiling now.

Three hours later, I'm with Mom, Abby, and Izzy, whom Abby pulled out of school early for this trip, and we're in Vegas—the beauty of owning a jet—and they're all watching as I try on dress after dress after dress.

I'm wearing a Versace with a single off-the shoulder

207

bodice when Abby shakes her head. "They've all been lovely, but. . ."

"What?" I bite my lip. "Do I look fat already?"

Izzy laughs.

"Why is that funny?" I frown.

"You make half the kids in my high school look fat, Aunt Helen," Izzy says. "You have the self-control of an army of monks."

"Are there monk armies?" Mom asks. "Because I thought they were pacifists."

"They're all lovely," Abby says, clearly trying to keep us focused. "But none of these are quite right."

"Why not?" The dress attendant looks downright irritated.

"You need to wear that black dress," Abby says. "That's the one that made you say yes." She shrugs. "It's the right one."

"A black dress?" the attendant asks. "Are you kidding?"

"My aunt is epic," Izzy says. "Boring wedding rules don't apply to her."

As if a teenager saying that makes it true, I realize Abby's right. I wanted what I wanted, and I was made to feel small. But now that I'm here, I realize that I had reasons. I am who I am.

I'm epic.

I can wear that black dress if I want to, and that's the one that made me feel ready to have a baby and marry David. So what if no one else understands? So what if they think it spells our doom? I know the truth and no one's opinion matters. Well, David's.

And maybe Abby's a little.

But she gets it now.

On the plane ride home, with the help of Abby, Izzy, and occasionally my mother, I choose my bridesmaids. David had texted that he had four groomsmen picked out, but he assumed we'd also include Steve. I stress out about it for a while, but in the end, I give up. I'm not including Amanda—she went on dates with David, for heaven's sake. Donna liked him, so she's out too. I wind up choosing Mandy, Izzy, and Whitney. Abigail will be my matron of honor, and as long as Steve doesn't throw a fit, that's enough. If David wants to, we can include Beth and Ethan. My superhumanly loyal nephew hasn't wavered once in his affection, so I'm assuming she'll be around for quite some time.

Izzy's writing this all down on a notepad, and she bursts out laughing.

"What?" I ask.

"So in the wedding, we all walk down the aisle, right?" She lifts her eyebrows.

"Right," I say. "Then you stand next to us as they marry us." Now I'm worried. Am I missing something? "That's what Abby said."

"That's right, I think," Izzy says. "And you said that David's groomsmen are his best friend from college, a friend from business school, and two old friends from Korea, right?"

I nod.

"That means they're all roughly his age." Izzy's smirking still.

"Oh." It hits me why she's laughing.

"You'll be putting your married sister next to one, her two kids by the other two, and a grandma by the last one."

"Oh, it's fine," I say. "They just have to stand next to them for photos." But now I'm smiling too, because Mandy is going to throw a fit.

"Can I be there when you tell Mandy?" Izzy asks. "I actually feel sorry for that guy she's walking next to. Can you imagine all the jokes she's going to make?"

I can, and for the first time, as I chat with my niece, I can actually picture the wedding. It will be messy. People will complain. Abby might grab a poker, though I hope she doesn't impale anyone, and it'll be *mine*.

I'm smiling as the plane lands outside of sleepy little Manila, and I realize that, in spite of my mom coming, in spite of a pregnancy I didn't want, in spite of a lot of things. . . I may be more excited right now for my future than I ever have been in my life.

I'm certainly surrounded by more people who love me than ever before. I'm starting to realize that the two things may even be connected.

20

MANDY

Maren may not be perfect, but I'll give her this. The diva knows how to clear a room.

And now that Amanda and Emery and Maren are finally out of my hair, not badgering me with questions and making me relive my past, I actually miss them.

It's late enough in the morning that I'm starting to wonder where the heck Tommy is. He said he'd be back this morning to sign the papers. He said I'd see him soon. Abigail has already worked her magic and sent me a file with the papers I asked her to draw up. I print them off.

It's ten forty-four, and he's still not here.

I call the retreat, but everything is miraculously in order there. Our general manager actually has the audacity to act *annoyed* with me when I start asking about booking numbers going into the holidays. Once I hang up, I decide it's good that he's not here. It gives me time to catch up on things around the house.

I wipe the counters, even though they don't need it.

I sweep the kitchen floor, which Jed keeps quite clean already.

I even scrub the toilet, because now that Helen has been here, it's actually been used. So, you know. That's a relief. Can't have things getting yucky.

I'm washing my hands when there's finally a knock at the door. It could be UPS, needing a signature, or Helen, who has again lost her key, or any number of other people, but for some reason, I'm positive that *this time*, it's not.

This time, my racing heart is sure that it's Tommy.

I check to make sure the paperwork is sitting on the coffee table in a perfect stack, just as I knew it would be. There's even a pen lined up right next to it. If I stick to the plan, he can be in and out in under thirty minutes, even with an appropriate amount of meaningless small talk.

So why are my hands shaking as I swing the door open?

Why does my heart leap inside of my chest when I see him standing on my porch, holding a bouquet of flowers—bright, beautiful Indian Paintbrush mixed with purple cone-flowers. He's wearing khakis and a button-down shirt—much nicer than anything he wore when we were kids, but a combination I saw a lot when I stayed with him. His hair's neatly brushed, and his bright, clear eyes are trained directly on my face.

"Good morning," he says.

"It's nearly afternoon." I open the door a little wider. "You made me wait." I might be more annoyed than I wanted to admit.

"I thought you might be busy," he says. "I've been walking up and down Main Street, trying to give you however much time you might need."

I laugh first, but it's a near thing.

He's shaking his head. "I should've known you'd still be an early riser, even now."

I shrug. "Anyone out here, born and raised, will rise with the dawn."

"I may not have been born here," Tommy says, "and I

know we weren't born on the same day, but I've never been one for sleeping in, either."

I wave him through and take the flowers, careful not to let our fingertips brush. "You didn't need to bring these," I say. "We already agreed on terms, and I have the papers here, ready to be signed."

"Terms?" Tommy frowns. "Oh, right."

"You do still want to sell, right?" I step back. "Or, now that you're here. . ."

"Now that I'm here, what?" He walks past me, but his eyes never leave my face. "Am I having second thoughts?"

"I know your dad died here," I say. "And I know you were forced to leave by your mother."

He shrugs. "I could have come back, but there wasn't anything for me here."

That stings a little, but I know he doesn't mean it as a slight.

"Are you hungry? Maybe it's all the walking, but I feel like I could eat a whole cow right now."

"Oh." I think about my pantry. "I have some soup or. . ."

"Let's go out and eat. Do you have enough time to do that?" He's looking at me so intently that it's a little unnerving.

"Sure," I say. "I mean, yes. Let's go." I grab my jacket and turn toward the door. "The Gorge Reel and Grill is open now, or—"

"That sounds fine," he says.

"I can bring the papers," I say belatedly. "Hold on. Let me grab them."

He shakes his head. "No rush. I can sign after we eat."

It's not wrong. It's just *weird*. "I guess so." By the time I finish locking up, Jed's morose face pressed against the glass pane in the frame around the door, Tommy's already walking toward his rental car.

"Wait up," I say.

On the way there, he tells me about his flight over, apparently not a very smooth experience. Between the chatty tween obsessed with Taylor Swift sitting next to him for the first leg of the trip and the angry gay man complaining about the baggage fees for the second, he didn't even need to tell me about the guy who spilled soup all down his pants. He'd already earned my sympathy.

"You'd think you would have been in a terrible mood yesterday," I say. "I'm sorry it was such an ordeal to get here."

"I kept the prize in sight." He's pulling into a spot in front of the Gorge, but when he cuts the engine, his face turns toward mine, and I realize. . .

Is he talking about me? Am I the prize?

Surely not.

"All right, we're here." He opens his door and climbs out.

I have to scramble to catch up.

"You'll have to tell me the best thing on the menu," he says as we walk inside. "Although to be honest, I'm unlikely to be very picky right now."

"Still hate mustard?" I arch one eyebrow. "Or have you finally seen the light?"

He shudders. "You're still delusional, I see."

"Miss Saddler," Jasper says. "You want the corner like always?"

I've been doing a few too many meetings in here lately, but their coffee's the only local brew I like. "Sure."

The second Jasper's gone, Tommy tilts his head. "Miss Saddler, huh? You weren't kidding before."

"Kidding?" I frown. "About what?"

"You never changed your name to Brooks." Tommy's rubbing his hand along his jaw, the tiny hairs on his chin rasping as he does.

My blood runs cold, realizing how close I am to being outed by a random waiter in a grill. All it would take is one question by Tommy in front of Jasper about why I didn't take my husband's name. Everyone in this town has been gossiping about me for years. They all know I've never been married. If Tommy had kept up with even a single person from here, he'd already know too.

Jasper has returned, blessedly handing me a cup of coffee without my asking. "And what can I bring for you to drink, sir?"

"I'll have a water, please. Because coffee at lunch?" Tommy's frowning. "I can't imagine that's very healthy."

"I'm not really supposed to give it to her," Jasper says with a wink. "But since she didn't have any for breakfast. . ." He shrugs. "Her doctor said one cup a day, and she usually sticks to it."

"Your doctor?" Tommy looks alarmed now, his hand crushing a napkin into a wad. "What kind of doctor?"

"Her cardiologist, I think," Jasper says.

"I forgot how you hate tips," I mutter.

Jasper pretends to zip his mouth closed and walks off.

But it's too late. I can already tell that Tommy's not going to let this go. "I had one small cardiac event, and it was resolved. I had not one, but two procedures to deal with the problem, and they're monitoring it now. Everything has been cleared out, and I'm fine." I pat my chest. "Fit as a fiddle."

"Pardon my doubts, but I've seen plenty of fiddles that didn't look fit at all," Tommy says.

Before I can argue, he's reaches over and snatches my coffee mug right out of my hands. "Let's switch drinks. My doctor's a quack who keeps going on and on about fish oil, but so far I've had not a single problem with my ticker. So I'm going to step in here and help you out."

He's not prepared for me to yank the mug back, so I manage to take it back as simply as he stole it in the first place. "Don't get between me and my caffeine," I say. "Not if you value your fish-oiled life."

He laughs. "I didn't say I actually take any of it."

"That's a relief. It's a gateway drug. Before too long, they'll have you taking collagen, and then multi-vitamins. It's all downhill from there."

Tommy rolls his eyes, but I can tell he still gets my sense of humor. Just like when I went out to stay with him, we slide back into the same easy, comfortable relationship we had back in high school.

It's funny how everything can change in sixty years. . .except the things that really matter. Those don't even shift. After we eat, he wants to go for a walk. "You didn't get enough walking around this morning?"

He shrugs. "I did a lot of reminiscing, and I guess I want to reminisce with you a little."

"That sounds a little cryptic to me," I say, but when he stands, I do too. Instead of forcing him toward his rental car, I amble along beside him.

Main Street *has* changed a lot in the intervening years. I wonder how it would feel for me, if I left and only now returned. It's not so much that it's bigger, but it's definitely more modern. We still had tie posts for horses back in the sixties, for heaven's sake. They were mostly a relic of an earlier time, but they were still there. Now the streets are littered with cars. Shiny ones, bikes, scooters, and even the occasional motorcycle. The antique tie posts have been replaced with chrome bike racks.

"The school looks the same," he says. "And the general store hasn't changed much. Neither has the diner."

"The best things haven't changed," I joke.

"But you have changed in some ways," he says. "I think those women and their kids have softened you."

"Amanda," I say. "And Abigail."

"You must have been devastated before they came back to live here." His voice is quiet. "You'd lost Jed. You'd lost everything."

Right. Jed. I lost my husband of decades. I sigh heavily,

wishing I hadn't made up that story to begin with, but if I hadn't, he'd have come out here and told Jed I was in love with him. I couldn't stomach the idea of him coming out for that, and a lie felt easier than telling Tommy *or* Jed how I felt.

I should tell him the truth now, though.

I know I should, but when I open my mouth to say that I was never married to Jed, my hands tremble. I run through what I'll say in my mind as we walk. First, I'll tell him that I didn't want to force him to come back. I didn't want him to be stressed about me, either. Then I'll explain that when Jed died, it was just the loss of an estranged neighbor. Nothing more.

But I can't do it. Tommy's eyes are so bright, his expression so fond. He's been reminiscing about a life I never had. He's come to see an old friend he doesn't know at all. Some things don't change. He's right about that.

Apparently, once a coward, always a coward.

"Mandy?" Dolores is watering her plants outside her strange little house, like usual. She must have dragged them inside when it snowed, and now they're back out because the sun is here. The bright spots of fall color are actually pretty nice.

I raise my hand to wave.

"Who's that with you?" She squints. "Is that. . ." Her jaw drops.

"Wait, little Dolores Gibbens?" Tommy asks. "Is that really you?"

"It's Dolores Jenkins now," she says. "Tommy, right? Tommy Collins, director of champions. I never thought I'd see you again in this sleepy little town. You were always destined for great things."

"I suppose I'll be a big disappointment then," Tommy says. "I lived a quiet life, just not here in this particular small town."

"Well, we missed your shining personality for all these

years." Her hose has been spraying on the same pot full of mums for nearly a minute now, and the water's pooling and running over the side, taking a lot of potting soil with it. I could tell her, but I'm having too much fun watching her swoon over Tommy. "You sure aged well." She's eyeing him up and down like Jed the pig looks at a Thanksgiving turkey.

Tommy nods, trying to come up with something nice to say about her, I suspect. Poor Dolores looks a little unhinged, with her knit sweater, crocheted fingerless gloves, and a weird sort of open-topped hat, white hair careening out and down her back in all directions like the feathers of a cockatoo.

"Well, if you're in town for a while, I'd love to get together and catch up," Dolores says.

Which is funny, because she was years and years behind us in school. It's an obvious ploy to snag a date. I can't help a snort.

"Or, maybe not," Dolores says. "You're clearly busy already with Mandy."

"He's not," I say. "I don't know how long he'll be around, but he won't be busy with me. He just has to sign a few papers and our business will be done."

"Ah, yes, Amanda Saddler, real estate mogul," Dolores says. "While I've crocheted and gardened, Amanda has been busy, buying up everything that goes up for sale in a hundred miles."

"You don't say," Tommy says. "I'm not sure I knew that."

"Oh, yes," Dolores says. "She's the richest woman around here."

"Really?" Tommy lifts his eyebrows. "A widow of means. Perhaps that's why she's been too busy to even call me lately."

Dolores frowns and I realize that I have to shut this conversation down.

"Well, we better get going."

"It has been a very long time," Tommy says, "but I'm happy to have a bit of her time now, given how busy she is."

"Busy?" Dolores asks. "Do you mean with her resort? She just started that—"

This conversation is a ticking time bomb.

"I have a meeting later, actually. We should get going." I drop one hand on Tommy's elbow. "I'm sure you two can find a time to chat very soon."

Dolores might even be a great match for Tommy. He said he was pretty lonely now that his wife has passed. If Dolores wouldn't be sure to tell him all about Jed and my real past, I'd almost consider setting them up, but as it is. . . I steer him back toward the Gorge Grill and practically shove him at his car. That's two near misses in less than two hours.

I need to get these papers signed and send Tommy Collins packing, or he's going to find out just how pathetic I really am.

But when we get back to my place where the papers are waiting, there's another car parked in the drive. Lately my house feels like the parking lot of the True Value.

I prepare myself, because I know Amanda's not going to be happy with a handshake and a brush off. She's going to hang around until she's made a complete nuisance of herself, and if I'm not very careful, she'll slip and spill my lie. Probably not intentionally, but I wouldn't put it past her to tell him as payback.

She's still angry about the whole pretending-I-was-dead thing, and she knows I was with Tommy while she thought I was gone. Sometimes, when she gets upset, her rational thought just goes AWOL.

"Uh, it looks like my—Amanda Brooks, er, Dutton is here."

Tommy's smile is broad. "I'm excited to meet her. Anyone you're willing to fake your own death to set on the right track must be an amazing person."

"It did get her head back on straight," I say. "Although, my idea might have been a bit extreme."

Tommy laughs. "You really haven't changed in sixty years. If there was ever a person I knew who would fake her own death so that her loved ones would live a happy life, it's you."

I'm not sure that I like how he's implying that fooling others is some crucial part of my character, but it bodes well that he doesn't find it despicable. Just in case he does find out the truth. "Well, brace for impact. Amanda is a lot."

"All the best women are."

But when we climb out of the car, it's not Amanda who hops out of her BMW SUV.

It's Maren. "I want to live with you." She folds her arms and huffs.

"Maren," I say. "Does your mother know you have her car and skipped out on school?"

She rolls her eyes. "Well, she took mine to get an oil change, supposedly, but I think she just took it so I'd be stuck. Well, joke's on her. I walked home and found her keys." Her nostrils flare. "Any way to control me, she'll take." She shakes her head. "I can't handle her anymore."

"You did just sue her," I point out. "She might be justified in being a little irritated with you."

She throws her hands up in the air. "She won't let me record an album, and not because I'm a bad kid. Because my stupid *stepdad*'s an alcoholic!"

I don't think I'm brave enough to tell Amanda, but I almost agree with Maren. "She's blocking you from doing that because she loves you, though. Plenty of kids have it much worse."

"Do you know the attention span of TikTok?" Maren starts pacing, and as if the wind is on her side, it's whipping her ponytail up into the air. "I have, *maybe*, another month before they forget about me, and then it's game over." She shakes her head. "If I don't get this album recorded soon, I may never have another chance."

"Well, your parents are fairly well known," I say, "and—"

"My parents are ancient," Maren says, "and they're pushing their stuff off on me." She's still shaking her head. "You have to help me. You're the only one they listen to."

"Abigail might be a better—"

"Aunt Abby's worse than they are!" Maren's shouting now. "She's the one who moved the whole thing to *Utah*." She says the state name like she would say *poopy diaper*. "Mom probably got the whole idea from her. She wanted to force her own son to go to college when he didn't want to, just so she wouldn't be embarrassed. They don't *get* it. Life is short, and you have to do what you want to do *now*. They think they can make us like them, but they can't. We have to be who we are."

"I mean, life isn't really that short," I can't help saying. "Look at me. I've been around forever."

"Speak for yourself," Tommy says. "I'm eighty-two years young."

"But that's why you lied to Mom, right? Because she needed to live her life, just like me."

She does have a point there.

"Actually," Tommy says, "that's why I'm here, too."

"What?" Maren, sensing another possible ally, turns to face him. When her eyes widen and her jaw drops, I realize that she may not have even noticed he was here. She's not usually quite *this* self-centered, but she does have a lot going on. "Whoa, you must be Tommy!" Her mouth makes a tiny o. "You're the guy Mandy liked who moved away and never came back." She whistles. "So now it's time for *you* to seize the day, too." She steps a little closer. "Let's do it together. You start dating Mandy, and I'll record my album."

I'm going to strangle her. "Maren Brooks, you will get in that car and go home, right now."

She glares at me for a moment, and then tosses her head. "You're just mad that I told him you liked him, but I'm doing you a favor." Her head snaps back to Tommy's face. "She liked you during the play, she liked you during prom, and she liked you during that gameshow thing." She shakes her head. "Life is short, Mandy. Live it." Then she climbs back in her mom's car, revs the engine, and screams down the driveway.

I whip out my phone and send Amanda a scathing text. MAREN JUST CAME BY AND TOLD TOMMY I WAS IN LOVE WITH HIM. SHE WANTED TO LIVE WITH ME. IT WASN'T HARD FOR ME TO TELL HER NO.

Maren's Amanda's problem again, but now I have my own mess to deal with, thanks to her.

"Is it true?" Tommy's eyes are staring at me intently when I look up, and my breath catches in my throat.

"What?" I swallow.

"What she said? Did you—were you in love with me?" I can't tell whether he's smirking or smiling, but either way, I feel ragingly uncomfortable.

"She's a teenager," I say. "She is so hot and cold. Trust me. You can't believe anything she says. One minute she's ready to burn down the house and make an album, and the next she's bawling in the corner because she dropped her phone in the toilet and her life is over."

Tommy doesn't laugh. He doesn't even so much as blink. "Amanda Saddler, for once in your life, just tell me the truth. Did you like me back then?"

"I—" But I can't do it. I've been lying to him for so long that I don't even know where to start. If I tell him I liked him . . . I don't even know what I want. My heart soars at the thought that he might like me. That he might have liked me then and still like me now.

But if that's true, then he'll stick around, and I'll have to confess that my whole life, all the things I've told him, and written to him about, everything I've said, they were all a lie.

Wouldn't it be better, with as old as we are, with as established as we are in our lives, if we just let things go?

"Do you know why I came here?" He raises his eyebrows.

"To sign the paperwork," I say. "To sell off your parents' farm and finally be done. You told me before."

He shakes his head slowly and steps closer, his eyes still fixed on mine. "No, that was an excuse."

Now my heart's stuttering, and it should *not* be stuttering like that. "It was?"

"My wife was the sister of my best friend Henry. You met him, remember? When I left here, I had lost my dad, and I had lost you, my only real friend. I was a mess. He was the first person I met, and he was my age, and he became my new best friend right away. We didn't have much in common, but he was quiet and calm and I needed that. Twenty-five years later, his sister moved back to live with him after her marriage ended, and you were married to Jed, and after measuring literally every woman I met to you, I was lonely and miserable. She and I were miserable together for a while, and it was a little less depressing that way, so eventually, we got married."

I met Henry when I went, and I knew he had been married to Henry's sister, but he didn't tell me the rest. It almost sounds like I'm not the only one who didn't tell the whole truth.

"When she died a decade back, I was sad. I was lonely, but I wasn't wrecked. She was a very good, very solid companion, and I missed her. Her brother died two months ago though, Mandy, and that broke me, because I realized that we're running out of time." He inhales sharply. "You had a lifetime with Jed. I know that was what you wanted, but I spent a lifetime missing you. And now you're here, and he's gone, and I just had to come out here and find out. . ."

"Yes," I finally say, my heart beating so loudly that I can hear it in my ears. My hands are trembling, and my palms are sweating, and I feel like I might vomit, but the words can't be held back any longer. "I did like you back then, Tommy. I liked you a lot, and I was going to tell you that before your dad died, but then it was too late." My words are so soft, I can barely hear them myself. "I liked you more than I liked Jed. I think I always have."

21

MANDY

Tommy moves faster than a man in his eighties should be able to move, his hands finding mine. "Mandy." His eyes drop to my mouth. "Mandy."

"That's my name, unless you wear it out," I say. "But you should know that I didn't let *anyone* call me that after you left. No one in town, not my other friends, no one."

Tommy's brow furrows.

"It hurt just hearing it after you left," I whisper. "But then, when Amanda came, it was too confusing having two Amandas, so I finally starting using it again." I force a smile. "I thought it was sort of fitting. Every time Amanda, Abigail and their kids call me Mandy, it makes me think of you."

"Did Jed always call you Amanda?" he asks. "He didn't talk to you much when I was here, but he did call you that to me, the few times you came up."

"He did," I say, the reminder that he still thinks I was married to Jed a little painful.

I start casting around in my brain for ways out. Maybe I could move to Montana. He might never need to know. But then, how would I see Amanda and Abby and their kids?

Maybe we could live in Montana, and he could stay there when I come out here for visits. Maybe. . .

"So." He drops my right hand and brings his free left hand up to my face, brushing the side of my cheek. "Does that mean. . ." His eyes lift to mine, and they're nervous.

It makes me smile. "I guess it means we're dating."

His smile is so broad, it transforms his entire look. For just a moment, I see the Tommy I knew. His eyes are the same, even if his face is now wrinkled and his hair's lighter. "That makes me *so* happy. You have no idea."

The bubbly feeling in my chest is ridiculous, but at least my heart's beating properly. "Me, too."

But the wind's picking up, as if it can tell something big has happened, and my hair's whipping around my face. "Maybe we should go inside." I realize that sounds almost indecent, and I can feel the heat in my cheeks. "Just to talk, of course."

Tommy's smile is wicked. "Of course." His eyes dart down at my mouth.

I feel equal parts ridiculous and excited as his head lowers toward mine. I'm not some teenager, excited for my first kiss. But I kind of *am*, since I never was married. I never even had a proper boyfriend, at least, not as an adult. So when Tommy's mouth finally brushes against mine, it's probably the most exciting moment of my entire life.

My cardiologist would hate this.

But I won't forgo it. Not for anything.

The wind whipping around my face is spinning my hair into a disaster, I'm sure. Tommy's mouth presses against mine, his hand tightening on my hip, and joy bubbles up in my chest.

When he finally releases me, he's smiling. "How about now? Do I still have to stay at the hotel?"

I swat his chest. "Of course," I say. "You know I'm not that kind of girl."

He's smiling, but I can tell he won't push it.

"And actually." I start for the front door.

Tommy slides his hand down mine and interlaces our fingers, falling into step beside me. "Yes?"

"I'm not sure how dating will work. I suppose, with Amanda and Helen to run the Retreat, I could move to Montana. I'd just need to come back here once a month or so for a few days or a week."

"Don't be ridiculous," he says. "You already know that with Henry gone, I don't have much tying me to Montana. I'm happy to move here."

Move here.

Just like that.

"I would never ask that of you." We've reached the steps, but when I start up, he doesn't. I turn around, tethered to the ground by his hand's hold on mine.

"You don't have to ask me," he says. "I'm offering. You have Amanda and Abigail and a life here. You have friends and family, and I would never want to be responsible for taking that from you. In fact, I want to be a part of all of it." He's beaming. "I'll move here. I'd love to move here."

I have no idea what to say. There's no way he can *move* here without finding out that I was never married to Jed and that I never traveled around the world, but I can't imagine he'll feel the same way about me if he finds out I've been lying to him all these years. Until about ten minutes ago, my plan was to send him back to Montana as quickly as possible, but now. . . He wants to date me. He wants to move here. He wants to be a part of my life, and *I* want that, too.

But there's this huge lie stuck between us. A lie I'm not brave enough to disclose. Because what if I lose him again?

I have to somehow convince him to move back to Montana and be happy with occasional visits. Seeing him occasionally is better than not at all, right?

Right.

"Well, we can talk about it." With enough time to think it over, I'm sure I can come up with some way to put him off. Some thing that will call him back home. Some reason why he can't just up and move here.

When my phone rings, I'm almost relieved. I release his hand and whip it out. When I see it's Amanda, I cringe a little. I just sent Maren packing, and then told Amanda I was mad at Maren for outing me. But without Maren's nudge, would Tommy have confessed how he felt? Would I?

"I have to take this." I hit talk.

Tommy walks up the steps and sits on the porch, patting the swing next to him.

But I'm worried about what Amanda might say. If I'm too close to him, he might hear whatever she spouts off about. I haven't noticed any hearing aids, so like me, Tommy may hear just fine.

"Hello?"

"I'm so sorry," Amanda says. "Maren has been a total mess, and—"

"It's fine," I say. "Tommy actually. . . Well. Let's just say it's fine. We can talk about the rest later."

"Oh." I can hear the smug smile in her voice. "Well, that's interesting."

"Sure," I say. "It is, but you needed something, right?"

"I hate to ask, since I'm guessing you're with him now," she says. "And it's a long story, but I'm stuck at Gold Strike, because Maren's car needed an oil change, and then I realized I hadn't finished the packets for the corporate retreat, so instead of waiting, Eddy drove me over here."

"Which is how Maren was able to swipe your car."

"She did what?"

"Maren came by here," I say. "That's how she—you know."

Amanda swears under her breath. "Well. Now I'm more angry than before, but I'm still so sorry she did that. I can't believe she's cutting school again and acting out, but I'm also a little glad. I mean, it'll only help us with the case."

I sigh. "You need me to pick up Emery, right?"

"Her play practice was canceled, but she didn't find out until after she'd missed the bus. The director's still sick. At this rate, they'll have to cancel the show."

"No problem," I say. "I'll go get her. But maybe tell her what Maren said when she came to visit me earlier." I'm hoping she'll pick up on my subtle reminder to tell the girls not to be an idiot around Tommy. In this particular case, Maren's overshare worked out, but I'd rather she not spout off about anything else. "I'll have Tommy with me."

"Of course," Amanda says. "I'll remind her to keep her mouth shut."

When I hang up, Tommy's watching me with dancing eyes. "You are so beautiful."

I roll my eyes and wave one hand at him. "Stop."

"I mean it, Mandy. In all the years I've been alive, I never met anyone else as pretty as you. Never." He stands. "So we're off to pick up a granddaughter? Or is she a grandniece? I'm not sure what they call you."

I try not to grimace. He's thinking grandniece, because of their relation to Jed, my deceased husband. But in reality, Emery calls me grandmother because I'm the grandmother of her heart. Adoptive, not legitimate. "Emery's a doll. You'll love her."

"And she's in a play?"

"It's one you know," I say. "*The Christmas Carol*, actually. She's Scrooge's love interest back in days of Christmas past."

Tommy's eyes light up. "No one ever seems to do that one these days."

"Christmas isn't PC." I sigh. "Most of what you and I were taught is now embarrassing, outdated, offensive, or all of the above. Or hadn't you heard?"

"It's a real shame."

This time, we take my car. "I doubt anyone would even produce *The King and I* these days."

Tommy's shaking his head as we pull out onto the main road. "I do think it's a shame. So many great stories that have fallen out of fashion."

"They're doing what we did," I say. "Trying to make the world a better place."

"Sometimes it feels like a place I don't even recognize." His voice is soft, his eyes on the road. "But when I'm here with you, it all makes a little more sense." He drops his hand on mine on the center console. "I can't tell you how happy I am to be here. I'd live in a cardboard box if that's where you wanted me to be."

"I do think you might be happier in Montana," I say. "There's no rush, either way. We can talk about it."

"Yes, we can talk," he agrees.

Thank goodness. We pass Dolores Jenkins' tiny house on the way to the school, and he asks about her. I tell him about her great love and then how she lost him, and how strange she's gotten since.

"Humans aren't supposed to be alone," Tommy says. "We need other humans. They tell us when we're being crazy. They help us remember what matters." His hand squeezes mine.

"Amanda and her kids have done that for me. Before they moved here, I was turning into a caricature of a person."

"That's why," he says, as I pull into the parking lot of the school. "That's why I can't stay in Montana. I want to be here with you and with your people. I want to spend every single moment I have left by your side."

My eyes must be wide as I put the car in park.

"Or something less intense," he says. "But I really don't want to waste time, and that means I need to be where you are, and where you are is here."

"Where I need to be is picking up Emery." I hop out, but

I duck back down so he can hear me. "You wait here. I'll be right back."

But he's already climbing out. "I'd like to see the theater again."

I can't deny him the chance to revisit. I've seen it countless times since he left, and I never fail to think about the plays we did together. Especially *The King and I*.

"Did you really like me back then?" Tommy's hand is braced against the top of the car, but his eyes are on mine.

"I was going to tell you," I say, "but I heard you shouting at Jed, telling him we were only friends." I close my eyes and inhale. "I felt really stupid after that."

He laughs. "I can't believe how much I sacrificed back then."

"You were a good friend to Jed," I say.

"Forget that idiot. I did it for you," he says. "Because it's what you wanted. I knew he was all you wanted."

We were both stupid. I can't help thinking about all of that again as we walk in through the side door of the theater.

Emery's not supposed to have practice, but she's on stage, reading out her lines as Belle, Scrooge's fiancée. "Oh, Ebeneezer, I have no money." She sighs. "But can you love me anyway? Can you love me as I am?"

Young Scrooge is played by the boy she likes—she told me when she was cast. He's suitably handsome, and I'm distracted enough that I don't even think about the fact that the rehearsal is, in fact, happening, when it's supposed to be cancelled.

"That's not what you say," the boy says. "You got the line wrong, I think."

"But it sounds better," Emery insists. "The lines they gave me were so blocky." She looks pained.

"You can't change the lines," the boy says. "You have to read what the script says."

"Who says we can't?" a woman holding a large bowl asks. "Mr. Hammerly isn't even here."

A half dozen other kids weigh in, but none of them can agree.

"Are you supposed to be practicing?" I finally ask. "Emery's mother told me to pick her up."

"If we can't even get the first act done before Thanksgiving," Emery says, "there's no way we'll be able to do this play." She's frowning. "We need to find someone to substitute for Mr. Hammerly until he's better."

"I could step in until he's back," Tommy shouts.

"Who's that?" Emery shields her eyes against the stage lights. "Eddy?"

Tommy strides down the aisle toward the stage, his shoulders square, his head held high. Within a few moments, he's completely taken over. No one is squabbling. No one is lost. He's making decisions, cleaning up dialogue, and the kids are excited and animated.

"Who is that?" the principal asks.

I startle a bit. "Oh, Tommy's an old friend of mine. He's in town for a bit. He owns a farm down south of town, but he was planning to sell it. Now I'm not sure."

"Does he have a theater background?" Principal Miller narrows her eyes. "He looks competent."

"He's directed a lot of community plays," I say. "And he used to direct plays in this theater when we were in school. Under the direction of our theater director, of course."

Principal Miller smiles. "Think he'd be willing to stick around long enough to get this one done?"

"I doubt it." Because if he sticks around until Christmas, I'm doomed. "But maybe he can do it until Mr. Hammerly comes back."

"Mr. Hammerly had a stroke," Principal Miller says. "He's not coming back for a while."

I close my eyes. "Emery will be devastated."

"See if you can convince your friend to step in," Principal Miller says. "Or the play is off."

By the end of the rehearsal, I'm not sure I could drag Tommy away with a drop net, zip-tied hands, and a team of draft horses.

Which leaves me in a bad spot.

If he stays, I'll see more of him, and Emery will be delighted. But there's no way he won't discover that I lied. He's going to find out, and then what? Last week, I'd have said that him discovering my secret would be disappointing, but ultimately not a big deal. But now, after a few heart racing moments, it feels like everything has changed. He likes me. He always did.

And all those wasted moments weigh on me.

If I had been honest earlier, then what? He might have come back much, much sooner. If he didn't think I was married to Jed, would he have come back for me when we were young? How different would our lives be?

I'm not someone who usually wastes time and energy on regret, but it feels like this is unavoidable. No matter how I look at it, I'm going to have to confess my sins to Tommy and beg for his forgiveness. But will he still like me? Or will he despise me for lying to him?

On the flip side, as Emery climbs into my car, chattering happily about the play and how Tommy's ideas are already so much better than what they had in mind, how can I be so selfish that I ruin her pinch-hitting director?

I sigh.

"What's wrong?" Tommy drops his hand over mine again.

My heart swells, and I want to cry. I manage to rein it in, barely. "Nothing." I shake my head, trying to dispel the tears that are still threatening. "I'm great."

Emery wades right back into the fray, talking to him about some ideas she had for costumes.

"You have a real knack for this," he's saying as we reach

her house, which is barely two miles from the school now that they've moved in with Eddy.

"You know, I really could have walked," Emery says. "That's why I told Mom not to worry."

"We were happy to come get you," Tommy says. "And it was great fun working on that play."

"Actually," I say, "the principal was hoping you might be able to fill in for Mr. Hammerly for a while." I don't really want to tell him, but I feel like I have to. I'm not sure I've ever been quite this conflicted.

"Really?" Tommy's eyes light up. "I would love to."

"Why?" Emery looks worried. I know theater is the one thing she really likes about school. Without it, she'd try to hide in her bedroom at home and never go out.

I don't really want to be the one to tell her, but. . . "I'm not sure whether it's going to be announced, so you may need to keep this quiet at school, but Mr. Hammerly had a stroke. He won't be coming back anytime soon."

"Oh, no." From the rearview mirror, I can see Emery's hands on either side of her cheeks. "That's terrible."

"I'd be happy to fill in for this play. And if they're happy with my work, maybe I can keep helping after that."

"Do you mean it?" Emery's leaning over the seat, her hand on his shoulder, clearly already unbuckled. "That would be amazing."

"Do you think your friends would be alright with such an old guy as their new director?"

"You're not that old." Emery's a sweet kid. "But anyway, you're way better than Mr. Hammerly was. He's also the art teacher, and I think he likes art way better."

"Well, I'd be thrilled to have something to do. It might keep me from making Mandy crazy."

"Wait." Emery's eyes widen. "What do you mean?" Then her eyes drop, and she's staring at Tommy's hand where it's resting on top of mine. Her voice goes supersonic, like her mother's is prone to do. "Oh my gosh, are you two together?" She's bouncing up and down in the car, and then before I know it, she's bawling.

Actual tears, running down her bright red face.

"You have no idea, Mister Collins," she's blathering. "When she told us those stories, about you and Jed, and I just almost cried then, because you two are clearly perfect for each other, and I am just so happy that you're here and you're together, and I am so glad that you still like plays, and this is, like, better than Cinderella or Mulan or, like, Sleeping Beauty, too."

Oh, my.

"Well, I'm happy that you're happy," Tommy says.

But clearly he's over the moon. He's beaming wider than he was when he told me he'd liked me way back when. If I said I wasn't happy to see Emery's excitement, I'd be lying too. It's always been contagious and this is no exception. We do manage to drop her off, but only after a few more minutes of excited gushing and well wishes.

By the time we leave, I've made a decision.

Tommy's a good person. If I tell him the truth and he decides he can't forgive me, he might stick around, at least through the end of this play. And that would give me some time to convince him that I made a mistake, but that he should give me another chance.

On the drive back to my house, I make benign chitchat as best I can, but really, I'm planning how to come clean. I need to tell him the truth, and I'm going to do it.

Tonight.

"I have some steaks in the freezer," I say. "With as windy as it's gotten, we should check whether there's a storm front coming in. If there is, we should stay in tonight. I could cook a few potatoes and steam some broccoli. . ."

"Are you asking to make me dinner?" He squeezes my hand.

"I suppose I am." I turn down the drive, and again, there's a car in the drive.

"Your house is very popular," he says. "I can't believe you thought you could move to Montana."

He's right. It was a ridiculous idea. But this time, the person who owns the car pops right out. Helen doesn't let other people drive her overpriced toys. She's waving as I park.

"Hey, there," she says. "You're still around, I see."

Tommy climbs out and leans against the door. "I'm hoping to stick around for quite some time."

"A smart man," Helen says. "Very smart."

"We were about to go in for dinner. Are you here to stay, or are you moving out?" I'm not sure which I prefer. If she's around, I could put off telling him for another night. I'd have a buffer to help me manage it.

But on the other hand, she could slip and say something. Even though I'm planning to come clean, I'd rather do it on my terms than have it sprung on him.

"I have dinner plans," she says. "But I'll come in for a bit. I have a question to ask you." She shivers.

The poor woman insists on wearing clothing that looks like a work of art, but it's not ever very sensible. You'd think someone who lived in New York for so long would be able to dress properly for cold weather.

Helen also looks nervous as we go inside, which I can spot easily, because there's no one on earth more nervous than I am right now. We've barely stepped through the door when she blurts out, "You already know my secret."

She's never been someone to beat around the bush. "Yes, I do." I fold my arms and sit on the sofa. Tommy takes the seat next to me. "What did you decide to do about it?"

"I don't owe anyone an explanation." She huffs.

My heart sinks. "Helen, I know you have spent your life—"

236

"You don't know," she says. "No one does. So just let me talk."

I sit back, placing my hand on Tommy's forearm. He's shifted forward, dropping his elbows on his knees, like he'd like to lay Helen across his lap and spank her. I understand the sentiment, but I'm not sure he could even manage it. Besides, I know her well enough to know that even if he did, it wouldn't help.

"Go ahead, then." I arch an eyebrow, preparing myself for the worst.

She drops into the chair across from me with a sigh like she's tired. Bone weary, really. "I'm keeping the baby."

You could knock me over with a feather—no, with a piece of lint.

"You are?" Relief floods every part of my body. I had been debating in the back of my mind whether I needed to rouse the troops and call Abby. I'm glad that wasn't necessary.

"It wasn't part of the plan, but Abby has had a lot of detours, and she seems happy about hers."

"If you're saying that gorgeous man, David, is a detour, then sign me up." I can't help my smile.

Tommy's scowling now, which is adorable. To have a man getting jealous over my ridiculous appraisals of men half my age is very entertaining.

"I didn't decide because of Abby or David or even you," Helen says. "I decided to keep it for me." Now she leans forward in the chair. "But that leads me to my next question."

"And now I'm truly interested," I say. "I was nervous for you before, but you have my full attention." I can't help my smile. It's been a strange and wonderful day.

"Will you be a bridesmaid?"

"Oh, absolutely not."

"Please," she says. "David has dozens of friends, and the man has so many groomsmen, I have no idea how I'll find enough people to stand next to them if you say no."

"How many boys are you thinking will escort me?"

Helen's smirk is calculated. "I was counting on at least two."

"I'm not some kind of court jester," I say.

"And I'm not really the typical blushing bride, either. I think with your help, we can make this wedding something people will remember."

"Is that your goal, then? Memorability?"

"It's a start." She shrugs. "I'm only getting married because we're having a baby—no other good reasons to *get* married. If I have to do it, the wedding ceremony may as well be interesting."

"That's not the only good reason to get married," Tommy says.

"What?" Helen asks. "What else you got?"

"You could want to send a message to the world that this is your person, forever."

"I think the fifty percent divorce rate might undercut that message," Helen says.

"But marriage is valuable, no matter how long it lasts," Tommy says.

"Agree to disagree," Helen says.

"Don't worry," I say. "Helen and I regularly disagree, and she's still here, asking me to be her bridesmaid."

"Well, no matter how you look at it, my marriage won't be very traditional," Helen says. "My wedding gown is black, my maid of honor will probably have a baby on her hip, and David and I are currently arguing over which resort will host the ceremony."

"It should be at ours," I say. "It's so much prettier."

"He says his has better views," Helen says, "but he's actually pushing for us to do it at Gold Strike."

"He is?" I frown. "Why?"

"We'll have to move quite a few guests that are booked

away from whichever resort hosts, since we want to do it soon," I say, "and he would rather we eat the cost, that devil."

"Are you sure he's not messing with you?" That seems like something he'd do.

"I don't think so," Helen says. "He's let me have my way on everything so far. I really thought he'd balk about the black wedding dress."

"If I were ever to get married, I think I'd like a black wedding dress," I say. "It would be cost economical—it could double as my shroud when I die." I can't help my cackle.

"If you were *ever* to get married?" Tommy asks.

I freeze.

"I think that's a great idea," Helen says. "At this age, people are going to comment on it, so you may as well be in on the joke."

"But you've been married," Tommy says. "Why did you say *if*?"

"When were you ever married?" Helen shakes her head. "No one in their right mind would be willing to put up with a lifetime of this misery." She's smiling.

But Tommy's not.

"I think Tommy's talking about my wedding to Jedediah Brooks," I say.

Helen's laughing even harder. "As if."

"Tommy, I have something big to tell you," I say slowly. "And I meant to do it after Helen left, but I guess there's no time like the present."

Helen's not laughing anymore, somehow grasping that the tone has shifted. "You know what?" She stands. "I'm going to put you down as a yes, and I'll see myself out."

I don't argue with her.

Once the door has shut, I continue. "You started pressuring me years ago, threatening to come back here and tell Jed how I felt if I didn't do it myself."

"I was hoping you'd tell me you didn't like him anymore," Tommy says. "It was stupid, I know."

I look down at my hands, weathered and worn. "I was scared that you might really do it, so I lied." I look up, forcing myself to stare into his eyes. "I didn't ever tell Jed that I liked him, and we didn't get married, and I never traveled the world either. In fact, I made all of those things up for one reason. I was fond of Jed, and when he cut me off, it hurt. I found out after he died that he'd fancied himself in love with me for decades. But all that time, the guy I really liked. . .was you."

22

HELEN

Back in business school, I thought I was *so* lucky, meeting someone like Oliver. His family was impressive. His parents were picture perfect. He was gorgeous. And he liked *me*.

It wasn't until after he stole my idea that I realized what a bullet I had dodged when he dumped me.

When I saw him again, I got a little nostalgic, and for one very stupid second, I actually wondered if I was making a mistake, putting my effort and time into someone like David Park. Someone who wanted things that were fundamentally different than what I wanted.

But David has always been willing to lead me to water, and he's always been patient waiting for me to drink.

Oliver has been impressively consistent in an entirely different way.

"He did what?" Abby asks. "I'm going to castrate him."

"Not kill him?" I lift my eyebrows.

"No, I want him to live with his misery for a very long time," Abby says. "And I want to make sure he can never ever make any more little monsters like him while he suffers."

I place my hand on my belly. "Like the one I'm growing right now?"

"Yours won't be a monster." Abby's face softens like it always does when she looks at my stomach. "Yours will be an angel."

"Not this again."

Abby rolls her eyes and changes gears quickly, as usual. "What's our plan then, if not castration?"

Oliver alerted the board about our plan to force a vote, when he knew I didn't have enough votes yet. By my calculations, I'm still one percent shy of taking the company for the price I want—a price that will make us all a lot of money.

"There's not much we can do," I say. "Except talk to the shareholders about what I think they should do and how it will benefit anyone who votes with me." I shrug. "This is how this kind of thing goes. He'll forfeit his share of the gains if we can prove he disclosed after signing that agreement, and we'll do what we can to repair anything we can."

Once Abigail has lined up a sitter for her little guy—Beth is proving to be very willing to help out in a pinch when I throw money at her—we both hop on a jet and head for California. We go over the particulars of the speech I'll make to the board on the way.

"You're ready," Abigail says. "After that speech, I'd hand over my votes *and* my retirement fund to you."

"It's about time," I mutter. "It's offensive you have that money invested in REITs."

"They consistently outperform the market."

"So does your sister, by a much larger margin." I narrow my eyes.

When we land, there's a car waiting, and even so, stupid Oliver has already assembled a quorum and is talking to them when we land. At least I recognize a lot of faces around the table when I walk in the door.

"We have the required quorum," Oliver says.

I wonder what the current CEO offered him for turning on me. "That makes things easier for me."

Abigail hands me my stack of proxies. "I represent forty-nine percent of your outstanding shares. And you've gathered most of the others here."

"But it's too late for talking. You're late. We're about to vote," Oliver says.

"Under section 16f, a majority shareholder can speak before any forced vote, as long as there was less than twenty-four hours notice given," Abigail says.

I love having her with me. "And I'm going to exercise that right." I can tell that Oliver's ticked, but he can't stop me. None of them can. I just need to get at least two percent of the people gathered to switch to my side, and they'll have to accept my tendered purchase offer.

The CEO's a very stormy looking older man with eyebrows that look like little white caterpillars. He moves out of the way very slowly, like he might be able to hold his ground by refusing to yield the podium. But I don't need a microphone to address the people gathered in this board-room. There aren't even sixty of them. It looks like a town hall meeting in Manila.

"My name's Helen Fisher. Some of you have heard of me, either from Oliver, or perhaps from reading Forbes. You surely know that I'm famous for making a lot of money out of companies that were formerly foundering."

"Which is why we're confused at your interest. Our company is doing fine," the CEO says. He's clearly Gonzago's man.

"We won't let you steal from us," a blonde in the back says.

"I wouldn't dream of it," I say. "In fact, as you may already know, I've been buying your shares at market value for quite some time now. I personally own twelve percent of your company. If I were planning to steal from you, would I place myself in exactly your position?" I arch one eyebrow. "I also own another thirty percent through my group—a company that I own nearly outright myself."

"So what do you want?" the same blonde woman asks.

"I would like to wrest control from this man right there." I point at the CEO. "For the past three years, he's been badly mismanaging things, and your company has underperformed as a result of that management."

"You get monthly numbers," the CEO says, his caterpillars bobbling wildly. "You know that's not true."

"I don't read the Bible much, but my sister was just telling me about a story from it, one that you might know already. In the New Testament, Jesus tells a story about some master who gave his servants gold pieces. One of them buries the gold, but doesn't lose it. One turns two gold shares into four, and one turns five into ten. As you already know, Jesus rewarded—"

Abby clears her throat. "The master in the story rewarded."

"Right," I say. "The master rewarded those who turned two into four and five into ten, but he punished the man who sat on the buried money. That's essentially what your CEO here has done." I nod at Abby.

She passes around the packets we prepared. A few people have to share, but most of them have one to themselves.

"This is my plan for the company, which most people in my position would *not* share. You can look over what I intend to do, the numbers we project it will yield, and what we hope to accomplish in the next twelve months. I believe they speak for themselves." I lean forward and drop my palms flat on the table. "I never bury my gold."

I let them think, murmur, and review for a moment.

But just as the CEO is standing up, ready to dicker over some line or another, I resume. "Compared to the rest of the market, you've barely kept apace with what your company has long been worth. I'm suggesting that instead of treading water, we double our money." I straighten. "Or. . .how do you think Jesus would feel about us tripling it?"

Abby looks a little pained at my abuse of her analogy, but no one here seems too upset. In fact, a few of them are cheering. In the end, the vote winds up being close to sixty percent in my favor. I'm smiling when I stand up. "I'm delighted at the trust you've placed in me."

Abby's hiss, however, is a little distracting.

"What?"

She points at my chair.

And I realize that where I was just sitting, there's a puddle of blood.

For a baby I didn't even want, I'm surprisingly nervous as I'm rushed to the ER and then straight up to labor and delivery. Abby's texted and called everyone by the time I've been seen, and David's on his way to LA.

Abby's downright terrifying when she wants to be, and apparently when my baby's future is in question, she wants to be. She never raises her voice, but a woman with an ultrasound is checking my belly five minutes after we reach the room.

"Good news." The woman shifts the wand and points. "There's a steady heartbeat, and the fetus looks good. I'll wait for the attending to tell you more."

"You're not even a doctor?" Abigail looks disgusted.

"I'm a third-year resident," the woman says. "I am a doctor."

"Then what are you worried about?" Abigail says. "What do we have to wait for the real doctor to come tell us?"

The woman sighs, and I almost feel sorry for her. "Bleeding during a pregnancy isn't always a concern, but it's not usually good."

"Well, a quick internet search would tell me it's not good, if I didn't already know that much," Abby says. "But I figured after seven years of training, you'd be able to tell me whether it was placenta previa, a placental abruption, or something worse."

"It's not an ectopic pregnancy," the resident says.

"We already knew that," Abby says. "It's not our first ultrasound."

"I'm actually a general surgery resident on a rotation," the poor woman says. "So if you could just wait for a bit—"

"Next time, lead with 'I know less than you,'" Abby sighs. "It'll save us all some time."

It takes about ten minutes for the terrified resident to track down the attending, but once she's in the room, she grabs that ultrasound wand and starts whirling it around like some kind of wild west gunslinger with his favorite pistol. "Alright, your baby's attached high, so there's no risk of placenta previa, and your baby's vital signs continue to be very good. I'd like to monitor you overnight, but I think you're going to be just fine." She tilts her head as she puts the wand down. "Did you work out today?"

"Could that have caused it?" I frown. "I went for a jog this morning, but I've done that almost every morning of the pregnancy, and it's been ten hours since then."

"Did you drink anything or eat anything out of the norm?" She frowns. "Or were you under a lot of unusual stress?"

Abby laughs.

"This isn't funny," the attending says. "In a woman your sister's age, stress can be very dangerous to a pregnancy."

"The woman you're scanning is Helen Fisher, and she's made Forbes' list of top ten billionaires to watch for over a decade," Abby says. "An unusual day would be one without stress."

"I did fly out here this afternoon and attend a board meeting where I had to convince shareholders to vote for me over the current management," I say. "The vote was unexpected, and we didn't know how it would go."

"Well." The woman stands. "I'm going to recommend that you try and take it easy for the next few months, unless you'd like to lose this baby and start over."

My heart sinks. "This is what I was afraid of," I say. "This baby is already slowing me down." But really, I'm terrified. Could I, with my normal, daily life, kill this little child? Would it be my fault? Because I live and breathe stress constantly?

"Helen, do not let that woman browbeat you," Abby says. "Bleeding in a pregnancy isn't your fault." She leans toward me and drops her hand on my arm. "You're going to be just fine, and so is your little one."

"But it wouldn't hurt if I took it easy for a while."

She smiles. "No, it wouldn't hurt."

"Well, then Oliver did us a favor," I say. "I had another few weeks of meetings planned, but now I can just process the paperwork for this forced purchase deal and then focus on the boring work of getting that company turned around."

"Yes, just that." Abby pulls out her laptop and starts clicking, clearly already working on the documents we promised to send. "You should try and take a nap before everyone gets here."

"Everyone?" I ask.

"David says his parents insisted on coming. Steve wanted to be here, and if he's coming, apparently the kids wanted to come too."

It's going to be a zoo. "So much for low stress."

"Having family around is always a good thing," Abby says. "I promise."

She winds up being right. David and his parents bring about five hundred pounds of food when they arrive, and Steve and his kids bring cards and camp out in the corner of my room, shouting and laughing as they play some variation of Uno that I've never seen.

Nathan practically screeches when he sees his mother.

"Thank goodness," Abby says. "I left my pump on the plane." She ducks into the bathroom, apparently not keen on nursing in front of David's shell-shocked parents. For two people who claim to like children, they're not very natural with Abby's mob.

"How many kids do you have?" Mr. Park is looking at all the blonde heads in despair.

"Five," Abby says as she walks out. "But Ethan stayed behind to deal with stuff on the ranch, so there are only four of them here." She smiles. "Don't worry, though. They're easier to process when they come one at a time."

Now I'm the one coughing. "And in our case, we'll only ever have just the one."

"For now, anyway," David sits next to me on the bed, patting my legs. "We never know what the future holds."

"Oh, I disagree. We know just what it will hold. This one little baby and no more."

"A few months ago," he whispers, "you'd have said it would never hold this one."

I roll my eyes, because. . .he's right.

There's a tap at the door, but it's just a courtesy. The attending from before walks in without waiting for a response. "We did some routine bloodwork when you first arrived, and now that it's back, I wanted to find out whether you wanted to know the gender of the baby." She's hovering in the doorway, like I should be ready to answer her right away.

So I do. "Yes."

"I'm not sure." David hops to his feet.

"Why would we not want to know?"

"Don't you think it might be fun to do, like, I don't know." He glances around the room, and then he starts to pace, hopping over Uno players and bags and discarded shoes as he moves. "People do parties for this stuff nowadays."

"We have a party here right now," I say. "Look around."

"But they, like, blast pink confetti out of cannons and stuff," David says. "We could do something like that."

"Out of a cannon?" I can't help laughing. "Is that something you've been longing to try?" I glance back at the attending. "I think we would like to know. Then we can start shopping and setting up the nursery in the right colors."

"That's another thing," David says. "We still haven't decided where we're going to live once we're married."

"You know what?" the doctor says. "I'll come back."

"No," I say. "Don't. Just tell us."

She glances at David, which is infuriating. I'm the one growing the baby.

But thankfully, he nods. "Go ahead. I just like messing with her." His smile reminds me why I love him. He does love messing with me, and he takes my irritable behavior in stride, too.

"It's a boy," she says with a grin, and then she ducks out the door.

Like she didn't just drop a horrible bomb.

I know that, with this many people in the room, I should pretend I'm pleased, but I just can't. My face appears to be frozen in shock.

"Whoa," David says. "What's wrong?"

Okay, shock, and apparently also disappointment.

David hops back up on the bed and drops an arm around my shoulder. "You're the one who wanted to know." He sounds half concerned and half entertained. "Should I go order a cannon?"

"This isn't funny." I shove at him.

"I'm sorry," he says. "But I'm glad we didn't record that. I'm sure our future son will be sad when he finds out you were this upset to have a boy."

"I was sad when I found out Nathan was a boy," Abby says. "The girls' clothes and shoes are so much more fun."

"We can have another one," David says. "Even if this spontaneous pregnancy was a fluke, we could purposely—"

I shove him harder this time. "Stop." I've calmed down some, but that joke has passed its expiration date.

"What's so upsetting?" Mrs. Park asks from the corner where she's been hiding. "You don't like boys?" She arches one imperious brow. "Or are you sad about the dresses?"

"Who cares about dresses?" I feel tears threatening, and I just can't do that. Not with all these people around.

"What is it, then?" David asks.

"I like boys just fine, and I couldn't care less what the baby wears," I say. "But I have no idea what to do with a boy. I don't play ball or watch sports or. . ." I trail off, not even able to think of other little boy things. "My own baby's going to hate me."

David laughs. "That's ridiculous. He'll like what you like, and I happen to *be* a boy, so I'm more than willing to lend a hand whenever you need ideas of how to connect."

It takes me a few minutes, but I do calm down. David's telling me the things he did with his parents back in Korea, and Gabe's telling me all the things he and Nathan like, and Steve even pipes up with how much fun it is to bean his infant son in the head with squishy balls. When Abby waltzes back into the room, I do a double take.

"When did you even leave?"

Abby's lugging a huge bag. When Nathan sees her, he practically lunges out of Izzy's arms to the hard tile floor.

"What is that?" I ask, staring pointedly at the large white paper shopping bag. "Where did you go?"

"This is now a gender reveal party," she says. "In honor of that, I popped downstairs before the gift shop closed. The bad news is that they were fresh out of confetti cannons." She makes a face at David. "But I did manage to grab a few things I thought might cheer you up." She reaches into the bag and what she pulls out is tiny, light blue, and it has grey ridges all down the back.

I'm squinting. "What is that?"

She hands it to me, and I flip it over in my hands before realizing it's a dinosaur sleeper for a newborn. It may be the cutest thing I've ever seen. "Aww."

The next thing she pulls out is a baby bunny nightlight. "All babies sleep better in a room with low lighting, boys or girls." She winks.

Steve takes the bag. "I call dibs on giving her the tiny fox." He whips out a fluffy brown fox plush. "Plenty of boys still want to snuggle." As if he can understand what Steve's saying, Nate drops his head on Abby's shoulder and closes his eyes.

"Ooh." The kids have gathered around, and Izzy reaches into the bag and grabs something. She offers it to me.

It's a pacifier with a mustache on the top. I can't help laughing. "That is pretty cute."

"And I know I didn't buy any of this, but this is called a soccer ball." David pulls a squishy orange ball out of the bag and tosses it to me.

Gabe opens his mouth. "That's not—"

Whitney shoves her hand over his face before he can finish. "Hush."

"It's clearly a basketball," I say. "I know that much."

"If he inherits my athletic ability," David says, "you won't need to know much more than that."

"Oh, please," I say. "You're decent at sports."

"But between the two of you," Abby says, "he's bound to be a huge nerd. Better than anyone else I know, you're both amply equipped to raise a nerd."

By the time Steve takes the kids to a hotel to sleep for the night, I'm feeling better. About the bleeding, about Oliver and his attempt to destroy my takeover, and about the baby being a boy.

"Should I stick around?" David asks. "Or are you going to be sleeping?"

Abby left with Steve, at my insistence, so she could nurse her little guy in peace, and for some reason, staying here alone kind of freaks me out. "Do you mind staying?"

"I'd prefer it," David says. "But you're Miss Independence. I try to keep you as happy as I can."

"To keep from getting your head bitten off?" I'm smiling so he knows I'm teasing.

"I do like my head," he says. "It keeps my neck in line."

"Is there room on your plane for all those kids?" Mrs. Park asks.

I snap my head toward the door where she and Mr. Park are standing. "Of course," I say. "It seats twenty."

"If you don't mind, we may head back to Utah tonight."

"Of course. You should," I say. "I really appreciate you mobilizing your jet so fast and bringing Abby's family along as well. I know they can be a little much if you're not used to big families."

Until I got used to being around them, they used to wear me out, too. Sometimes they still do.

"I was worried," Mrs. Park says. "My husband and I both were." She steps closer. "We were hoping to convince you to move to Korea to raise your child."

I have no idea what to say to that.

"But now, after seeing the family you have." She shakes her head. "Our son has joined a beautiful family." Her smile's sad. "We'll try to come and visit often so that we aren't strangers."

David's parents may be overbearing, and they may be irritating in their insistence that he do things their way, but they clearly care about him, and they're more insightful than I expected. Their culture is one where the woman leaves her family and joins the family of the man, typically, from what I've studied. It's nice to hear her say he's joined a nice family.

Once they leave, David drags the sofa a little closer to my bed and lies down. I feel a little bad. He's far too long to sleep on the short little sofa the hospital provides. "You should have gone too," I say. "You won't be able to sleep there."

"You know, in Korea, my people often sleep on mats on the floor." He smiles.

"You're lying."

"I mean, I didn't ever do that." He's smiling more broadly. "But you know, our people often do."

I throw a pillow at him. It seems fair, since I have three, but it's also gratifying to smack his smug face. "I love you," I say.

"I don't think you'll ever truly comprehend how much I love you," David says. "I know how much you've changed your plans, and I know you're doing it all for me."

"And for me," I say. "Most of my plans are great, but the one where I never had a kid needed an overhaul." I think about that moment when I saw the blood earlier today. "I'm not sure I've ever been so afraid as when I thought I was miscarrying."

"Me either." David stands and squeezes in next to me on the bed.

"You better not try to stay here all night," I grumble. But I'm already turning just a hair sideways so he can curl up behind and beside me.

And when I fall asleep, I haven't let him leave my bed yet. There are so many things in my life now that were all wrong for me before I met him. Now those very same things are the best parts of my life. I'm thinking about how certain people can completely alter the trajectory of our lives, if they're the right ones.

Like Abby did when she was born.

I'm blessed that David careened into my orbit and knocked me sideways, and I'm beginning to understand how blessed we both might be to have this little boy joining our family.

I wanted Abby.

I didn't realize I wanted David for years and years.

And I almost made a huge mistake with this baby, one that I would have regretted, maybe forever.

While I will forever champion the right for women to choose, I'm glad my family and friends helped me find the right path for this pregnancy while there was still time to take it.

23

MANDY

No matter how much you love a particular food, if you eat it too often, you'll probably get sick of it. If you really, really eat too much, you may find that your love of that food turns into hate. It's a pretty simple concept for most humans to understand. I mean, we've all listened to our favorite song so many times that it started to make us cringe. We've probably also eaten so many Pringles that we had to avoid the chip aisle.

At least for a few days.

The harder lesson is that in life, no matter how good the day, that joy never lasts.

If I hadn't been quite so happy about Tommy's revelation that he had liked me all this time, I wouldn't be so upset when he leans over, snatches the stack of paper at the end of my coffee table, and stands. "I think it's time for me to call it a night." His nostrils flare as he inhales, and his chest rises and falls.

Then he walks across my family room and out the front door.

I want to chase after him. I want to shout and beg and tell him how sorry I am, but the man I know wouldn't be swayed by any of that. Or at least, the boy I knew wouldn't have been.

He didn't flip out on me, because that's also not his way.

Tommy's going back to his hotel, and he'll read through the paperwork, and he'll think about what I said, and he'll make some kind of decision. He'll have to decide how upset he was by my news, and how delighted he was by my other revelation, and then he'll weigh out which one is more important. Until he has, all the arguing in the world won't help.

But unlike Jed, he's not pretending I'm not alive. He was polite, and he was calm, and he will remain that way. He's been gone a few moments when a ding from my phone reminds me of something important. The message is from the principal, asking me to pass along an email he's sending to Mr. Collins, and offering him the terms under which he could take over for Mr. Hammerly.

I waste no time forwarding the email, and then I take a screenshot of the message and the email and text it over in case he's not consistent about checking his email. It could also get caught by his spam filter, since I'm not a very frequent email contact, and I'm quite sure Principal Miller has never emailed him at all.

I KNOW YOU'RE UPSET WITH ME, AND I DON'T BLAME YOU, I text. BUT IF YOU CAN SPARE THE TIME, PLEASE STICK AROUND LONG ENOUGH TO HELP EMERY AND THE OTHER KIDS.

Two very long hours later, he replies. I WOULD BE HONORED TO DIRECT THEIR PLAY, AND I'M WILLING TO TEACH THE ART CLASSES TOO, AT LEAST UNTIL THEY CAN FIND A BETTER REPLACEMENT.

And just like that, I have an 'in.'

Of course, the very next day, I'm thrown into a panic. Amanda's busy dealing with Maren, who's now boycotting school entirely, and that leaves me to manage a reservation mix-up at the retreat while Helen flies across the country for some last-minute work thing.

When I hear that she's spotting, I nearly break down crying.

How can all the good things in our lives be so precarious? My tears won't help her, especially if they keep me from cleaning up the problems here, so I keep right on working, unraveling the nightmare of the clerk who apparently spent the two months she was working for us stoned, and by the next day, I hear that Helen's been released and is coming home. I'm able to message back with a party emoji and the message that, ALL THE RESERVATION MIX-UPS ARE FIXED. AND THE NEW CLERKS ALL PASSED THEIR DRUG SCREENS.

Hallelujahs all around.

Only, I haven't heard from Tommy, and it's been a day and a half.

I'm not proud of myself when I text Amanda and offer to pick up Emery, but sometimes you have to take any chance you can get.

I miss Tommy's face.

Which is pathetic.

When did I turn into such a dope?

"Hey, Emery." I wave as I walk into the back of the theater.

She's not the only face that turns toward me, and my stomach flips and then flops when Tommy meets my eye. He nods, and then he looks back down at the script in front of him, his little red pen darting across the page to change things here and there.

Emery jogged, so she's already reached me in the back. "Mr. Collins is *amazing*," she says. "He's so funny, and everyone loves him. They're so jealous that he's dating my grandma."

I can't help darting a glance his way, but if he heard her, he didn't react to it. "I'm not sure we are dating," I whisper. Then I drop my voice even lower. "I told him the truth two days ago, and I haven't heard from him since."

Emery blinks. "But. . ."

"But what?"

"I introduced him at yesterday's practice as my grandma's boyfriend, and everyone cheered and laughed, and he didn't say anything to contradict me."

"What would he say?" I whisper.

If I could crawl into a hole right now, I'd do it.

The joy I would usually feel about her telling people that I'm her grandma evaporates at the thought that Tommy might have been irritated, or worse, furious. What was I thinking, picking up Emery? "It's not like he'd renounce me in front of the whole cast." He's far too nice for that.

"I guess," Emery says. "Or maybe he's just taking time to think things over, but he still feels about you the same way he always has. That's my guess."

I shrug like I'm nonchalant, even though my mind is now spinning out. "Maybe." That night at home, my traitorous fingers check my phone incessantly, hoping that she's right.

But he never texts.

The next day, while I'm in the True Value shopping for more broccoli and green peas because my cardiologist insists I eat them daily, I glance down at my purse for one second, and when I look up again, I almost run into him. I expect him to ignore me, but he doesn't.

"Mandy."

He's holding one of those pathetic little plastic baskets, and all he has in it are three sad-looking TV dinners.

"What are those?"

"I was worried I might run into you at Brownings or the Gorge," he says.

That makes me laugh. "No chance of that. I've been hiding at home."

He laughs, too. "I suppose fate had other plans this time around."

"Listen," I say. "The last thing I want to do is make your life miserable while you're here. You are only here to help out my granddaughter."

"But she's not," Tommy says. "She's not related to you in any way." He frowns. "She's Jed's great-niece, but you had nothing to do with him."

"From the moment those two women came into town, they've been like daughters to me," I say. "Sometimes the family we choose is dearer to us than the people we're born to love." Or at least, I like to think it's true, since I don't have any children of my own. It *feels* true.

"The gas station attendant tells me that you *bought* Abigail and her son Jed's ranch back. Did he really leave it to a charity?"

"Worse. That idiot left it to an *alien* foundation like a complete crackpot." I suppress my urge to swear. It's not especially ladylike, which is fine because I'm not much of a lady, but it doesn't seem like the best time to advertise that fact. "I was just repairing his idiocy."

"Some things really never change." Tommy's half-smiling.

"I'm so sorry." The moment I say it, I know it's a mistake.

Tommy's face darkens like the rolling clouds of an impending storm. "I can't, Mandy."

"I waited two years for Jed to forgive me," I say. "He never did."

"I'm nothing like him." Now he looks even more upset.

Nice work, Mandy. "I know you aren't. So when the play is done, if you're still upset, please go home. Don't feel bad about it, either. No hard feelings from me."

"It's not that I—" He sighs. "I'm not angry, or not just angry, anyway."

"Your TV dinners are going to melt and they'll be even

worse than they already are," I say. "You don't have to explain anything to me right now. Just go." I step aside.

"Oh, well, now that I know you're hiding at home, I don't have to eat these." He chucks them back into the bin. "Thanks for suffering so I don't have to."

I gesture at my mounds of broccoli. "Actually, it's years of delicious bacon I have to thank for my suffering. I'm supposed to eat these blasted greens with every meal, which is fine during the summer when my garden's in full bloom, but it's really obnoxious over the winter, when I'm stuck eating wilty junk they bring up from Mexico."

"At least it's not all canned." He pulls a face. "I hated canned pears the most, I think."

"It's just that they're so good fresh. . ."

"And so mealy and stringy and gross canned." Tommy's smiling. "You know, I didn't even know I like pears until I was an adult and tried a fresh one for the first time. Why did our moms use exclusively canned fruit?"

"I think transportation was harder," I say, just a little proud of myself for making him smile about fruit. I can't help being optimistic as I turn to march up the aisle and pay. My cause can't be totally hopeless if he can smile during an awkward exchange in the grocery store.

Or maybe the fact that he's already getting over his upset indicates he didn't feel that strongly about me in the first place. I pause, thinking things through slowly. Should I be hoping it takes him a long time? Deep feelings are harder to sort out, right?

"Mandy." Someone grabs my elbow.

I'm pretty sure it's Tommy.

I shouldn't be so desperately hopeful, but I can't help it. My heart swells with it as I turn and confirm that it is him.

"Yeah?" My voice is embarrassingly breathy, like I'm auditioning for the role of Scarlett in *Gone with the Wind*.

"I'm not angry at you as much as I am at myself. Instead

of pushing you to tell Jed how you felt. . ." He releases me and steps back, his head down, focused on his now empty plastic basket.

That's when I understand. If he had told me how he felt, instead of writing to threaten me, we wouldn't have wasted all this time. "I'm embarrassed," I admit. "The whole thing is embarrassing."

"It shouldn't be. Your family taught you to lie," he says.

My jaw drops.

"Your dad was kind of famous for it."

That stings, but it's not untrue. He never stole, but he'd boast about unbelievable things with the best of them. And when he got drunk, it was even worse. "That's no excuse."

"I ruined our lives, not you." He steps closer, shaking his head. "I messed this up, and it's hard for me to live with that."

I look up at him, the stupid burgeoning hope soaring. "You—I told you I traveled."

"I knew that part wasn't true, at least not after you got married." His lip's twitching. "Jed wouldn't even go on the field trip to San Francisco, and his mom kept offering to pay for half the class if he'd go."

I forgot about that.

"He never went to see his brother, either. At least, not when his parents went out to visit Clyde at school. I asked him why once, and he said, 'if it can't be reached within one tank of gas of here, I don't want to see it.'"

His impression of Jed is *so* spot on, I can barely handle it. Once I start laughing, Tommy does, too.

"If you can forgive me for being an idiot, I can try to forgive myself," he says.

"I'm the idiot."

"You overheard me trying to be a good friend to you," he says. "If I could convince Jed I didn't like you, I thought you had a chance of getting what I thought you wanted. And also, if I told him I liked you, when you did get together, he'd make you stay away from me. At the time, that felt like the worst of all possible options."

"But you were never in the way of him and me."

"Everyone in town thought you and Jed were star-crossed lovers. If you had any idea how many people told me your tragic story." His hand's clutched so tightly around the handle of the basket that I'm worried he'll break the flimsy plastic.

"I'm sorry about that," I say. "But we weren't really *star*-crossed. We were just cross."

His lip twitches with suppressed mirth.

"I don't want us to be cross," I whisper. "I was too happy the one day we were straight."

He drops the basket then, and he yanks me away from mine, pulling me tightly against his body. I'm sure everyone in the store is covering their eyes or making puking sounds, but I'm giddy as a lamb in a field in springtime when he drops his head toward mine. "I love you, Mandy Saddler, and I don't want to waste any more time eating television dinners alone. I want to spend the rest of my time right here."

"In the grocery store?" I grimace. "Because that could be awkward."

He's smiling when he kisses me.

And it's just exactly the kiss I've always dreamed about. I forget about the world around me, about where we're standing, about why I'm here. Nothing matters except his arms around me, and his breath on my face. Until he finally releases me, and I realize that my top denture has come loose and is now falling down on top of my bottom teeth.

"I better go check out," I manage to mumble. "Why don't you pick up some food and meet me at my place."

Ours may be the strangest romance ever told, but I like my romance with a side of laughter. So when he gets to my house with two burgers, one patty made with disgusting black beans he insists are heart healthy, I tell him thanks, and then

I confess why I shot out of the store like a calf from its first hoof trim.

I know I picked the right man when he laughs so loudly that Jed squeals and heads for the back door. Sizzling chemistry is great, but someone to laugh with matters so much more, and I'm old enough to realize that.

Thank goodness that Tommy and I have both.

❦ 24 ❦
DONNA

No man is perfect, but I swear the ones who are awfully close always have a few things that they hide until after you're married. In the case of my adorable husband, it's that he likes to camp out on the toilet and read.

Sometimes for an hour.

I wish that was a huge exaggeration.

It is not.

"Will Earl, I love you to the moon and back, but if you don't get out of that bathroom right now, I'm going to cut off your big toe."

He shoots out, yanking his pants up as he hops. "Why my big toe?"

"What else could I cut off? You wouldn't care about the small ones." I'm smiling as I shove the book basket back into the corner. "You can read all you want, but stop doing it in my bathroom. Capice?"

"It's the only time Aiden doesn't walk in on me every five minutes."

He's not wrong about that, but I wish he was. Aiden has gotten progressively more annoying, probably because the house is now marinating in babies and their crap is just all over.

As if my thoughts summoned them, one of the babies starts to cry. I know good mothers are supposed to know who's crying from the sound, but I swear Althea and Andrew made some pact up in heaven, and they sound *exactly* the same.

Andrew should be quieter, since he's, you know, months and months younger. But the lungs on that kid are impressive. As if he's already engaged in some kind of sibling rivalry, he's made it his life's purpose to out-scream her.

"I think that's Althy," Will says.

"I thought we decided not to call her that."

"No, you decided I shouldn't call her that. I never agreed." He's smiling as he dries his hands and heads out in a search and rescue party, calling back at me over his shoulder, "You almost ready to go?"

Before setting the time on their wedding, Helen actually texted me to find out whether there was a time that would be easier for me. As if there could *be any* time on *Thanksgiving Day* that would be convenient to attend a wedding when someone has two babies.

"We told them ten a.m.," I say. "We can't be late, and I know that. I'm almost done."

But we were doomed from the start. When you have two babies, one of them is destined to poop right as you're ready to go. And the one thing I didn't think to do was buy two black dresses for my six-month-old, so when Althea's diaper explodes, splattering poop all over her first one. . .I have limited options.

Our family does show up wearing black, as requested, except for Althea, who's wearing her next-nicest outfit, a rose print, white floofy dress her grandmother bought her. As Will swings her car seat through the door of David's retreat in Dutch John, I can't help noticing that we stand out. Not me, and Will, and Aiden. Even Andrew looks pretty good in his little faux-tux.

But our bright white and pink baby looks like the fairy that showed up for Maleficent's ball. For some reason, that thought really cheers me up. "This really is like Maleficent's wedding," I hiss.

Beth and Ethan hear me, and they start to laugh as well. "It so is," Beth says. "And who does that make Althea? Is she Aurora?"

"Aurora?" Abby's just walking through the door, and she's clearly looking for someone, but we've distracted her, as usual. "Is there someone here named Aurora?"

Ethan's laughing so hard that he can't even explain, but Beth does.

To my surprise, Abby chuckles. "It is a little like Maleficent herself is getting married. She could have at least done something with her black wedding dress and bridesmaids' dresses other than adding crimson as an accent color." She's still smiling when she snatches an enormous bloodred bouquet of roses out of a vase and ducks back through the door at the rear of the ballroom.

As I glance around us, I realize it's not just the bridesmaids. Everything is black and red. It's absolutely elegant, but it's also pretty dark. The walls are draped in cloth as dark as pitch and then covered in the tiniest, cutest, pure white twinkle lights. Dark red floral arrangements drape dramatically down the middle of each panel. The aisle where Helen will presumably be walking is the only space that's white, and the fabric walkway is *so* white, that I worry everyone will stain it black with the soles of their shoes.

At the front of the room, there's a large raised platform, and it's covered in more crimson roses than I've ever seen in my life. They're also larger than any roses I've ever seen, all half-open, as if some insane florist stood over millions of red flowers, shouting, "No, no, no," and then, "Off with their

266

heads!" over every closed or open red rose that dared to exist.

Actually, knowing Helen, that might be precisely what happened. She's got the kind of money that most of us can't imagine, and she's not afraid to spend it.

One of the side benefits to being a touch late is that we don't have to wait around long before the orchestra—yes, a full orchestra on Thanksgiving Day—begins to play.

Andrew decides to fuss at all the new noise, loudly, so I have to pull him out of his car seat, which means I'm distracted for just a moment. By the time I have him on my lap and have the wherewithal to look up, Helen has nearly reached us.

Her dad's not walking her down the aisle.

I should have expected this, but it's Abby. Helen's wedding gown is entirely black, and the dress is much simpler than I anticipated it would be. The skirt's sheared, and asymmetrical, but it's full too, almost like there's a small petticoat underneath it. Her heels are predictably tall, and deep red. The bodice is simple, slightly asymmetrical as well, and the top's beaded with something bright that's sparkling like little red diamonds. They look like they're cascading down the front, thicker at the top and splayed outward near the base of the bodice.

She's holding the largest bouquet I have ever seen. The flowers Abby retrieved were clearly just a bridesmaid's bouquet.

The contrast between Abby and Helen is a marked one. Abby's wearing an almost identical dress, but it's blindingly white. The same tiny, bright red stones sparkle across the bodice, also cascading down like they're frosting dripping down the sides of a warm cake. Only, against the white gown, it's clear what they are.

Rubies, or maybe garnets?

They must be one or the other.

It *is* Helen, after all.

And I won't lie—the effect is visually stunning. When the two of them reach the front, Abby extends her arm, handing Helen off to David, who's wearing a gorgeous black tux with a black shirt and a red tie that just matches Helen's shoes and stone accents. He looks worthy of Helen, in all his haute glory. His tux is clearly made by some snooty designer, and his raven hair gleams in the light of the chandeliers overhead.

He's also beaming as he helps Helen up the stairs and to his side.

As the rest of the wedding party works their way to the front, I can't help admiring the contrasts Helen worked in. The first bridesmaid is Izzy, and she's in black like Helen. The next one is Whitney, who's in white like her mother. Beth is in black again, with Ethan on her arm, and finally Mandy stalks her way up the aisle, with not one, but two attractive groomsmen holding her arms like she might fall forward on her face any moment. Her white gown looks absolutely hilarious, like she's part of some parody of a wedding for a comedy act.

Once she reaches the front, she yanks her arms free. "Thank you, young men. You're nearly as steady as a walker, but you don't listen as well." Her eyes are flashing, and I can tell she's loving this. Her scowl is just part of her act. I'm sure she's complained convincingly through every step, all while everyone knows she's enjoying it.

At least none of the bridesmaids other than Abby are sporting ruby-frosted bodices.

It makes me feel a little better about not being chosen that I didn't miss out on forty thousand dollars' worth of bling. I'm sure Helen left me out because I have a baby on both arms, but it's a little depressing that everyone's up there who comes to our girls' nights other than me, and Mandy had *two* escorts. Helen really should have asked someone else. Amanda was out, since she and David *dated*, so that would be awkward in the extreme. She could have asked me, though. We could have left the babies with Will's mother if she had.

"Welcome," a very large, very black man says, pulling me out of my head. "The first time I ever met Helen, she started an argument with me about the ethics of insider trading." He spreads his hands. "In fact, you might even say she single-handedly drove me into the clergy."

The audience, which contains a lot of Helen and David's business friends, chuckle.

"I never in a million years imagined that David Park, the kindest business student I ever taught as a professor at Harvard Business School, and Helen Fisher, the most cutthroat, would decide to marry. But here we are, proving that strange things you'd never imagine could be just around the corner, because God's hand is everywhere doing His work."

Helen and David are looking at each other like two kids staring at their Christmas stockings. It's actually pretty cute.

"Sometimes, things we never imagined become one of the most amazing things we've ever witnessed. I spent some time chatting with these two in anticipation of marrying them. It was strange that they came to me, their former ethics professor turned pastor, but I feel quite flattered to have been asked. And after talking to them, I feel there have rarely been two people more ready for this sacred commitment."

The rest of the ceremony's pretty much more of the same, with him complimenting the two of them like they just created an endowment at Harvard in his name, and everyone in the audience eating it up. Finally, he asks them if they have vows to share.

"Of course," Helen says, at the same time David says, "That's not really our thing."

Helen's brow furrows, and it feels like the room actually darkens as a result of her displeasure. Maybe she *is* Maleficent.

Until David bursts out laughing. "Got you."

When Helen cracks a small smile, the entire room takes a breath.

It feels like the market would plunge hundreds of points if he really had displeased her. I don't envy him the future he chose. It stresses me out even thinking about it.

"I'll go first," she says.

"Of course you will, you overachiever." But David clearly worships her.

"It's to give you a few more minutes to make yours up," she jokes. "But you know, that's one of the things I love most about you. You don't have to agonize over what to say when it's time to speak. You always say the right thing at the right time, somehow. You always know, not just what I want to hear, but what I need to hear."

Helen's softer when she's looking at David. Like a lion, gazing at her tamer.

"You've always known what we both need, together, and you've always been patient enough to wait for me to see it, too. But I think today, on the day we're getting married, the only thing I need to say is this." Helen pulls something out of her bodice. "You know that Abby spent four days drafting this up, and then you signed it without reading it. Now it's my turn to do my part. I never did sign it." Her lip curves slightly. "But today, I thought I'd do this."

She takes what is presumably their prenuptial agreement. . .

And rips it in half.

"I don't need contracts to keep me safe with you. I don't need to protect my assets, however considerable they are. I had my sister Abby walk me down the aisle, because I hate the idea of my parents giving me to someone. But I love the idea that whereas before I had just her on my side, now I have you as well. I love the idea that our interests have just merged in a way that goes beyond corporations or stock values or anything else." She drops her hand and entwines her fingers with his. "David Park, I promise that no matter how angry I get, or how scared I am, or how desperate I may be to close a deal, I will always be by your side, from now, until the end of my life."

David cups her jaw with his hand and kisses her then, the whole audience in awe just a little.

It does feel like the lion tamer just stuck his head in the big beast's mouth. I'm not the only one holding my breath. But he does release her, his face still intact, and then he starts talking. He never looks away from Helen, but we can still hear him, mostly.

I suppose looking away from a lion is a good way to get mauled.

"Helen Fisher, I've been in awe of you since you schooled Professor Sims on the production cost of her sample company on day one of Financial Accounting." He shakes his head. "We all knew you were something special, but I had no idea quite how special." He drops his voice. "Or that you'd ever look my way."

"I almost didn't," Helen says.

"Thank goodness that idiot looked so bad that I looked good by comparison." He runs a finger along her jawline and tucks a hair we can't see back into the beautiful pile of curls on the top of her head. "You've shone like the sun since we first met, and I promise that, like the sun, I'll always turn toward you as the center of my universe."

When they kiss this time, it's pretty epic.

"Get a room," someone shouts.

It takes me a moment to realize it was their priest.

I'm not the only one laughing about that. A few moments later, when their ceremony's finally done, Helen says, "Can I just throw the bouquet now? It's so heavy that I don't want to carry it for another minute."

It's not a shock to anyone in the room when Beth catches

it, except for maybe Beth. She's blushing so furiously that her face nearly matches the roses. Ethan's family claps so loudly at her success that I almost feel bad for her, but I can't. Not when she's clearly being so warmly welcomed by a family that knows how to love outsiders.

If possible, the reception under the large tents outside is even more grandiose, and positioned so that just behind us, the Flaming Gorge is framed up in nearly every photo. With the massive heaters they've brought in, I'm not even cold. I'll give Helen and David this. I know they planned this wedding in a few weeks, but it looks like they spent a year making every detail perfect. I suppose it's no shock that two people who run resorts can plan a spectacular event.

Even the turkey, dressing, potatoes, and more pies than I could ever count are all perfect.

"I know this is usually my sister's thing," Helen says, as she stands in front of a stunning cake almost as tall as she is, frosted with a chocolate so dark it's nearly black, and decorated with deep red blooms that cascade artfully down one side. "But since it's my wedding, she says I have to do this."

Abby's rolling her eyes from behind the long table laden with exquisite food.

"I was going to hold this wedding a week before Thanksgiving in the hopes that my baby wouldn't be showing yet." Most of her business acquaintances gasp, but everyone in Manila has known for weeks. "But then I started to worry that some of you might try to stick around until Thanksgiving."

People do laugh, which is a relief.

"But seriously, for years, almost every Thanksgiving, I would make the trek from wherever I was, to wherever Abigail and her family were. I knew I was welcome, and she always did all the heavy lifting of making this a holiday that we would enjoy. This year, since she has a baby, I thought I'd take some of the work off her plate." She spreads her hands wide. "I'm happy all our friends and family chose to be here to celebrate and give thanks for the beautiful life David and I have chosen to make out here in the middle of nowhere."

"There's nowhere else I'd rather be," David says. "And as a big thank you for all of you from the two of us, we've had the largest boxes we could acquire of chocolate covered cherries placed under every single dining chair." There's a sparkle in his eye as he says it.

I remember Helen's generous gift at Thanksgiving. . .that got everyone drunk. It's also clear that Helen knew nothing about this part of their plan, because at first she looks a little annoyed. But when Abby starts laughing, Helen rolls her eyes.

"I'm sure there will be times I'll regret getting married," she says. "We regret even good things now and then—that's human nature, to second guess. To regret. But when I do, I'll look back on this beautiful wedding, and the joy David always brings with him to everything we do, and I'll smile, because this year and probably every other year, being shackled to him is my greatest blessing in life."

When he kisses her this time, everyone cheers.

And as soon as it quiets down, Gabe shouts, "Uncle David, do the cherries have beer in them this time?" The room is entirely silent, most people probably having no clue what he's asking. "Or no?"

But as people realize that there's a prior event the cherries are commemorating, the laughter starts, and it grows and grows.

"These are most definitely *beer* free," David says. "And when you eat them, I hope they fill you with the same joy I have in this moment."

And as I stuff my face with some of them later, they kind of do. But what's even better is that when I grab a blanket and start to nurse Andrew, Althea notices. And she starts to cry. Once Andrew's done, Will hands her to me so I can hold her up against my breast one more time, as I have done over and over without success.

This time, surrounded by people and sounds, she latches.

For the first time, I successfully nurse my darling baby girl, and after I'm done and I'm cleaned up and presentable again, she insists that I take her back. I rock her, in spite of the noise and chaos of the reception, or perhaps because of it, until she falls asleep on my chest.

Althea still cries more than most babies, and sometimes I still feel disconnected, but moments like this remind me that she's my treasure. All our children are different, much as Helen and Abby looked just right in black and white respectively, but they're each more glorious for their differences.

If today's wedding showcased anything, it's that: there's great beauty in our unicity. It's something I never learned while I was living in a miserable home, and I certainly didn't learn it while married to the loser, but I think we're all learning as we go, together.

It's glorious to watch our little community thrive.

On our way out the door, Abby slides something into my bag. "What's that?"

"Just another party." She looks almost weary, which is saying something for Abby the Energizer Mummy.

When I get to the car, I open the card, and I can barely breathe. "Will." I bang on his arm.

"Easy, Lennie," he says.

I doubt he knows that he's making reference to Steinbeck. He's just copying me, and it kind of makes me love him more. "Helen's having a little boy. This card is blue."

"That's great?" He stops the car and turns to face me. "Can you imagine what a terror those three will be? Nathan, this kid, and Andrew?"

"I'm a little worried about Althea. She'll be all alone."

"Please," Will says. "I'm just worried about her future

husband. Can you imagine dealing with Aiden, Andrew, Nathan, *and* this kid?"

"I mean. . ." But I realize that he's right. This is our family. It makes me smile, imagining the four of them terrorizing the boys who love Althea.

"Aiden will be giddy," Will says.

"About what?" Now I'm lost again.

"About the shower." Will grins. "He loves elephants."

Our friends are so ridiculous that he might be right. Surely the circus won't come out again, but. . . "I'm sure whatever they come up with will be amazing."

Will clears his throat. "Can I make a suggestion?"

"What?"

"Maybe order them a gift now. Something nice."

I'm hitting him again as he pulls back onto the road.

"Also, no stuffed animals this time. You suck at picking those." Will may be squawking about how hard I whap his shoulder, but he deserves it for mocking me. Abby's baby shower was stressful squared.

When I get home, it takes us a while, but we get the babies both down for bed, and Aiden too, and I'm almost asleep when I hear the quiet whisper. "I'm the blue dukey demon, and I'm coming for you."

That's all the warning I get before a demented blue hamster beans me in the head.

I leap out of bed, wide awake and fuming. "I'm going to kill you." I snatch the creepy blue poop stuffed animal, and I run after Will. We may be the exhausted parents of two tiny babies, and we may feel like we're run ragged most of the time, but my husband still knows how to make me smile in all the best ways.

❧ 25 ❧

AMANDA

I'm not sure anyone has any idea what to expect when they arrive at Helen's baby shower. I should've known it would be fine—it's being thrown by Abby. She's not prone to Helen's excesses.

Most of the shower is completely normal.

Abby invited all the usual suspects, like Donna, Beth, and Mrs. Earl. A few of the people from town who aren't terrified of Helen also came, as well as me, of course, and Mandy. But there are a few others that we might have wished didn't come.

Abby's mother, for one, and David's mother, who still hasn't gone back home. I don't envy Helen all that mother-in-law time. I suppose that's one of the perils of having a mother-in-law who usually lives a twenty-hour flight away. When she does come to visit, she camps out for an extended period.

It's been a long run of weeks for her, surely.

And then there are also a few of Helen's. . .friends seems like a strange word for the dean of Harvard's business school, a famous talk show host, and CEOs of some of the biggest companies in America. Even so, we're all stuck making small talk and decorating onesies in Abby's family room with them. Thanks entirely to Abby, no one seems too very awkward about it.

When we start to open gifts, the difference between us becomes a little more obvious. "Here," Helen says. "I'll start with this one." She grabs a beautifully wrapped box I saw Mrs. Earl carry in.

"That's from me," Will's effusive mother says. "If you don't like it, you don't need to feel obligated to use it. I won't be offended."

After Helen unwraps the box, she pulls out a crocheted baby blanket featuring adorable fluffy white clouds on a blue background. It's sure to look like crap almost as soon as the kid starts spitting up, but I can get some really cute photos with it before then, if I remember.

"That'll go well with my gift," I say.

Helen glances around. "I. . ." She frowns. "Which one is yours?"

"I didn't wrap it," I say. "I'm going to do a newborn photoshoot for you."

"Oh, no," Beth says. "I was going to give her a photoshoot."

"Trust me," Abby says. "One of you can take photos in the first week, and one can do them a month later, and she'll love both."

"Absolutely," Helen says. "Thank you so much."

"I have to leave soon," the dean of Harvard says. "But I wanted to give you this." She winks as she hands Helen an envelope.

"What's that?" Beth asks. "I hear the best stuff comes in cards."

I try not to cringe.

"Oh, it's just a letter for a friend," the dean says.

She's almost out the door when Mrs. Earl presses. "Surely it's more than a letter. What is it?"

"Oh, well," Helen says. "I think—"

"It's an acceptance letter for little baby Fisher-Park," the dean says. "Whenever that child is ready, Harvard Business School will be waiting for him."

"Not until he's graduated from Stanford undergrad," Helen's mother says.

The two women are glaring at one another, clearly upset over the school an unborn child will choose to attend. I'm definitely out of my element here, having only ever attended an unimpressive school haphazardly.

"Open mine," Abby says, thrusting a box with little rabbits all over it at Helen. "You'll like it."

Helen opens the box, and I'm sort of praying, softly, that it's not some epic gift. Abby's already thrown her a baby shower with adorably cute decorations and food, and she's been the perfect host, all while pulling double duty on legal work every time Helen feels lousy, and helping plan the wedding.

Plus, it's a week and a half before Christmas.

Please, please, let her gift not make me feel even more inadequate.

"I didn't have a lot of time," Abby's explaining.

As Helen pulls out the oversized, double-thick swaddling blankets, I'm a little annoyed. She only had *just* enough time to sew her little nephew not one, or even two, but *three* swaddling blankets? I suppose it could have been worse. It's not the custom quilt she made for Donna—for *both* of her babies.

"I did start a quilt, but I haven't had time to finish it yet. It'll be done before he's born." She winks. "You'll have to tell me his name before then, though, or I'll never be able to embroider it before he comes home from the hospital."

There it is. An embroidered custom quilt, in process.

After everyone oohs and awws over the blankets I know are great—she made them for me with both of my girls, and

278

they were the best—it's time for a few more silver-spoon gifts. But finally, the shower's over, and it's time to go home.

"I know most of you need to leave, but for anyone who isn't done partying yet," Abby says. "We have a special surprise."

A. . . what? Somehow, in the past two hours, Steve and Ethan set up a whole host of decorations, including a beautifully made wooden backdrop made from a bunch of different colors of distressed wood plank. Adorable baby items have been attached at artful locations, and the words 'Fisher-Park baby' are spread across the top of the whole thing. It's nice, this time of year, that Steve has a covered arena they can use. I can't help wondering how much it cost to bring in a dance floor that's covering the better part of it.

There's even a live band that has just started playing songs at the far end.

"I invited your spouses and significant others to join us," Abby says. "I hope you don't mind." She winks at Helen. "But I wanted to show my sister that once you have a baby, it's okay to still do fun things. Adult things." She shrugs. "So if you're so inclined, let's dance!"

The band is pretty decent, and maybe that's why it takes me not one, but *two* songs before I realize who's singing.

Maren.

Abby evades me for nearly five minutes, which is good. It gives me time to consider that if I kill her, there won't be anyone who can defend me on the murder charges.

When I finally find her, I'm still pretty upset. "What could you possibly be thinking?"

She shrugs. "About what?"

"Maren?" My hiss comes out a little more deranged than I'd like. People around us are staring. "She does not need encouragement!"

"It was my idea, actually." Eddy steps out from behind the arena support beam and wraps an arm around my shoulders.

"Traitor," I say. "Don't tell me you've switched to their side, too."

Mandy, Abigail, and Steve have all approached us at different times to suggest that we should let Maren record her album. Thankfully, Abby has done exactly as promised, gotten the venue transferred to Utah, and she's awfully close to having the whole thing dismissed.

She's done all that while taking care of her own baby, her other children, keeping her husband happy, and handling all of Helen's legal work. My hero-worship notwithstanding, I'm still royally ticked. "We've been over this and over it."

"Have we?" Eddy asks. "I feel like *they've* been over it and over it, and we've just ignored them."

"Our friends need to learn when to butt out." I can't help stomping my foot, but my heel hits the dance floor hard just as the song ends, and now everyone's looking at me. Now's the moment. I should order Maren to quit singing, and if it ruins Abigail and Helen's party, well, they deserve it. They can't tell me how to parent, and just because they disagree doesn't mean I'm wrong.

The whole world can disagree with me, and I still won't back down.

That's what it means to be a mother.

And that's when it hits me.

The whole world, or at least, *my* whole world, does disagree. Mandy told me that holding Maren back would just make her resent me. Abigail told me that with our guidance and support, which Maren has been asking for, she would be safe. Much safer than Eddy ever was. And Steve even worked up a plan for how an adult from our family could go with her for every single event the label wants, from recording to marketing and social media.

The whole world thinks I'm wrong.

Am I?

For the first time since this madness started, I figuratively stand down. Instead of shouting and stopping my daughter from performing, which she's clearly enjoying, I shut my mouth and I listen to her. I watch her.

Maren's next song is about her dad.

Her dad was pretty lousy even when he was alive, so I'm shocked she'd write a song about him. . .until I realize it's *not* about him. It's about Eddy. She's singing about how her dad chose her. Her dad's always there for her. Her dad supports and uplifts her. He never judges.

And he always forgives.

That's definitely not Paul. She's singing about Eddy, and it's all the kind things she never says out loud.

Is it possible that she expresses the feelings and thoughts she can't bring herself to say. . .in her music? Are these more than just inane pop songs? Could she, at not-quite-eighteen, be an *artist*?

I hate that I've missed it.

I've been *blind*.

But I'm seeing it now. Abby walks up and slides her arm through mine. I wait for it, but the I-told-you-so I've been dreading never comes. "It's hard," she whispers. "So, so hard."

"What is?" I force myself to turn and look at her perfect face.

"Watching them grow up."

A tear forms in my right eye, and it slides its way down my cheek. "She's still a baby."

"It hurts when they don't need us anymore," Abby whispers. "But don't worry. They always come back, because they will always need us in some ways. That part never changes."

"Not me—she doesn't." Now there's more than one tear. "She hates me now, and even before, she knows she drew the short straw."

Abby drops her head on my shoulder. "That little girl knows how blessed she is."

As if she can hear us, Maren launches into a cover of "I'm

not Lucky, I'm Blessed." By the time it ends, I've definitely wrecked my makeup.

"I hate this," I say.

"Admitting when you're wrong?" Abby asks. "Or letting her go?"

"Option C, all of the above."

"A few years ago, you couldn't have done it," Abby says. "I'm proud of how you've grown."

It takes me a few more minutes to compose myself, and another ten minutes after that to be ready, but by the time Maren's done with her set, I'm prepared. When I tell her I'm sorry, when I tell her she can record her album, Maren leaps into my arms, her hands wrapping around my ribcage.

No one ever actually tells me that they told me so, even though they all did.

And I never do feel much better about the record label. I won't trust them until the day I die. But when I think about how my family now boasts connections to the dean of Harvard's Business School and a half dozen powerful CEOs, I can't help smiling.

I might have come from a trailer park, and my parents might still be willing to trade me in for a pack of double-mint gum, but my daughter isn't like that. My daughter has an army of people behind her, all of us willing to attack and destroy if she's threatened.

I'm not sure I could hope for anything more than this, to have created a family that's so much more than the one I was born into. It's the American dream, really, to grow a life for your kids that's better than you ever imagined it could be.

And I'm living it every day.

❧ 26 ❧

MANDY

The first snowstorm of the year hits right before Emery's performance. I'm honestly worried that it'll be canceled, but the snow flurries let up just in time, and Horace gets out his plow, and the roads are cleared by early Saturday afternoon.

HOW'S IT GOING? I text Emery, because watching Tommy type out a text is a very special kind of purgatory. He refuses to wear reading glasses, so he keeps shifting the phone farther and closer and peering at it, pecking at the buttons one single letter at a time, then backspacing and starting over.

Luckily, they have *just* enough time for the dress rehearsal if there aren't any hiccups. I know Emery *and* Tommy are both nervous. I try reminding them that it's not Broadway, and they shouldn't worry, but that doesn't go well. Apparently performing a play for a hundred of your closest friends is way more pressure than performing on Broadway.

Who knew?

Helen swings by to pick me up in her new four wheel drive BMW, as if that's really all-terrain. I sigh, but I don't argue. Trying to win a fight with Helen on a good day is futile. But trying now? When she's pregnant-cranky?

It's a death wish.

"Hey, Mandy," David says, as I use the side of her car to anchor myself while I climb into the back, batting at his hand.

"I don't need help," I say. "I told you that."

"Did you know that even breaking a hip at your age makes you seventy percent more likely to die in the month after it happens?" Helen tsks. "Just let us help you, you cantankerous old woman."

"Mind your business, you whale of a pregnant harpy," I say.

Other people are appalled by our banter, but we've discovered that saying the things we're both thinking actually helps us not hate each other. We're both laughing when Helen tears down my drive and skid-slides onto the main road.

"If you insist on driving this ice skate, you could at least wait to hit the gas until you're on the professionally plowed road," I say.

"Where's the fun in that?" Helen loves driving in snow, and David's too afraid to take the wheel away from her. It's a strange relationship that I don't think anyone really fully comprehends.

"Have as much fun as you want if it means you're going faster," I say. "You showed up five minutes late, and I still need to pick up those flowers. The post office crapped out on delivering them."

"You live in a place where flowers are delivered by the post office," Helen says. "That's your fault, not the post office's."

"That and a *blizzard*," David says. "I think Emery might forgive you for showing up empty-handed."

"I'm not empty-handed," Helen says. "I don't give people flowers that have been *mailed*."

"What did you get her?" I know I shouldn't claw the back of the seat of someone who's driving, but if I were to clip an artery with one of my claw-like nails in my distress, well, no one could blame me. "Just tell me."

Helen smiles, angling her face to be sure I can see her in the rearview.

"You're evil," I say. "I'm not defending you anymore."

She snorts. "As if you ever did."

"You can't show me up with my own granddaughter. You're not even related to Emery."

"She's my sister's niece, so I'm actually more related to her than you are, you wacky old biddy."

"As fun as it is, listening to you two fling insults," David says, "in the interest of surviving to the play, I'll just say that Helen was sent a bunch of swag for a company that boasts a line of jewelry last month. Among the things they sent, there was a lily pendant, and she's giving it to Emery."

"What's this pendant made of?" I ask.

"Diamonds." Helen's beaming. "Beautiful, high-quality diamonds."

"You can't—"

"It's a flower," Helen says. "Which is what you give someone who has successfully performed in a play. Only, this one she can wear and keep."

My hands clamp down on the back of the chair again, but I wish they were around her neck. "Helen Fisher Park—"

"No Park," David says. "She's not taking my name."

"Actually, maybe I will," Helen says. "I like how sophisticated that sounds. Helen. Fisher. Park." She glances over her shoulder. "Say it again."

I really might strangle her.

But we're just pulling into the parking lot, and I remember that we're here for Emery. She'll love the necklace, and that's what matters. "Wait," I say. "What about my flowers? We need to pick them up. They said they're holding them for me until I get there because of the storm."

Helen shrugs. "Do you really think they matter?"

David pokes her shoulder. "Stop."

"Why?" Helen's grinning like the Cheshire cat. "This is so much fun."

"Abby already picked up the flowers," David says. "She texted Helen earlier. She had to get something for the baby, and she saw the box. She'll have them—"

But Abby's already tapping on the glass, a baby on one hip, flower box on the other.

I snatch it from her and peel back the lid, only to realize that they're all brown. "Oh, no," I say.

"I think the weather wasn't really the best for them," Abby says. "The Post Office thinks maybe they froze while they waited. I guess their heater kind of couldn't keep up with the temperature drop."

"Or they threw them in the warehouse." I bare my teeth, but I manage to keep from growling.

"Don't worry," Abby says. "I brought you something better." She winks as she hands me a tin.

The smell hits me before I can even open it. Lemon sugar cookies, Emery's favorite. "Thank you." I hug Abby. It's not a diamond necklace, but I know Emery will love them. "But wait, what about you?"

"I got her flowers," Abby says. "Izzy's taking floral design, remember?" She gestures back at the auditorium. "I'd have offered you those, but Emery saw Izzy making them, so she'd know they came from us."

As if she won't know the lemon cookies are from Abby. "It's great," I say. "Thank you."

Moments later, with Abby's arm through mine so she and David will stop fussing, I shuffle through the doors and find my way to the seats Ethan's shamelessly saving. With Beth, Donna, Will, Aiden, most of Abby's kids, Amanda, Eddy, and

Dolores Jenkins, we take up the majority of the second and third rows. Only Scrooge's family is in front of us, and they're all pretty short.

Just before the curtain opens, Tommy comes out front and introduces himself.

"My name is Thomas Collins, and I'm delighted to be filling in for Mr. Hammerly to help your kids bring you this year's Christmas play, *A Christmas Carol*," he says. "I haven't lived in Manila for more than sixty years, but the kindness you have all shown me upon my return reminds me why I loved it here in my childhood. I hope you will enjoy your kids' production of this play even half as much as I enjoyed helping them put it together." With that, he bows.

And we all cheer.

I love seeing how much everyone else loves the man I love.

And the play itself, well. It's the cutest thing I've ever seen. I know a lot about what happened behind the scenes, like Scrooge getting appendicitis ten days ago and being replaced. . .with a third grader.

Tommy told me they had two choices. He could step in and play Scrooge, but he would be the one old man in a children's play. I knew he'd do a flawless, believable job, but I also know his delight is in producing and directing, not in acting. His second option was to use Gabe, whose speech delay was still a struggle, but who had a mind like a steel trap. He memorized lines without a second thought, and he's a natural up in front of people.

I told Tommy that everyone loved Gabe, and of course I was biased, but I thought a third grade lead would make it even more endearing than ever before.

Boy, was I right.

The audience *loves* Gabe.

I've never seen a kid with a better sense of comedic timing. Things that weren't even supposed to be funny are hilarious when he says them, and you can tell Gabe means for them to be. He scowls, harumphs, and stomps around with complete skill and utterly precious audacity.

The scene with him watching as Emery dances with a 'younger' Scrooge is belly-splittingly funny.

I've never seen this play performed as a comedy, but it was a stroke of genius, and the audience loves it. Then, somehow, at the end, Gabe manages to bring it down a level, and play things entirely seriously. I'm so proud of him when, at the very end, he focuses hard and actually articulates most of his r's.

"I don't know what to do," Gabe says at the end. "I'm as light as a feather, as happy as an angel, and as merry as a school boy." Then he winks.

We can't help laughing, all of us with lighter hearts.

"I'd also be as giddy as a drunken man." He mutters under his breath. "If only I could find some cherries."

The audience roars over that, most of them having heard the story of the cordial cherries from Thanksgiving last.

"A merry Christmas to everybody, and a happy new year to the world." When Gabe bows, the audience stands up and claps and claps.

I may have struggled with delivery on the flowers for Emery, but I'm confident that I'll win with Gabe. I robbed the pile of Christmas gifts I've been hoarding, ordering something new to replenish it, so I could give Gabe the Charizard Lego kit I know he wants.

I did check with Abby to make sure they weren't planning to get that for him. I can't stand people who wreck other people's plans. I'm hoping my overexaggerated distress about Emery's flowers distracted Helen, because I really want to beat her for once, and she didn't even mention a gift for Gabe. Maybe she didn't realize he was even in the play. He was a late addition.

After the curtain closes, I grip either side of my seat so I can get up and move down the row faster than Helen, but the lights in the auditorium don't turn on. Instead the curtain opens again, only the kids aren't wearing their Christmas Carol costumes, so it's not an encore.

They're wearing what looks an awful lot like. . . *The King and I* costumes instead. And Maren's standing at the front.

When she starts to sing *Shall We Dance,* my jaw drops nearly to the floor, and as Ethan comes out wearing King Mongkut's clothing, I can barely believe my eyes.

"Some of you may know that when I lived here last," Tommy's saying from the corner of the stage, "this very same group, the Manila High School theater program, performed a musical called *The King and I.* Amanda Saddler played Anna Leonowens, and through a bizarre stroke of luck, I played King Mongkut." Then Tommy drops down, with some difficulty, to one knee. "That's when I fell in love with her for the first time, I think." He's beaming. "I was too stupid to do anything about it then, but now I'm older, and I'm also a great deal smarter." He pulls a box out of his pocket and flips up the lid. "I want to ask Amanda Saddler if she will marry me. I thought this would be a good time to do it, with all her family here, and with some of them featuring spectacularly in a Christmas production." He's beaming.

And I realize that the nicest diamond here tonight. . .isn't for Emery. It's for me. I wonder whether Helen knew, whether she was keeping me riled up to keep me in the dark.

I heave myself out of the chair, and I embarrass myself thoroughly when I join Maren for the last few lines of the song. Then I stop, and I reach for Tommy's hand, and I say, "Yes, King Mongkut. I will happily marry you."

When he kisses me, the entire room erupts. There are lots of groans and ewws from the kids gathered around, but there are more than a few hoots and hollers and quite a lot of clapping as well.

As Tommy leads me off the stage, insisting like Abby and

Helen and David that he hold my arm in the process, I'm smiling like a halfwit. Uncontrollably. Unceasingly.

"I should also tell you that I've been offered a full-time job at the high school." Tommy's chest is puffed up in his suit. "Since you said yes, I think I might just take it."

"Oh, no," I say. "Poor Principal Miller." I shake my head. "He must be going senile already to offer you a job."

Tommy pretends to scowl, and I lean my head on his shoulder. He's learning how to fit in with this family fast.

"I don't think many people wait as long as we did for their happily ever after," I say.

"Most people are boring. At least no one can accuse us of that."

He's right. They can't.

"I was thinking," he says. "Maybe we ought to get married the day after Christmas."

"You have lost your mind," I say. "That's ten days away."

He pulls me into his arms, and he presses a kiss to my brow. "Amanda Saddler, you and I have wasted enough time, don't you think? I don't want to waste another single moment."

I can't argue with that.

So I don't.

❧ 27 ❧
ABIGAIL

It feels like a million years have passed since the day I sat in my office in Houston, chatting with the lawyer on the phone about Jed's passing. When he told me that my kids had inherited a massive cattle ranch in the middle of nowhere, I had absolutely no intention of even visiting here, much less moving everything out and building a life in the world's least populated area, surrounded by cows.

I've always been someone who thrives with a plan for her future.

Once, during law school, a renowned psychologist came by to speak to us. He asked all the law students to raise our hands if we set goals, made plans to achieve them, then enacted the plan, modifying it as required until we reached our goal.

More than half the class raised our hands. Mine shot up before anyone else's because that was a perfect description of how I live my life. Neither luck nor fate was allowed to interfere. With each course correction I would find the most logical path forward and keep on going.

Then that man dropped his bomb: less than one percent of the human population does that. Most people *intend* to do things, but somewhere between setting the goal and getting it done, things break down, never to be recovered.

I remember being absolutely flummoxed at that, until I started thinking about some of the other people I'd met in my life. The dry cleaners who helped me be presentable for moot court regularly took longer to deliver than they promised. Sometimes they even lost things outright. The fast food people screwed up every order in at least one major way. Grocery store baggers fling things around like they're all indestructible, and packing stuff I'm purchasing is literally their only task. Generally speaking, the entire mill of humanity around me struggles to do even the most basic of things they've chosen to do as their life work. For the first time, I started to understand that perhaps those people weren't just the underachievers I'd always thought of them as.

Maybe they were just wired differently than I was.

I proceeded along my way, though, unperturbed, focused, until the day when luck intervened in a big way. For the first time, in spite of my ability to make plans, enact them, and see them through, I was left without a way to fix my plan.

I was alone, widowed, and miserable.

But with time, I made a new plan. I powered through. I think that's why luck had to intervene again. Because my way needed a course adjustment. Maybe not for me. Maybe not for all of my kids, but for at least one of them.

Ethan has always been my hardest child. From the second he was conceived, he turned my life upside down. But I'm a firm believer that God knows what each of us need. Some people need a hand in making plans, in enacting plans, or in adapting them. Others need a hand with letting go.

Manila, Utah, its people, its climate, and the life we have built here have been a perpetual lesson for me in letting go. I've learned to allow life to surprise me with the possibilities that open up anew for me every single day.

When the day of Mandy's wedding dawns, I haven't yet

taken all my Christmas decorations down, wrapped them up, and packed them into boxes. Usually I make sure that happens on the afternoon of Christmas day. After an entire season of clutter and extra gifts, something about piles of paper and trash sends me over the edge. My kids hate it, but we pack things up almost as soon as the gifts are opened.

But not this year.

My beautiful baby caught some kind of cold on Christmas Eve, and he did not sleep well, which means I didn't sleep well. So when I finally got him down for a much-needed nap on Christmas Day, instead of marshaling the troops and cleaning up like I always do, I slept.

And so today, on the day after Christmas, while my hands itch to finally put decorations away, when my husband returns home weary from yet another long night shift, I kiss his forehead, and I start to ready the kids for another wedding.

"It hasn't even been a month since Aunt Helen's wedding," Gabe grumbles. "I hate wearing suits. They're so itchy."

"I think I figured that one out," I say. "I cut the tag out—ripped it out, in fact, and then I stitched the shirt back up."

"Really?" his eyes light up. "You ripped a hole in it, and then you stitched it back up? So now it's like a zombie shirt?"

"Sure," I say. "Let's hope the zombie shirt can behave itself today."

He's smiling as he jogs to his room.

I'm halfway through applying my makeup when Nate starts to cry.

"I got it." Izzy breezes in, her short blonde bob as perfect as ever, but a little fluffier than usual.

"You actually blow-dried it for once," I say.

She shrugs. "Miracles do sometimes happen." She winks on her way out, already bouncing Nate up and down, his squeals following her out. I've never met a kid who likes babies more than she does.

"Not too much bouncing," I call after her. "The last thing we need is to have him up-chuck the carrots he had for breakfast all over the place."

"I'll stop before I get him dressed," she calls back.

There aren't many things in this world I can rely upon as universal truths, but Whitney and Izzy squabbling is one of them, and Izzy taking care a baby with competence and a smile is the other. Apparently it's just when kids hit ten or eleven that she starts to get annoyed by every single thing they do or say.

It feels like a miracle, but Steve emerges from his nap without being woken up, all blinky and slow-moving, right as I finish marshaling all the troops. Ethan and Beth have arrived, both in their own cars, but dressed in corny coordinated outfits that never fail to make me smile. Moments later, Steve ducks into the shower, and I make him a steaming cup of instant coffee.

It's ready just as he comes out, suit on, but tie hanging loose around his neck. "Is everyone ready?"

Whitney salutes. "Horses fed sir, chickens have full water and food, and the dishes are. . ." She glances sideways at Gabe.

"Done," Gabe whispers. "Even the stupid silverware."

Our puppy yips as we lock her into her crate, but she always stops once we reach the door. "Who has the gift?"

It almost killed me, taking a break from Helen's baby quilt to make Mandy's quilt in the week right before Christmas, but I managed to finish it just in time, if finishing at three a.m. counts as being 'in time.'

"She's going to love it," Steve says. "Trust me."

I know Helen will get Mandy something lavish and ridiculous. Amanda will know just what she's been wanting. And Donna will stress to the point of misery and get her something weird.

It's just what we do.

But my role is to make something special and heartfelt, and it's starting to feel like a contact sport, with all these weddings and babies piling up one right after another. "The seams aren't great," I say, "but it's done."

"She'll understand." Steve sips on his coffee and then blows on it again.

"Or she won't even be able to see that they're crooked," Izzy says.

Whitney jabs her right on cue.

"What?" Izzy says. "She's ancient. Everyone knows old people can barely see."

Steve's laughing. "How long until we're ancient?" He rotates his right shoulder slowly. "Because my shoulder feels like an antique already."

The drive to the wedding is so short that we're not even late, which is nice. It might even be the best thing about small towns. We're all shivering as we dart across the parking lot and duck into the long hallway that leads to the ballroom of Gold Strike.

It's clear as we walk up that Amanda has outdone herself with the decorations, and we're not even inside yet. The long, normally white walls are plastered with a series of hilarious signs, and every one of them screams Mandy.

Amanda nailed this part.

They say things like, "Marriage: when dating goes too far," and, "Those who fly solo have the strongest wings," and, "The older I get, the more everyone can kiss my petunia." Every sign makes me smile, and I suppose that's the point.

Part of me wonders whether Amanda put a little extra energy into this because it's the wedding she wanted and just didn't have the bandwidth to do after giving her first setup to Donna. Mandy and Tommy gave her carte blanche on budget, decor, and entertainment, with one stipulation.

"There will be no bridesmaids," Mandy had said. "I enjoyed that farce for the last few weddings, and it was nice

to be included, but everyone at my wedding is an *old* maid."
She had cackled like mad, and then said, "Actually, that should
be our theme. *Old* Maids."

As we step through the double doors into the ballroom
itself, every guest is issued an 'old lady hat,' each one bigger
than the last, or more piled up with flowers. "These aren't
optional," the woman passing them out says. "All women have
to wear them."

"What about us?" Steve asks. "We don't get anything?"

The woman points over her shoulder at where a few feet
ahead, there's a man passing out striped canes. The hats and
the canes each have little tags saying, "Thanks for joining
Tommy and Mandy as they tie the knot. Better late than
never." Then they're all marked with the date, which would
be easy to remember in any case, being the day after
Christmas.

"Ooh," Gabe says. "This is awesome. I call Nate's stick."

"It's not a stick," Steve's explaining fruitlessly. "It's a cane,
to help you walk."

"But I already walk fine," Gabe says. "So do you."

"It's a joke," Steve's saying.

"Jokes are supposed to be funny." Gabe's frowning. "This
is just weird."

I let Steve worry about that one as I look around.

There's a deck of Old Maid cards in the center of each
table, and the floral tablecloths are perfectly fussy. Each
table's set for high tea, with floral china, and large, stacked
tiered trays laden with cakes, sandwiches, and little treats.
There are also disposable cameras in little piles all over, which
must be Amanda's version of old school, but I have no idea
where she'll get the film developed.

There are photo booths on either wall, all taking only
black and white photos, with props that look right out of the
1920s. The wait staff are dressed like candy stripers, though

296

I'm not sure what that has to do with old maids or even being old.

All in all, it looks more like a reception than a venue for a wedding ceremony, which is probably exactly what Mandy asked for. There will be no long line of people, no pews and rows, and no waiting in boredom. She told us to make sure that when she walked in, it's already a party.

I'm ready to do my part, and it looks like everyone else is too, because at that moment, the band starts to play. Maren's apparently singing, again. She waves at me and blows Steve a kiss, and then she launches into her first song. After two or three more, Eddy actually climbs up the stairs and joins her. They actually sound pretty nice, and they keep the volume low enough that people can still talk.

Aiden and Gabe race around the room, waving their canes a little too exuberantly until Will reaches out and yoinks them both, hiding them under the table until an unspecified 'later.' If he's smart, they'll disappear forever. Several of the roaming kids are working out how to use a disposable camera, which is entertaining, but they're frustrated that they can't figure out how to see the photos they've taken.

"You can't see them," I explain. "You don't get to see them until you take them in and pay to have the film developed."

It makes no sense to them, but once I explain we did it because it was our only option, they look exceptionally unimpressed. "You're kidding," Izzy says. "That's so dumb. How could you know whether you got a good photo?"

I shrug. "Why do you think we have so few great photos of Mandy and Tommy?" I toss my head at the beautiful, blown-up images Amanda hung on the wall. They're actually lucky they have anything to work with, after Mandy's stupid barn fire.

But looking at their smiling faces, youthful and fresh, I can't help smiling in response. Life marches on, but there's beauty in all the stages of it. It's too bad that you really only learn to appreciate it as you draw nearer the end.

Suddenly, without warning, Mandy bursts through the back doors, blinding us all as the light from the midday sun backlights her and Tommy both. "Let's get this party started." I can hear the smile in her tone. "Who wants to see a wedding?"

She and Tommy march through the middle of the cheering guests, dodging errant chairs, skewed tables, and heedless of the flashes of instant cameras from the right and the left. They look happier than probably any other couple I've seen.

As Mandy passes me, I can't help saying, "What a gorgeous dress." I tilt my head. "You look just stunning."

Because she does.

Instead of a slinky dress, or a big puffy dress, she opted for a Jackie-O style midi-skirt. The hem hits her mid-calf after flaring from the waist outward, and the bodice itself is both modest but also fitted, showing that even at eighty, she's still got an impressive figure.

She sashays her hips and smiles. "I had to show off my ankles. They're my best feature."

"I formally disagree." Tommy chuckles. "But you do look amazing."

When they reach the front of the room, the same pastor who gave the sermon for Mandy's father and mother's funerals, the same pastor who taught a sermon every Sunday, stands up and welcomes us all.

"I am so happy to be here this fine day after Christmas, with two of my favorite people." Pastor Michael spreads his arms out wide. "For Thanksgiving, we were able to celebrate a wedding not far from here, and here we are, not even a month later, celebrating another."

We're all feeling that pain, Pastor Michael.

"But today's a very special wedding indeed. Two very good

people who were apart for a very long time are finally being joined." He isn't brief, like Helen's former professor was. He's not the most eloquent either, but he is familiar, and he cares.

He's also a friend.

When he reaches the part about vows, he says, "I know you two said yours would be short and sweet, but however long they are, now's the time to say them."

"I promise never to lie to you again," Mandy says. "And I promise that I'll always eat my vegetables so I can be with you as long as humanly possible."

He presses his hand to her heart and smiles. "I'll hold you to that. I know where they keep the broccoli down at the True Value."

Mandy rolls her eyes.

"And I promise that if you ever do lie to me again, I won't pretend to believe it."

Everyone who knows about Mandy's weird decorations laughs.

"I also promise that from now until the day I do die, you will be the only thing that matters to me. I will steam and prepare broccoli until our whole house reeks, and I'll love every minute of it." He leans closer and presses a kiss to her cheek. "I'll even pretend that your ankles are your best feature, if that's what you want, though anyone with eyes knows it's your—"

"Okay," says Pastor Michael. "Let's keep this PG."

"Is this the part where I can kiss my bride?" Tommy asks.

"We already did that part," the pastor says. "But if you want to do it again."

Tommy doesn't wait for more of an invitation, kissing Mandy with the energy of a teenager. This time, he even dips her. I'm a little worried that his knee might give out and they might both crash to the ground, but they're both fine when they finally do come back up for air. Once they straighten, Tommy reaching over to repair Mandy's ruffled hair, Pastor

Michael rolls his eyes and mutters something like 'this is not the right order,' but then he finally says, "I now pronounce you man and wife."

We all cheer.

Clearly doing things in the right order hasn't been their forte.

In fact, if I've learned much in my last few years here, it's that the order of things matters a great deal less than the love and emotion with which something is done.

So when I give Mandy my gift, out of order and at the wrong time, right after the ceremony, I don't worry about making people wait. I don't worry about what others might think.

I look only at Mandy as she opens the box slowly, lifting the quilt I made out reverently. I chose my favorite photo of each of her favorite people, and with each friend or family member I identified, the quilt got bigger and bigger. I can't think of a better testament to the love people here have for her than this.

"It should easily be big enough for your king size bed," I say.

"Tommy." One utterance of his name, and the man turns away from the person he's chatting with and toward his new bride.

His strong hands grasp one end of the quilt and help Mandy spread it out so she can see all the blocks with all the faces she loves. Maren, eyes closed, hands on a guitar, singing. Emery, a rapt smile, riding her dark bay. Gabe with his hand up and a self-deprecating smile, winning everyone's heart during the school play. Steve, wearing scrubs, distracted by a patient. It's a snapshot one of his colleagues sent to show me that he's wearing the scrubs Whitney embroidered, but it's probably my favorite photo of my hot, hard-working husband.

I even included a photo of myself.

Amanda took it on the day I fell asleep, waiting for Mandy's procedure to be over. In the center of all the photos, there's a large block that says 'Love,' but it's spelled out with one handprint from each of the people in the images. Izzy, Emery, and Whitney all helped me embroider names on each individual handprint.

"It's to represent—"

"I know," she cuts me off. "Love isn't a feeling. It's something we build together."

When she looks up at me, her eyes are full of unshed tears. "Thank you, Abby. In many ways, you built all of this. We certainly couldn't have done any of it without you."

I shake my head. "I wish I had embroidered you something else," I say. "You said on your notes, 'better late than never.'" I can feel tears welling up in my eyes, too. "But I think some things are better when they're late. It's the only way we appreciate them fully."

When Mandy pulls me tightly against her body, I know she gets it. She loves Tommy as much as she does because of the lost years. I love Steve as fiercely as I do, because I know what it feels like to lose the first love of my life.

It's easy to think that our mistakes lessen our lives, but really, they *lesson* our lives so we can learn to do better with each day we're granted. In so many ways, it's the temporal, finite nature of our lives that makes each day so very precious.

There are no guarantees.

As the sun sets and another beautiful day winds to a close, I find myself very, very grateful for the twists and turns that have led us to this bright, happy, and very full place. If any one person wasn't here, it wouldn't be quite so very beautiful, which is the real joy of family.

***

I hope you enjoyed The Lookback and the whole Birch Creek Ranch series. It was a lot of fun to write them! If you'd like to grab a FREE bonus chapter that shows the birth of Helen's baby, you can do it by joining my newsletter here: https://BookHip.com/FMAJXHP

(And don't worry. If you're already on there, you won't be signed up twice unless you use a different email address, of course.)

I had such a fun time writing this last book, but I was sad to be finishing too. Because of that. . .

If you've read my Bridget E. Baker titles, specifically the Russian Witch's Curse (horse shifter) books, you may have already noticed something. . . I've decided to cross this series over with that one. Namely, the fourth horse shifter book will feature characters from Birch Creek Ranch.

Gabe was carrying around a heavy bag at Mandy's house... and it had books that will come up in that fourth horse shifter book. SO if you have any interest at all in reading more about the Birch Creek characters, you're in luck! You would start the horse shifter books here, with the first book, My Queendom for a Horse. You won't see the crossover until book FOUR, so be prepared for that. <3 They are fantasy romance, but they are clean books like these. No language or adult content.

OR if you'd rather stick with my B. E. Baker titles, that's fine too! I have two other contemporary romance series out now. The Finding Home series (complete with 9 books), starting with Finding Grace, and The Scarsdale Fosters series (being written now—three books are already out), starting with Seed Money.

Feel free to come find me on social media if you haven't yet, or follow me on your favorite platform! Thanks so much for all the kind words and reviews. Your support means the world to me.

ACKNOWLEDGMENTS

My big thank yous always go to my readers, to my editor, to my author friends, and to my family. You guys are really my bedrock. Always have been, and probably always will be. THANK YOU for being the most supportive, understanding, and amazing fans and readers and support team any author could ask for...

My husband, my kids, and my mom and dad have been my biggest cheerleaders, and they continue to be.

And I'd like to throw a little shade at my seven wonderful horses, who kept having lameness issues and problems that required large vet bills and time-consuming visits and slowed down my writing process. Get it together, guys. Start making better decisions. ;)

ABOUT THE AUTHOR

I have animals coming out of my ears. Seven horses. Three dogs, three cats, and thirty-ish chickens. I'm always doctoring or playing with an animal... and I wouldn't want it any other way. But Leo (my palomino) is still my very favorite.

When I'm not with animals, or even if I am, I'm likely to have at least one of my five kids in tow, two of which I'm currently homeschooling.

My hubby is the reason all this glorious madness is possible. He's the best parts of all the amazing men I write (although he's bald and his six pack sometimes goes into hiding because of cookies.)

That may be my fault, because I also love to bake and like to cook. I feel amazing when I find time to kickbox, lift weights, or rollerblade, but that doesn't always happen.

I'm also a lawyer, but I try to forget about that whenever I can, and I've succeeded in doing less legal work every year since I started writing. YES.

If you want to come follow me on social, be warned. The hubby has a weird sense of humor, and he's been known to frequent my Facebook group: https://www.facebook.com/groups/750807222376182

ALSO BY B. E. BAKER

The Scarsdale Fosters Series:

Seed Money (1)

Nouveau Riche (2)

Minted (3)

Loaded (4)

The Finding Home Series:

Finding Grace (1)

Finding Faith (2)

Finding Cupid (3)

Finding Spring (4)

Finding Liberty (5)

Finding Holly (6)

Finding Home (7)

Finding Balance (8)

Finding Peace (9)

The Finding Home Series Boxset Books 1-3

The Finding Home Series Boxset Books 4-6

The Finding Home Series Boxset Books 7-9

The Birch Creek Ranch Series:

The Bequest

The Vow

The Ranch

The Retreat

The Reboot

The Surprise

The Setback

The Lookback

Children's Picture Book

Yuck! What's for Dinner?

<u>I also write books under Bridget E. Baker. They're mostly fantasy romance, and they're all clean.</u>

The Dragon Captured Series: (dragon shifter romance!)

Ensnared

Entwined

Embroiled

Embattled

The Russian Witch's Curse: (horse shifter romance!)

My Queendom for a Horse

My Dark Horse Prince

My High Horse Czar

My Wild Horse King

The Magical Misfits Series: (paranormal humor!)

Mates: Minerva (1)

Mates: Xander (2)

The Birthright Series:

Displaced (1)

unForgiven (2)

Disillusioned (3)

misUnderstood (4)

Disavowed (5)

unRepentant (6)

Destroyed (7)

The Birthright Series Collection, Books 1-3

The Anchored Series:

Anchored (1)

Adrift (2)

Awoken (3)

Capsized (4)

The Sins of Our Ancestors Series:

Marked (1)

Suppressed (2)

Redeemed (3)

Renounced (4)

Reclaimed (5) a novella!

A stand alone YA romantic suspense:

Already Gone

www.ingramcontent.com/pod-product-compliance
Lightning Source LLC
Chambersburg PA
CBHW021031280125
20978CB00011B/43